2

Dario Lisiero

JUSTICE UNFINISHED

4

Dario Lisiero
Justice Unfinished
ISBN 978-0-6151-9189-8

"Wow... I don't even know where to begin! The way you incorporate elements from history into your stories is amazing. I keep having to look things up on Wikipedia -- like Paul Marcinkus and Emanuela Orlandi. Also the connections between Atticus Bitter, Ephemeris and Rambo and the way the .... made Angie and Heloise ..... and Titus gay was so clever! I actually read through it twice and only picked up on the part about Titus the second time. There are just so many details that you add in... very clever! ... Can't wait to read your next book -- I hope it won't be 5 years again!!!"...

"By the way, I am really enjoying it. You are a superb writer!"

Jessica Keet

PREFACE

1.- God's palingenesis

"The one who sat on the throne said, '*Behold, I make all things new.'*"(Revelation 21:5)

However, before this apocalyptic palingenesis, something catastrophic, never seen before or after, will occur.

"*Immediately after the tribulation of those days, the sun will be darkened, and the moon will not give its light, and the stars will fall from the sky, and the powers of the heavens will be shaken.*" (Matthew 24:29)

According to the inspired Word, these will be the ultimate and final events of our universe. The last generation of humans will witness, among horrors and indescribable sufferings, the total destruction of everything.

After this ruinous event, a very new entity will ensue—"*I make all things new.*"

What this newness will be like is impossible to imagine or conjecture. The only thing we can assure is that nothing will subsist from the previous world.

The innumerable treasures, so jealously preserved in museums, libraries and monuments will end up as dust and ashes. The memories of celebrated thinkers, inventors, conquerors, etc. will be erased from the consciousness of the entire universe.

A black hole of complete emptiness, invisible and imperceptible, will reign supreme. Silence and eternal oblivion will constitute its essence.

Apparently, the Divine Maker is not interested in preserving, perfecting, even with "*a radical cure,*" the old, perishable cosmos.

God does not work along the lines of vastly improving preexisting things; He creates new things from basically nothing.

Unlike nature and man, this is the divine "*modus operandi.*"

2.- Nature transformation and evolution

"*Natura non facit saltus.*" Nature does not make sudden jumps. This ancient wisdom clearly suggests a certain continuity in the natural process of transformation and evolution.

Nowadays, this ancient axiom, even if challenged by the unexpected outcomes of several sciences (for instance evolutionary biology), nevertheless maintains some grain of truth.

For centuries, thinkers and laypeople alike have considered nature the root and measurement, the reliable source and origin, of all moralities, law and justice.

Nature, according to this old way of thinking, possesses within itself a preordained set of laws and values, embedded by the Divine Maker since the inception of creation. To follow nature implies obeying the Supreme Reason.

Besides an aura of correctness and orthodoxy, nature presents itself as something solid and permanent, the antithesis of novelty and uncertainty. Natural things are better, superior and more reliable than processed or manufactured ones.

According to our ancestral wisdom, to alter or modify nature from its course is detrimental and ultimately harmful.

Despite an impressive array of noble attributes and virtues, if we carefully study nature over its history—spanning billions of years—we discover its germane and genuine essence, as the biggest force and manufacturer of **transformation and evolution**.

Lifeless and formless things, thanks to this inherent thrust, have taken shape and come to life, generating countless species in the three main kingdoms: mineral, vegetable and animal.

Nobody could ever narrate or dutifully explain the inscrutable life of this magnificent and unobserved laboratory. It is so extended in time and space that no one could ever witness and record it. Just the simple fact of trying to imagine it, provokes vertigo.

Only some vestiges are left, so scarce and undecipherable, that not even the most intuitive mind can penetrate their inner secrets and discover the mysterious evolutionary course that has taken place since the dawn of time, and continued through billions of years.

Modern man is slowly undertaking the journey back in time, in order to unveil the apparently forbidden kingdom of this natural force, where the marvels of evolution have taken shape and keep transforming things with such lentitude that it is impossible to detect any mutation.

Will our scientists ever reach any assuring conclusion? Will they ever find any solid proof to this simple belief and assertion?

Despite these insurmountable difficulties, it does not seem out of human reach to capture some mutations and transformations that have occurred on our planet.

The total extinction of some species, such as dinosaurs, due to meteorological and geological changes, stands as a silent reminder of our changing habitat.

Add to this the formation of new landscapes, products of volcanic activities, water erosion, earthquakes and tsunamis and you will obtain an accurate picture of the constant turmoil this seemingly pacific planet is undergoing.

Moreover, not only our planet but the whole universe is in constant expansion and contraction, according to modern science. Contrary to its Latin name, "*firmamentum*," which means firm, solid, unchangeable, our universe is never static, always changing like a living organism.

Heraclitus was perfectly right when he wrote "panta rhey," ("all things flow"). **In other words, the essence of things is change**.

3.- Man's intrusive intervention

If these natural phenomena appear to be catastrophic for the conservation of the present *status quo*, infinitely more violent are the changes wrought by the greedy thoughtlessness of the technological man.

The many endangered species and scary climate changes are just a couple of examples of his brainless run toward the precipice of annihilation.

Man, with his unstoppable destructive action, provokes nature's fury that bursts suddenly into wildfires in California, devastating flooding in Louisiana and disastrous tornadoes in Oklahoma.

It is difficult to forecast or even predict with a minimum of accuracy these natural outbursts, but one thing is sure, they are out there, and they will become more frequent and certainly more unpredictable and dangerous.

Without subscribing to the doomsday predictions by scientists of an impending catastrophe due to ozone depletion, global warming, etc., we cannot fail to recognize the serious risks inherent in our wild and unbridled economic development, in the wasteful management of our limited natural resources, and in the contamination of our primary sources of life—water and air.

There is an enormous contradiction in technological advancement—making life easier and more comfortable through the creation of new products, while polluting our habitat to the point of creating miserable living conditions for its unfortunate dwellers.

Is this the price we must pay for progress and development? Aren't there any more humane ways of achieving similar results without compromising the future of every living creature?

The increasing awareness and legitimate fear of the calamitous effects derived from such a contradiction, do not stop multinationals and large corporations from pillaging the earth and poisoning the environment. **The green way is not their way.**

Is humankind doomed to self-destruction or self-annihilation? Alternatively, does every excess contain its own remedy, correcting its natural course despite our blindness and stupidity?

Whatever might be the suitable response to these pertinent questions and the drastic effects of this crazy run, be sure that man will inevitably pursue his dream of progress and transformation, stopping at nothing.

No moral imperative or religious restraints, nor civil laws or state prohibitions will obstruct our crusader from manipulating any possible form of change and transformation in the human composition.

We are not talking here of simply cloning human beings, or reconstructing limbs and essential organs, but of genetically engineering a new breed of people qualitatively different from the existing species.

At this very moment, there are scientists trying to create life. The new technology of creating protocells still has major hurdles to overcome. However, it has the untapped potential of altering our world in fundamental ways, ways that are impossible to predict.

Undoubtedly, this will constitute the most compelling and scary challenge, from which no scientist in the world will shy away.

Attempts to modify human behavior have been undertaken in the past, using powerful drugs for military or civilian use in secret government projects.

In order to achieve victory over our enemies it is imperative to count on fearless soldiers or fanatic subjects. Religious and patriotic ideology might constitute, in certain cultures, a more powerful stimulant than any other pharmacological product.

It is notorious, if not recognized and accepted, that religious and secular education, fostered by churches and states, engendered since the inception of time, still in our day creates a real manipulation of human behavior.

Whether or not this tampering through education is beneficial, or even legitimate, goes beyond our area of interest. The only thing we definitely hope to establish is that interference in human behavior is nothing new.

Whatever might have happened in the past through nature's fury or man's selfish attitude, we have seen nothing yet. For the future creators of the new superior human species will not suffice the usage of chemical drugs or religious-ideological indoctrination—it will be necessary to manipulate man's DNA, engineering a new type of being, capable of withstanding the fierce conditions of inhospitable planets and the unfathomable demands of radically different social structures.

The extraterrestrial survival will require—besides arduous physical training and rigorous scientific knowledge—a mental and psychological equilibrium, a balanced personality and an aggressive but non-conflictive attitude.

The new world must count on people without sexual deviations (a dormant sex drive) or religious dogmatism (a general, watered-down belief in God); they must be indifferent to the power structure of dominance and dependence (a real democratic society) and alien to the accumulation of material possessions (just a minimum of economic stability and security).

All the powerful and innate stimuli that configure our human identity and generate the excesses of our society must be somehow suppressed and eradicated with the clear intent of giving birth to an uncontaminated generation of galactic dwellers.

Utopia, myth, illusion, dream, craziness? Possibly, all of the above, or perhaps nothing at all.

Anyhow, men will never cease from imagining better worlds and will never stop in their efforts to create them with all the means at their disposal, whether they are licit or illicit, permitted or forbidden.

This is human nature: passive and inquisitive, intrusive and permissive, creative and destructive, dreaming and daring.

4.- Conclusion

God, nature and man seem sedulously occupied with changing and renovating all creations.

However, their methods, timing and outcomes differ radically.

God will wait patiently until the end of ages, and only then, when everything will be annihilated by an apocalyptic catastrophe, He will introduce his brand-new universe.

Nature, through millions or billions of years will carry out in the bosom of its invisible force, the gradual transformation of every single particle of our creation, eagerly pursuing an incredible evolutionary path, until some unforeseen event will truncate this chain of mutations and transformations.

Finally, **man**, callously disregarding God's and nature's methods and timing, since he does not possess their luxuries of infinite (God) or quasi-infinite (nature) time, and spurred by his insatiable appetite to reform, improve and create, will embark on a mysterious journey of unprecedented manipulation and alteration, not only of minerals and vegetables, but mainly of animals and human beings.

Where this will lead, nobody knows. The only certain thing is that man will stop at nothing in order to ultimately attain the coveted goal of improving and ameliorating whatever is subject to change.

Unlike God or nature, man will not respect any law or moral imperative, dictated by reason or religion.

Unlike God or nature, man's timing is here and now. His methods have not changed since time immemorial: whoever opposes his conquest will face extermination.

Will God or nature accept this intrusive arrogance, or will they fight back and in so doing utterly destroy the destroyer in the process? Nobody really knows, even if the prospective of ominous consequences looms on the horizon.

Our fictional story takes place in this blazing hot context, as a direct result of human manipulation.

Chapter I

One memorable morning, Heloise awoke feeling on top of the world. What a marvelous way to begin a new day! She had not felt that great since the merry days of her bygone childhood.

The energy springing from deep inside her being made her believe that everything was possible. Obstacles, fears, hesitations had lost their firm hold on her bursting personality.

How could she explain this surreal psychological state of mind? She looked around, almost intrigued by this rare phenomenon, but all seemed perfectly normal: weather, sunrise, city rumors and even the indistinct smell pervading her space.

Without wasting any time, she got dressed, fixed her hair and added a light touch of makeup to her face.

The large mirror standing in front of her reflected a gentle face with a subtle smile that could melt the hardest bureaucratic posture.

In her short working life, Heloise had learnt a simple lesson for survival: smoothness and civility were the only keys to people's heart.

Moreover, as a lawyer and a member of a large law firm in the capital city, those distinguishing qualities were essential.

Grabbing her portfolio, full of documents and legal papers, she locked the door of her apartment and walked straight to the elevator.

The short commute in her splendid Ferrari was unusually speedy. The traffic seemed lighter and less congested. The air was crisp and invigorating.

Human, nature and machine shared in the same jubilant concert of the morning's rebirth with an emotional song of gratitude.

In that extraordinary mood of empathy with nature, Heloise stepped into her office, feeling invincible.

Sustained by an irrepressible vigor, she began organizing her day and getting ready for a demanding court session.

To all appearances, it looked like a normal day; the only difference was the extraordinary charge of renewed optimism and emotional well-being that sprung from some unidentified source.

Was that an undeserved bonus or a totally earned reward for a blameless conduct? On the other hand, was nature playing a cruel trick on a poor soul, unaware of the blind dynamics and mysterious laws of our universe?

Heloise did not have the time or the desire to psychoanalyze herself, or to subject her intricate vital labyrinth of intellectual and emotional perceptions to a rigorous scrutiny.

Time was pressing and the impending arrival of her associates brought her back to the difficult tasks at hand. Could she disguise that euphoric state with a professional posture, or should she let her personality loose and shine immodestly?

Observing intently the wry faces of everyone entering the office, she perceived a subtle sense of guilt for not conforming to their gloomy facial expressions, so eloquent, even without uttering a word.

It was not the first time she had to ward off the environmental pressure, resisting the powerful forces of conformism and establishing herself as a unique individual.

In a society eager to please, it was neither a pleasant task nor a comfortable one to stand up and assert her uniqueness.

Our non-confrontational young lawyer, faced with the unprecedented dilemma of being herself or tolerating the unspoken rules of social behavior, chose a middle ground, toning down her overflowing exuberance, but allowing her expressive demeanor to emanate rays of light with soothing effects.

The outcome was quite unexpected. Every single colleague, in effect, after responding to the morning greetings and the usual exchanges of pleasantries, encapsulated himself or herself in an aura of selective mutism, isolating that poor creature, who did not pose any danger to anyone.

On the contrary, with her warm personality she was tearing down the invisible curtain of mediocrity behind which people felt comfortable and protected.

Under normal conditions, people could have genuinely assumed that some retaliatory measures were appropriate, but cleverly enough, Heloise, with her peculiar sense of composure and magnanimity, tried to ignore the silent treatment, quickly imposing her rules of fair play, so far removed from the little jungle in which she spent so many hours of her ordinary life.

There was no time to waste in petty office squabbles; more pressing matters required her attention.

She shuffled through the many judicial cases still pending. Almost instantly, she picked out of the stack the folder containing the defense of a young rapist, whose hearing was that very morning.

The alleged crime presented serious difficulties, concerning not the material act, which nobody was denying, but the victim's and perpetrator's characters.

The victim, a seventeen-year-old girl, notorious for her loose morals, used to conduct herself in a provocative manner and was aware of her significant impact on the excitable young males that unfortunately happened to be on her destructive path.

The perpetrator, barely eighteen and a cousin of the victim, was not very bright or educated, but despite this, he did not have any prior criminal offense. He was a first-time offender.

Heloise's defense would stress the diminished capacity of the youngster and the unsolicited provocation of the temptress, in order to obtain a lighter sentence for the offender, if not complete exoneration.

Could she succeed or would she face stiff opposition by the prosecutor and a veil of straight indifference from the unsympathetic jurors?

In similar cases, after accepting responsibility for the suspicious incident, it was an uphill battle to convince the jury of the victim's measurable share of accountability.

Heloise was perfectly aware of the thin ice on which she was treading. Honestly, she did not underestimate the perilous job she was taking upon herself.

Nevertheless, what frightened her most was her **physical and psychological makeup,** in which **libido, sexual instinct, fatal attraction and violent urges were completely absent**.

Unlike the rest of her schoolmates, playing flirtatious games and indulging in some romantic shenanigans, she never courted any boy, and she never felt any desire whatsoever to draw their attention.

Parents and teachers admired her irreprehensible conduct, portraying her as the supermodel of morality and seriousness.

Her total dedication to academic studies and extracurricular activities became legendary, converting her into a poster child for the perfect student.

If this image of herself was embraced and cherished during the high school years, the same image turned out to be cumbersome and inconvenient during her college education.

At that time, she began questioning herself seriously, whether the significant absence of passionate feelings for the opposite sex was normal or not.

How could she explain the absolute absence of sexual desires inside her little world, when from every corner of the universe and every angle of the global media, sex was the great motivator of the human race, and the biggest destabilizing factor in their daily life?

Had she been blessed or cursed by human nature? Would it not be odd to pretend to be better than anybody else, or simply normal when the whole world was marching in the opposite direction?

Would she ignore that awkward personal situation or should she seek professional help?

After a long period of torturing her soul to the point of shedding generous tears of desperation, she elected to accept herself as she was.

In the meantime, she would read as much as she could in specialized publications about sexual disorders and abnormal tendencies.

Surprisingly enough, after a lengthy period of tedious reading and deep self-examination, she did not come up with any earth-shattering discovery.

None of the sexual abnormalities listed or discussed in scientific publications she consulted, could expressly apply to her personal experience.

Nevertheless, there was something, within the broader realm of sexual pathology, which could have some bearing upon her singular life experience. That something was designated with a peculiar name—**sexual frigidity**.

The comprehensive description of that generic term, with which Heloise seemed to identify herself, appears very simple: "lack of sexual response in a woman." Too simple, maybe, to do justice to her intricate situation.

Despite the many doubts still tormenting the young woman and the inherent psychological maze, so perplexing and confusing, Heloise tried her hardest to be at peace with that uncomfortable persona and accept the handicap, seemingly hooked on her by nature, as an integral part of her life.

Still a persistent question emerged from time to time: was her sexual frigidity a result of her early rearing and sheltered upbringing, or something natural, as natural as the color of her eyes and the enchanting shape of her face? Or even worse, some diabolic tampering of her DNA, in order to obtain a new type of woman, impassible to the sexual storms of humankind?

Could anybody ever come up with a satisfactory explanation, and was there a real scientific answer?

For the time being, the uneasy mystery of the unwilling and frigid virgin will grow, the perplexities and uncertainties multiply, leaving a bitter taste and a feeling of general discontent.

If, on one hand, the significant absence of personal experience in this minefield of sexuality was intimidating and destabilizing, on the other, it would not dampen her high spirits, the same way her cheerful mood was not overpowered or weakened by her colleagues' sulky attitudes.

Heloise was fully competent and prepared to repel internal or external enemies with the same vigor and determination.

The young lawyer was a born fighter, who could not rest easily, unless her opponents beat the dust and retreated.

Recovering quickly from this self-examination, as if from a sudden flashback of past events on a steamy summer afternoon, Heloise wrote down some final annotations on her defense and after a perfunctory look at the clock, she was eager to rush to the courtroom.

However, something unexpected occurred. Her cellular rang. Surprised, she picked it up and answered with a hesitant voice.

"Hello, who is calling?"

"Hi, darling, it's Mom. How are you?"

Her voice sounded so different that Heloise had difficulty recognizing it. Startled, she responded,

"Hi, Mom. Sorry, I didn't recognize you. I'm fine. What's going on with you?"

"I'm calling because something terrible has happened. I confess that it's very difficult for me to put into words the grim news I'm about to share with you."

Heloise was becoming alarmed and stricken with fear and apprehension.

"Did anything happen to Dad?" Her dad was an elderly man, and she was constantly scared that something irreparable might happen at any time.

"No, fortunately nothing happened to Dad. He's fine. But your friend Angie passed away. She was found dead in her bed. They suspect suicide."

"Mom, Angie would never do such a thing! Not even as a last resort. She had her unresolved problems, like any other human being, but nothing in her life would justify such a desperate act."

"Apparently, that is the preliminary conclusion of the coroner. Maybe we should wait for his final report."

"Mom, I'm on my way to court, but I'll come home straight after that. As Angie's lawyer, obviously with her husband's and parents' indulgence, I want to pay my last respects to my dearest friend and witness the scene of that horrible event."

"Okay, darling, with pleasure I will take upon myself to inform that household of your intentions. See you soon."

"See you, Mom. I love you. Bye."

Heloise, pale and trembling, shut her eyes, reclined her head against the chair, and paused, trying to absorb the deadly blow.

Her exuberant mood had vanished, and her confidence had disappeared as if under a witch's spell. The very promising day was slowly mutating into a nightmare.

Angie had been like a twin sister to Heloise, a close friend, and a real confidante. Since kindergarten, through elementary and high school, up to college, they had shared almost everything.

Now her companion was gone forever. No more laughs, parties or silly tricks. No more enjoyable get-togethers, no more indulging in childhood and adolescent reminiscences.

Heloise could not come to terms with this suffocating reality; she could no longer look at people's faces as she had before. She perceived herself as diminished, lessened, almost halved.

It would take her a long time to reemerge from the abyss of desperation and confusion and retake full control of her life.

Still, in an awful state of mind, she performed in a robotic way the next steps. Without knowing how, she found herself in the courtroom facing an ecstatic judge and a bewildered jury.

Always attentive to the court's mood and the facial expressions of her audience, this crucial time she carried on her prepared defence mechanically, in the same manner as if nobody were present or listening to her.

It was not surprising that the young rapist was convicted and sentenced without extenuating circumstances.

This fact resulted in a serious setback for Heloise's professional reputation, and a serious blow to the firm's good name.

Would this regrettable episode come back to haunt her? Regrettably, yet naturally, nothing in life is without consequences, whether one likes it or not.

After that unusual session, an even more unusual departure took place. Heloise did not talk to her client or his parents, did not greet the prosecution or the judge— she just disappeared.

As her mind and heart were detached and unsympathetic during the defense, the same way her conduct appeared odd and unexpected now. It was clear that another Heloise, strange and cantankerous, was replacing the old one, charming and delightful.

The distraught young woman ran down the steps of the vetust justice building, as if a predator were chasing after her, turned on her car, and dashed to her dead friend's house, heedless of her disheveled appearance.

Upon her arrival, Angie's husband and relatives greeted her with an ill-concealed hostility. They definitely gave the clear impression that her presence was unwanted and unwelcome.

She did not take any offense or feel any resentment in the presence of that unpleasant reception. However, she failed to comprehend the motives behind their conduct.

Overlooking that situation of palpable tension, capable of creating anger and resentment, Heloise hesitantly stepped into the room where Angie lay lifeless. Looking at that pale face, motionless and destitute of expression, Heloise burst into silent tears.

Paralyzed by a sudden blow of agonizing pain, she remained petrified. Only hell, if it existed, could come close to the intense suffering she was enduring.

She would never again hear the sound of Angie's mellifluous voice, never again laugh in unison with her. That was the end of a marvelous friendship, cut short by a cruel destiny.

They were so different and yet so complementary at the same time.

Heloise was wise beyond her years, while Angie was wild beyond imagination. The first was shy and a little introverted, the second gregarious and popular. One kept away from parties, loud celebrations and goliardic manifestations, the other was the soul of all campus activities, from cheerleading to thespian entertainments. But above all, Heloise was ethically principled and morally unbending, while Angie was malleable under peer pressure and adaptable to all the changing conditions.

Yet, beneath her deceiving façade, Angie was hiding a turbulent reality. Like her dearest friend Heloise, she too was **frigid**. Her relations with the male species were superficial and outward at best.

In fact, her beautiful and luminous sky was often darkened by spells of a somber depression.

Socially adaptable as she was, she married a student, with whom she had a meaningless affair, pressured by both families. Obviously, the romantic affair had resulted in an unwanted pregnancy.

Those were the years of free love, sexual experimentation and disastrous relationships.

Angie could not move away from that generational push toward total freedom from any type of inhibition, despite her lack of sexual drive. Marriage was certainly the biggest mistake of her life.

Heloise will never forget the morning after, when Angie showed up for a study group, still blissfully unaware of her unintended pregnancy.

Her habitual, radiant face betrayed a weird expression of someone returned from a bloody battle where all the conventional ethical lines had been blown away, and the parameters of normal values lost forever.

Paradoxically, her shallowness of inherited character showed welcome signs of a painful awareness. She could not hide her uncomfortable situation, and her deep disappointment for an action considered liberating at the moment of carrying it out, but devastating after the fact.

Later on, when the tumultuous water of her overflowing river of thoughtlessness and carelessness had passed, a sense of relief eventually won possession of her intelligent mind, and she almost blessed her moment of insanity.

Being pregnant was perhaps the most rewarding mistake of her entire existence. Reminiscing the liturgy of the Holy Friday, she wanted to sing the sacred hymn "*Oh, felix culpa!*" ("Oh, happy mistake!")

She did not experience any particular attraction to men, but she wholeheartedly loved children, and to have one of her own was the most fulfilling accomplishment of her unruly youth.

Angie would have generously given her life to protect that little treasure hidden in her womb, and would have done the impossible to raise him or her after birth.

Her mood swings became less apparent, her conduct acquired some semblance of normality, and she definitely turned the page, starting a new chapter in her life.

Her passion for children sent her off to medical school to become a pediatrician.

Heloise remembered with fondness those months of pregnancy, and those years of Angie as a new mom. They became even closer and despite their geographical separation, shared their treasures of expertise, one offering legal advice and the other health suggestions.

For all of this and for her keen sense of observation, Heloise did not believe—not even for a split second—in the suicide theory. Angie had too much to look forward to, to end her life in such a cowardly manner.

Conversely, how could anybody suspect a family member of such an atrocious and violent crime? It would be preposterous, if not insane, to pursue such a line of investigation.

Nevertheless, the unexplained death of her friend was testing everybody's acuity of mind for a reasonable explanation, or at least an acceptable answer.

Unfortunately, the puzzle, with the passing of days and months, would acquire more twists and turns than anybody would have ever imagined.

Heloise, between generous tears and tremulous movements of her body, solemnly swore to her dear departed Angie that she would leave no stone unturned in discovering the real cause of her untimely death, despite what the coroner or any other expert said.

No one would stop her from uncovering the undisputed truth. She would conduct an unflinching crusade to find the underlying cause of that tragedy, no matter how painful it turned out to be.

From now on, she would add a new facet or dimension to her profession. She would anoint herself lawyer/detective and pursue with aggressiveness the illusive truth.

Before leaving that place of sorrow, she kissed the gelid front of her friend's inanimate body, offered her heartfelt condolences to the relatives, and very politely asked whether Angie had left any note of explanation or justification.

Without uttering a word, a relative showed Heloise the adjacent room, where the local police had just finished going through Angie's personal belongings.

No paper or note caught her anxious eyes, because there was none. However, something extremely familiar attracted her attention. Among the credit cards, one stood out of the pile due to its peculiar color and logo.

It was a familiar one, in fact she too possessed one, generously given to her by her father the day she passed the Bar exam and became a lawyer. Heloise would never forget her father's stern warning. Instead of encouraging her to use it frequently, as is customary, he instructed her to use it only in a dire economic emergency to try to avoid bankruptcy or total destitution. If used for frivolities or unnecessary goods, the anonymous institution would cancel it immediately and permanently.

So far, she was lucky enough to have a steady and sizeable income, without being forced to cast her lots on that last anchor of salvation.

Heloise was quite surprised at the discovery. Despite their privileged friendship, there were blind spots in their relationship.

The credit card's color was a rare light purple and the logo a stylized drawing of something resembling a medieval chastity belt with the letter C printed on it. The name of that plastic was most unusual too—**Moral Phalanx**.

The young lawyer had never tried to scratch beneath the surface of that alien-like card. Now, confronted with her friend's death, it was imperative to undertake a perilous expedition, using all the resources at her disposal.

She was not discouraged by the unjustified hostility surrounding her personal investigation, or by the animosity she could create along the journey. At this point, nothing would deter her from carrying out her noble mission and bringing closure to Angie's perplexing demise.

First thing she did, after returning to her office, was to sit down at her desk, switch on the computer, and search for the word "**phalanx**."

She had just finished inputting the recondite word in the search engine, when a colleague, by the fancy name of Brunilda, approached her and, all smiles and feminine finesse, said: "My condolences for the loss of your best friend. How did it go? Did you obtain any new information on the cause of her death?"

Polite, but carefully cautious, Heloise answered, "Thank you for your sympathy. And no, I did not get anything different from what the relatives and the coroner had already said."

"Let us hope for the best. Have a good day."

"I appreciate your interest, and I thank you again. See you later," Heloise replied.

Heloise returned to her search, not sure what to make of that spur-of-the-moment outpouring of sympathy from a senior co-worker.

Anyhow, among the avalanche of pertinent information given, she chose two definitions by the *Oxford English Dictionary*.

"A body of heavily-armed infantry drawn up in close order, with shields touching and long spears overlapping" and "A number or set of persons, etc., banded together for a common purpose, esp. in support of or in opposition to some cause; a united front; (also) the union so formed."

The first definition described accurately an ancient military formation; the second applied metaphorically the same concept to modern organizations, non-military in nature.

Since "**phalanx**" was modified by the adjective "**moral**," the implied meaning resulted in something peculiar: the mysterious society "**phalanx**" was conducting its battles not with real weapons, but with some other unknown arms, in order to support a cause, possibly the moralization of society.

All this was very puzzling. How could anybody make a society better in a moral sense by using a credit card, which, by the way, could be utilized only in a dire economic emergency?

Moreover, what was the significance of that stylized drawing, symbolizing an alleged chastity belt with the letter C printed on it? Was this the case of a criminal organization engaging in women slavery?

A good detective would not discard any interpretation or possibility. However, this last one appeared too far-fetched and overstated to be true.

If that credit card was any clue to a secret organization and its possible criminal intents, which looked very unlikely, the only effective way to discover it was to trace a credible map of potential candidates for that unenviable title.

This mad reverie was not helpful at all. Therefore, Heloise, depressed by the sudden disappearance of her friend and overwhelmed by the dark prospect of its causes, put a drastic halt to her brooding over the day's events, switched off her computer and went for a walk.

She wanted to clear her mind and heart. She desperately needed calm and serenity. Besides, she required guidance and expertise.

The following day, imbued with a more serene spirit and enlightened by better ideas, Heloise had an informal meeting with a police officer, an acquaintance of hers who dealt with criminal investigations.

During the lengthy talk, the seasoned investigator offered her some valuable hints.

First of all, Heloise should keep a low profile, to avoid suspicion, while searching for facts that do not square with the official version.

Secondly, she should arm herself with patience and shrewdness, suspecting the unsuspected. Only work and perseverance would reap the right reward.

Finally, no crime is ever perfect. There is always a hidden clue, a fingerprint, DNA, an indiscretion that can lead the investigator to the realistic solution of a case.

With this in mind, Heloise would embark on a personal crusade, never imagined or considered before.

The coroner's final report, as suspected, was no surprise to anyone. The cause of death was the result of a cardiac arrest induced by some hypnotic and sedative drug.

As Angie's lawyer, Heloise requested and obtained an independent examination. Unfortunately, the new medical examiner reached the same conclusion: death caused by an overdose.

The door to new findings appeared permanently shut and Angie's good name lost forever.

With nothing on her hands, but a strange and maybe insignificant credit card, Heloise had everything to lose and nothing to gain from that wild goose chase.

She was going, like a battering ram, against influential public officials (district attorney, police investigators, medical examiner, etc.), and what was even worse, against the reputability of Angie's husband and relatives.

The only cogent reason she had for that obsessive behavior, was her sincere love for her departed friend and her young orphan child.

She would wait a while before having an informal chat with the poor surviving girl. She could be, in fact, an unsuspected source of precious information.

Nevertheless, a conversation with her father, provider of the credit card, could not be delayed.

She had not been in touch with him in the last couple of months. Since childhood, their rapport had been intermittent, because of her father's hectic schedule.

What she remembered most, during the school years, were the short presences and long absences. She respected him, because he was a powerful man, but she was not sure of her feelings toward him.

He provided her with a splendid education, the finest things in life, and the security of being there for her, whenever she was in need of something. Without any doubt, he was the provident father of which any daughter would have dreamt or desired.

She adored him, without perhaps experiencing filial emotions and tender love. Scrutinizing the depths of her soul, she asked many times whether that was a byproduct of her sexual frigidity, or the direct cause of her father's deportment.

Digging into her past, she could not come up with a memory of a single embrace of affection, or even a warm kiss on her cheek.

This did not prevent her from consulting him, when the occasion arose. Now was the time to reconnect, and she did not hesitate to meet with him.

A telephone conversation would not be enough, because she planned to pour out her heart, and wanted to observe her father's facial expressions, listen to the inflection of his potent voice, and examine his body language.

If something turbid could surface, she would press until finding the undisputed truth.

As soon as they met, Heloise could not help noticing a change in her father's normal expression. It appeared something suspicious and hurtful was lurking in the back of his mind.

Asked about the credit card, in a very business-like manner, he gave her his official explanation.

"To be honest, I ignore the corporation behind the card. I found out about its existence through a very good friend of mine. He passed away a few years back. I was impressed by the new concept of a secure economic future, and I genuinely believed it could be a marvelous present for my only girl. That's all I can tell you."

"Do you know," insisted Heloise, "the meaning of the logo or the significance of **Moral Phalanx**?"

"Honestly, I never bothered about it up to this very instant. Me too, I would be curious to know what it represents and symbolizes. But why this sudden interest in a piece of plastic that has been in your possession for quite a while?"

"Oh, nothing, Dad. Just curiosity." By proffering those words, Heloise was fully aware of being untruthful to her father. However, she did not mind, knowing that perhaps he was first betraying her trust.

They kept chatting, jumping from one subject to another, the way people do when they find an unstable ground beneath their feet.

They departed amicably despite a deep dissatisfaction in the young lawyer and a great suspicion in the millionaire owner of a fast-food chain.

Reflecting after the fact, Heloise was positive that her father knew much more than he made known. After careful examination of his statements, she was sure he was lying.

Only somebody prone to lying would start his sentences with "To be honest" or "Honestly."

The biggest contradiction, however, lay in the fact that she was the only heiress to a multibillion-dollar empire, and thus did not need any card to assure her economic future.

To top that, her father's body language was more eloquent and explanatory than any of his deceitful words. She could swear there was more to that card than just a simple insurance.

Would it constitute the key to solving the mystery of her friend's death, or would it turn out to be a red herring, not worth pursuing?

Was she going over her head in a sterile pursuit of a deadly chimera? She was very baffled and in mental disarray.

If she could not trust her own father, who could she lean on? Certainly not Angie's husband or parents. Maybe some light could come from an unimpeachable source—the surviving daughter, Karina.

Angie's funeral was the perfect occasion to exchange a few words with the eight-year-old girl. They knew each other, and Karina felt a special attachment to Heloise.

Before the commencement of the obsequies, while they were waiting for the minister to arrive, the young lawyer inconspicuously approached the girl. She was holding hands with her maternal grandmother, and she looked terrific in her black dress with a white collar, a little hat and patent leather shoes. Her composure and dignified seriousness were touching.

She was glad to see Heloise, who in her young mind was her closest confidante, after her mom.

They exchanged a prolonged and emotional hug, as tears fell silently from their faces.

Still wrapped in that moving embrace, Heloise broke the magic of that crucial moment. "I'm so sorry, Karina, for your tragic loss. I don't have adequate words to express all my sympathy and sorrow. However, remember, I am here, and I love you immensely. Nobody can substitute your mom, but your grandparents, your relatives, and I will stand by you, always."

With a soft and emotional voice, Karina said, "Thank you, thank you very much."

Heloise, taking her gently a few steps back from her grandmother and some close relatives, with motherly persuasion, said. "Could I ask you a couple of questions?"

"Yes" was the simple answer from Karina.

"Do you remember anything out of the ordinary, the day before your mom died?"

That little, adorable face suddenly became less bright and a dark cloud seemed to obscure the serenity of her innocent soul.

"I was in my room," Karina began her brief recollection, "after supper, doing my homework, when an argument broke out between Mom and Dad. They raised their voices in anger, and I was afraid."

"Do you remember what the argument was about?"

"I heard the word 'divorce' several times and my father saying repeatedly, 'Never, never, never!'"

"I'm very grateful, Karina, that you answered my questions. I love you."

"I love you too," replied the girl, unaware of how invaluable her help had been.

The burial ceremony had begun, and the two mourners took their place in the front row. Karina was holding a beautiful rose, to be placed on her mom's coffin. She witnessed the short ritual without crying, but when she saw her mom being lowered into the ground, she could not refrain from her emotions. Hiding her face in her grandmother's bosom, she sobbed inconsolably.

Her mom was gone forever. Nobody was more conscious of that ineluctable fact than she. From now on, she would be an orphan.

They all left the cemetery with a huge emptiness in their hearts. However, before leaving, Heloise sealed her brief charged encounter with a kiss and a goodbye to Karina, and a handshake with the relatives.

Raw emotions were still boiling over, while driving in the direction of her apartment. Impatient to reach her destination, she did not realize the traffic was almost at a standstill, because of a terrible accident a few hundred yards ahead.

Moving at a snail's pace, she eventually reached the exact location of the crash and observed one of the victims being put on a stretcher by paramedics while a police officer was examining his documents.

What immediately caught her eyes was not the man's motionless body covered in flowing blood and the horrific scene with different people screaming, but the familiar color of a credit card, lying on the asphalt beside the investigating police officer.

She could not believe her eyes, as if it were a trick played by the reflection of the sun on the windscreen of her car.

Was she having an hallucination, where images and sounds generate spontaneously in the mind as the result of an altered mental state? Alternatively, was it a real physical object lying on the pavement of the highway as a reminder of a mysterious reality, unknown to profane eyes?

Heloise did not have a chance to verify the fact by stopping and questioning the local authority in charge.

She had to move on, and only later, through bits and pieces, she tried to compile a profile of the victim.

Painstakingly, she collected valuable information, starting with the name, profession and address. The local visual media revealed the primary data, while the newspapers somehow completed the picture.

The crash victim, who unfortunately breathed his last breath while en route to the hospital, was a young university professor by the name of Icarus Proctor. His teaching, on Foreign Policies, at one of the most prestigious universities in the country, was quite controversial, to say the least.

The dean of the faculty had quite a few headaches from conservative politicians and puritan academic authorities. Despite the many storms he had to sail through, he never withdrew or diminished his confidence in the rebellious lecturer.

With this information, Heloise had to positively establish the possession of that credit card by Icarus.

Through some difficult maneuvering and thanks to the help of friends at the police station, she received a list of Proctor's possessions.

Unbelievably, "Moral Phalanx" was right there in black and white with a big question mark. Apparently, the officer, who composed the list, was confounded by the weird name of the plastic and wanted to let others know about his overall feelings with that punctuation.

Heloise declared her mission accomplished and with some sense of satisfaction, she was ready to slay a hideous monster, hidden in some secret organization.

Upon reflection, she concluded that her life would soon change radically. In fact, two tragedies, with apparently nothing in common, could be tied to her destiny because of a piece of plastic.

Were these wild imaginations or sensible premonitions?

In the solitude of her apartment, Heloise took into her hands the "*Moral Phalanx*" and paused cogitatively for a long time, listening in her head to the whispering of ultrasound fantasies, in a flight formation.

Their movement was unidirectional, their insinuation univocal and their significance unmistakable.

Some secret organization existed out there, with precise rules and well-defined aims. It was imperative for the young lawyer/detective to sit down, gather all her strength, and begin her covert investigation with gusto.

During the few and far between intervals from her hectic professional activity, Heloise jotted down, in a black notebook with ruled pages, the minimum requirements needed for a professional institution to become the issuer of a credit card.

Since the very beginning, two main characteristics stood out: **economic power** and **religious activity**. Without those two elements, no organization could claim the paternity of the card. She could add some other attributes, like secrecy, purity, virginity, but they were not essential.

Among the numerous organizations that could fit into that definition, one emerged as a clear winner: the Catholic Church.

Could that be a valid clue to pursue, or was it simply an aberration of an overheated and delirious mind still in shock at the recent events?

Whatever the consequences, Heloise was determined to venture into very unfamiliar territory, and with the help of a young priest, who had proudly graduated in Rome, she would take her first steps into that venerable ground called the Catholic Church.

She was not Catholic, neither had she belonged to any organized religion, but despite her non-theistic and secular background, she nurtured a great respect and reverence for Catholicism.

For a profane eye, Heloise appeared utterly qualified for an impassionate research project into one of the most ancient and sacred organizations on earth.

Furthermore, her burning desire to undertake such an exciting journey was giving her wings.

As any young, inexperienced detective she pictured her search and discovery as marvelous and successful.

That memorable day, she went home tired and with overflowing emotions. Heart and mind were galloping, free of restraints, through the realm of infinite possibilities. Up in the blue sky, a gorgeous rainbow promised a rosy and hopeful future.

Chapter II

Mark Centurion, Heloise's father, was a man of great reputation in the business world.

After his brief encounter with his daughter, from whom he separated on good terms but with a bitter taste in his mouth, he solicitously called Brunilda, Heloise's senior co-worker and supervisor at the law firm.

Heloise, thanks to her physical proximity to Brunilda, overheard some isolated words of their conversation.

What caught her attention and awakened her curiosity was Brunilda's submissive, almost servile, tone of voice, and her mechanical repetition after every single pause of, "Yes, Mr. Mark; Yes, Mr. Mark; Yes, Mr. Mark."

She did not know of any Mr. Mark among her co-worker's bosses, relatives or acquaintances. Was there any connection between Brunilda and her father, Mark Centurion?

The link between the two was closer and deeper than anyone could have ever imagined.

In that unsuspected conversation, as a matter of fact, Mark Centurion asked Brunilda, who had been on his secret payroll for many years, to follow Heloise's every unexpected move and report immediately to him, even the most insignificant of her activities.

Heloise did not realize that Brunilda was at Angie's funeral, wearing a black veil over her face and a huge hat, making her indistinguishable among the crowd of mourners.

Heloise never suspected that Brunilda, with her mellifluous smile and sticky sweet manners, had been spying on her since her first day at work. Her secretive and ambiguous activity would remain concealed for a long time.

The dynamic young lawyer, with her sixth sense, never felt at ease and comfortable in her dealings with the senior co-worker, but she never smelled a rat either.

If Brunilda's activity was reprehensible, what could be said about Centurion's behavior? Which role was he playing in this drama—the caring and solicitous father or the ruthless and unsparing ideologue, whose only intent was to achieve his ambitious dreams of domination and controlling human minds and bodies?

So far, there were not enough elements to categorize the famous captain of industry. On the surface, he was all philanthropic, but in reality nobody knew him well.

His trajectory to stardom had a very humble beginning. Born from a family of scarce economic means, as youngster he had to deliver newspapers, mow lawns and flip burgers in order to scrape together a few dollars for his basic necessities.

By enlisting in the army, he could achieve some higher education, molding at the same time his character and future personality.

During his hard training as a cadet, his sergeant noticed an extraordinary intensity in him, and praising his efforts and achievements, jokingly, told him, "You can be more than a centurion, you can become a general."

In the roman army, a centurion was in charge of one hundred soldiers. Mark's rank in the military, according to his superior, would become much higher than that. Moreover, he was perfectly right, because during the Korean War, Mark Centurion reached the rank of Sergeant Major.

With the end of that war, the brilliant officer came back to civilian life. As he excelled in the army, so he sought success in business.

His rare intuition saw an opening in the fast-food industry, and he did not hesitate to consult experts in the sector. Counting on their cooperation, he put together a strategic plan.

The result was brilliant. Originally from Nebraska, corn and pigs country, he cast aside poultry and beef and concentrated on pork chops.

In his home state, he began with a handful of places, where with ingenuity and inventiveness, he perfected his recipe and marketing techniques.

In a short time, the swine franchise (by the fancy name of "Happy Pork Chop," and not "Centurion" as somebody had suggested,) spread like wildfire throughout the state. No wonder it took only a couple of years to be recognized by the stock market first as a national chain and later an international one.

The recipe concocted by Mark Centurion and his closest chefs was extremely simple. The prime pork chops were marinated in olive oil, Japanese vinegar, garlic and rosemary and grilled over a low open flame.

If the ingredients and method were not a mystery, the quality of the meat, quantity of the ingredients and timing of the whole process was certainly a heavily guarded secret.

Another requirement that contributed enormously to the rapid spread of the retail business was the creation of pig farms not far from the fast-food establishments. This ensured that the meat would never arrive frozen at the consumption table.

In view of this technique, the final product was a delicious one. The "Happy Pork Chop" always delivered juicy, tender and flavorful chops that would melt in your mouth, leaving an amazing sensation of lightness and satisfaction.

Mark Centurion was proud of his creation and the fast-food industry, at one of its annual meetings, bestowed on him the title of the "Supreme Master."

The discipline instilled in his chefs was legendary, because it was based on the army values of honor and sacrifice. Their selection and training was rigorous, and their salary so competitive that even seasoned cooks from famous restaurants were deserting their posts to join them.

Useless to say that advertising became outmoded and obsolete for the new fast-food chain.

The amount of wealth generated by this industry was staggering. Centurion could not believe his eyes. Pretty soon he topped the charts of the richest people on the planet.

While he was keeping a tight reign on his first-born industry, he was eager to expand and diversify into other sectors.

It did not come as a surprise when the gourmet guru poured his millions into the construction of fantastic hotels in the most spectacular places of the five continents.

He started in Kaanapali, Maui, with a grandiose project, the envy of the giants in the architectural world. The new construction would not only attract thousands of tourists, but it would also serve as a convention center.

Nature had endowed that place with moderate temperatures, sandy beaches, spectacular views of the ocean, and breathtaking sunsets with Lanai and Molokai as backdrops.

Like dormant monsters of the sea, they protected against hostile aggressions from any real or mythical creatures.

The opening of the Centurion Hotel (that was its name) was carried out with pomp and circumstance in the most imposing and lavish Hawaiian style.

Mark's wife, Magdalene, and daughter, Heloise, were there for the occasion, with hundreds of other relatives and friends, smiling and basking in the glory of an empire at its zenith.

However, Centurion's most astounding creation, still in its preliminary stages, was a model city, where crimes and vices were strictly banned.

Any aspirant to live in that piece of heaven on earth had to pass a rigorous physical, moral and ideological exam. A strict code of conduct would be enforced at all times.

The happy residents would benefit from the best educational system, most comprehensive healthcare system, safest police protection, most dynamic business development, most modern and nature-friendly housing, and the most spectacular city planning ever.

If something perfect, or close to perfection, could be achieved in this world, that was certainly it.

At its completion, that city, carrying the name of Mary (probably a reference to the Virgin Mary), would reject any official religious foundation. God would not be the cornerstone of the new community. As a matter of principles, it would tolerate any private and personal belief.

Even if not publicly known, famous Christian leaders were enthusiastic about this project, because tolerance for them equaled freedom to proselytize. Among the many prominent clergymen who gave their full support, one stood out, by the name of Paul Marcikkus (not to be confused with the historical figure Mons. Paul Marcinkus).

His unwavering backing raised serious questions within the Catholic Church, and questioned Marcikkus' real motives.

Notwithstanding the controversy, this creation, which resembled the New Jerusalem of the Bible, was something very special, that had never existed before, not even during the Middle Ages, where officially Christianity permeated every fabric of society.

The City of Mary would be a beacon of salvation and inspiration, in the modern ocean of corruption and perdition. It might also become a real awakening and a stimulus for many metropolises around the world, plagued by violence and decadence.

Feeding the masses with excellent and affordable pork chops might turn out to be a great accomplishment, but providing a safe and first-rate environment, where to raise a family was certainly one of the noblest missions ever embraced by man.

Centurion was proud of this achievement, and despite his poor academic background, he made every effort to elaborate a coherent doctrine that would support and justify his new world vision.

Life, first in poverty, later in the army and business, taught him so many valuable lessons that he strongly believed the time was ripe to put in writing the pearls of wisdom crystallized during his long career.

He was neither a philosopher nor a theorist, but a practical man seasoned in the crucible of pain, sweat and toil.

Mark was sure that his words would resonate in the minds and hearts of youngsters and seniors alike, because they were condimented in blood and not inspired by books or speculations.

Modern life was founded in fanciful myths and appalling misconceptions. He genuinely believed that it was one of his fundamental duties to uncover their fallacies.

Advertising was the most deceptive machine ever invented by man in order to shape and mold people's minds.

Centurion would create his own pulpit by becoming a public speaker, an inspirational motivator. Tirelessly, he would slay these modern monsters one-by-one, and like St. George, he would free the masses from their fear and enslavement.

This would be the last crusade of his life, the mother of all battles, and the apogee of his aspirations.

In Washington, D.C., it was a gorgeous Friday morning. Springtime was in the air. Nature was bursting out of its winter cocoon with boldness and the entire creation was singing praises to life.

Mark Centurion, at the Ronald Reagan Washington National Airport, was waiting for his flight to Los Angeles, where he would deliver his first motivational speech at the Staples Center.

Accompanied by aides, ancillary workers and bodyguards, he preferred for this ideological punch-packed trip to use public transportation rather than his private jet.

The image that he intended to project of himself was that of a modern prophet in opposition to a tycoon.

He was about to board Alaska Airlines when he received a curious phone call. "Hi, Mr. Centurion. Welcome to the City of Angels!"

The sarcastic-sounding voice did not allow any suitable answer. Without muttering a word and with a surprised look on his face, Mark closed his cellular and proceeded to take his first-class seat.

Nobody dared to inquire about the surreptitious call, and the numerous members of his entourage kept chatting garrulously.

A subtle veil of trepidation seemed to have befallen Centurion's exuberant mood. The confidence and self-assurance were gone, replaced by a more cautious attitude.

However, the intrepid fighter would not allow an anonymous phone call to spoil his once-in-a-lifetime chance to shine.

Fame can be ephemeral; however, the impact of a talk might be everlasting in somebody's existence. Centurion was there to illuminate, guide and spur to greatness.

When the aircraft began flying over the huge Californian metropolis, the view was breathtaking. The city was spreading without limit from the ocean to the mountains, from the planes to the unreachable horizon.

Could he touch, with his inspiring ideas, even one minuscule portion of that immense population? Would this be his inaugural step in a triumphal march, or his swan song? Success rested purely on his shoulders.

As an experienced soldier and perceptive businessperson, he knew that any battle to be fought would need an intelligent plan.

The general outline of his speech would not refer to religion or politics. Jesus and Caesar, Church and State, undoubtedly the two major forces to be reckoned with in people's lives, could have awakened raw passions and offered the flank for cheap attacks.

Besides, the presence of prominent religious and political figures in that multicultural and diverse audience, from the cardinal to the governor, the mayor to the police chief, would strongly suggest a neutral approach to any type of argument.

For his theme, Centurion would draw from the well of his touching life experiences, without the need of foreign sources, or made-for-TV dramas.

From LAX, he was whisked away in a caravan of luxurious limousines. In the Miyako Hotel of downtown an array of dignitaries and employees gave him the warmest welcome. Mark was staying at a Japanese hotel, for one simple reason. He loved and admired that nation's culture and traditions. Their proverbial manners and finesse did not need any personal recommendation.

Everything was proceeding smoothly. It was four in the afternoon. His speech was scheduled for seven at the Staples Center.

That modern facility was packed. You could breathe an air of extraordinary expectation. Unlike other renowned speakers, Mark did not charge a penny. The attendance was totally free. When he appeared on the stage and approached the pulpit, an enthusiastic ovation greeted him.

Encouraged by that sympathetic reception, he smiled generously at the crowd and repeatedly thanked all the participants.

With a clear and resonant voice, Centurion praised Los Angeles' great tradition of tolerance and patriotism.

Without indulging in his laudatory opening, he tackled head-on his favorite subject: **instant gratification** and the **defacement of education**.

One of the greatest fallacies of our culture, an undeniable byproduct of our fast-moving technology, is the immediate attainment and satisfaction of our desires and dreams.

If on one hand, progress, improvement and change are beneficial and advantageous; on the other, the instantaneous satisfaction of our impulses, by overstepping the rules of nature, vilifies the deepest meaning of life.

As in the agricultural world, where one must observe and respect the meteorological seasons in order to plant and harvest, in the same manner human existence has its periods. By disregarding them, the rewarding harvest will never reach its maturation point, leaving the rightful owner empty-handed and ultimately starving.

To put it graphically, we could ascertain with some degree of certainty that **instant gratification is the killer of expectation**.

Possession and fruition without expectation lead to total depravation of true joy.

Lack of expectation and real satisfaction renders human existence meaningless.

Devoid of purpose, life ends up in an unbridled and wild conduct, and in some cases, in suicide or homicide.

This is the surprising chain of direct consequences stemming from the premise of **instant gratification.**

How many stars, after a meteoric career and reaching the pinnacle of fame and riches, suffered total emptiness in their lives!

Deprived of meaning and totally empty inside, they plunged into the abyss of desperation. Neither fame, riches, nor potent drugs could bring them back from their living hell. Desperate, blind and out of touch with reality, the only way out was depravation or suicide.

Obviously, this is not the Hollywood ending glamorized by its "make-believe" industry.

This "instant gratification" mentality is reflected in what we call, for lack of a better word, the **defaced education** of many parents. With the best of intentions, they want to provide their children with all the things their parents could not afford.

Forgetting or neglecting the basic needs of their offspring—affection, closeness and quality time—they overwork and overburden themselves. The accumulation of money becomes their overriding concern in order to provide for their families, not only the basic necessities but also the frivolities and the mere superfluous.

Every single whim of their children is met with the definite belief of doing the best for them, resulting in the worst educational trap. As a matter of fact, willy-nilly, they fail to realize that their duty is to provide what is absolutely needed, while the rest should be optional and conditional.

Optional. Parents should be able to exercise their freedom of choice and not be compelled by the tantrums of insensitive and ungrateful youngsters.

Conditional. Parents should be wise enough to impose strict conditions. Children can obtain extra things upon completion of chores, good grades at school, acceptable behavior at home and outside.

Nothing should be forced on the parents or children. However, while parents need to make use of their authority and guidance, children must accept limits and boundaries.

The modern family's permissiveness creates new generations of undisciplined, spoiled and selfish citizens, incapable of dedication, sacrifice and tolerance.

If we disapprove of domestication and indoctrination as forms of education, we must encourage discipline, hard work and communication as the true foundations of raising a child.

Education has been **defaced**, initially by imposition and authoritarianism and today by *laissez-faire* and *laissez-passer*.

Our mission is to reconstruct the true features of this important component of the fabric of our society, as a surgeon reconstructs the lineaments of a patient's disfigured face.

This is a sublime mission, almost divine, because we strive to complete what creation and God have left incomplete.

Mark Centurion, as a prophet of old times, but without thundering or uttering terrible menaces, concluded his insightful speech with a clear warning.

"Our great nation has in itself the seeds for amazing success or dismal failure, for greatness or decline, for expansion or self-annihilation. Prosperity or self-destruction are in our hands. By rejecting the path of **instant gratification** and **defaced education**, we opt for life; by accepting them, we choose death. Let us embrace the hard way and the sun of salvation and glory will shine upon us. God bless our marvelous and predestined country!"

Such an inspired conclusion, neither pessimistic nor optimistic, but deeply realistic and motivational, drew a roaring applause.

The audience seemed to agree wholeheartedly with what was proclaimed from that profane pulpit; moreover, it appeared animated to arrest the crazy movement toward massive suicide.

Mark and his friends were pleased with these results and could not believe the laudatory comments in the newspapers and other media. It had been a resounding success, more gratifying than any military action or business venture.

Obviously, not all could be rosy. A few critics pointed out some inconsistencies and contradictions between Mark's vision and his material realizations.

The cold and distant relationship between Mark and his daughter was no secret.

Nevertheless, for a while, the general perception remained highly positive. His generous contributions to several humanitarian and non-profit organizations converted him into a splendid philanthropist, worthy of respect and admiration.

Still basking in the glory of his marvelous speech, he wanted to pay a brief visit to some of his fast-food restaurants in San Diego.

The weather was splendid, as it usually is in the Southern California coastal areas. The trip was turning out to be pleasant and relaxing. Nothing like a Californian freeway and a scenic view of the ocean to put you in a great mood.

The people accompanying him—close friends, associates and bodyguards—were still ecstatic at how things had turned out in Los Angeles, and their conversations could not be any merrier.

All of a sudden, a roadblock near San Onofre detained the caravan, and some police officers asked Mr. Centurion, with rude manners and a menacing tone of voice, to step out of the car and follow them.

The bodyguards, well trained for any type of occurrence, immediately smelled imminent danger. They started scuffling with those alleged officers, delivering them some serious blows and dragging Mark back to the car.

In a matter of seconds, rounds of gunshots were heard. Injured people began screaming, some falling lifeless on the hot asphalt. The scene was immediately evacuated. The assailants fled, leaving behind a bloody massacre.

Five were dead, two bodyguards and three attackers. Several sustained injuries of varying degrees, among them Mark Centurion, whose left leg received a couple of bullets, and was bleeding profusely.

The paramedics arrived quickly along with several police officers.

Mark Centurion and the other injured people were transported by helicopter to Cedars-Sinai Medical Center, where they received the best possible care.

On the ground, where the confrontation and shooting had occurred, astonishment and bewilderment were still the overriding note. Everything had happened so fast that nobody could make any sense out of that bloody mess.

The only thing people realized was the sudden change of atmosphere. When the bullets began flying in all directions, fear and panic replaced confidence and happiness, everybody ran for cover, except the bodyguards who engaged in mortal combat without hesitation.

It took just a few minutes to jam up the San Diego Freeway for miles, creating a nightmare for travelers and transit authorities alike.

The news had just hit the airwaves when the FBI took over the primary investigation from the local police, putting a lead on the dissemination of any shred of information.

Was it a kidnapping for ransom, an act of intimidation by envious competitors, or just a senseless road-rage shooting, so common in Southern California?

Who was behind this despicable action? Petty criminals, or an organized crime syndicate?

The national law enforcement agency's task was to find the motive and the mastermind, and bring finality.

Mark Centurion, who in his entire life never came so close to death, needed to know who his deadly enemy was. He could not keep living with the constant fear of a sneaky attack behind his back. Like never before, he came to the painful realization of his own mortality. From the pinnacle of fame and glory, for the first time, he looked into the eyes of death, into the bowels of total extinction.

It was a frightening experience that gave him a new outlook on life.

Thousands of miles away from the crime scene, Mark's family, through bits and pieces of news, learned the fate of their relative.

Heloise, his daughter, could not have been more shocked by the distressing event, while Magdalene, his wife, began crying inconsolably.

They were all still grieving over Angie's unfortunate suicide, when their hearts began bleeding again.

Their emotional anchor, their Rock of Gibraltar, was failing them, leaving their individual existences unprotected and at the mercy of giant, scary waves.

Heloise, her heart in her mouth, decided to take the first flight out of Ronald Reagan Washington National Airport. Her mother, terrified of flying, would take the train instead.

They hugged each other, kissed each other tenderly, and then moved hastily to their separate destinations. They had not received any official news yet, and they were already on their way to Los Angeles.

During the flight across the country, Heloise had time to reflect on her relationship with her father, always lukewarm and distant. Lukewarm because her father, a military man, never indulged in displays of affection. Distant as a result of her father's prolonged absences from home.

Was this the right moment to repair the filial relationship so tarnished by years of neglect? Should she take the first step? Would his age move her father's heart to reconnect with his lonely daughter?

Despite a burning desire to get closer to her progenitor, Heloise could not find straight answers or easy solutions.

Her mother too was reflecting on the same subject, with the advantage, traveling by train, of having at her disposal much more time.

Her marital relationship had been rocky, over the many years of that union. In the past, a few undisclosed infidelities threatened to end their stormy marriage. Only Magdalene's forgiving attitude saved Mark from a scandalous divorce.

Lately, their living together had acquired an air of normalcy and their affection had been sincere. Maybe his proximity with death could bring the two hearts even closer. That was exactly what Magdalene was hoping for.

She had been a good woman, an understanding wife and a solicitous mother. Even if nature does not automatically reward good people, certainly she deserved better treatment than she had received up till then.

Heloise, still with a sketchy notion from the news of her father's injuries, and fearing the worst, rushed to the hospital, anxious to see him and with dreams of a tender encounter.

Imagine her surprise to meet at his bedside two of her least favorite people, two grey eminences ("eminence grise"), whose presence instantly brought to naught her joyful expectation to reconnect with her father.

One was Brunilda Pusher, the senior lawyer and supervisor at her prestigious law firm, and the other, Brutus Barker (BB for short), Angie's husband and Chief Financial Officer (CFO) of Centurion's fast-food empire.

With her anticipations dashed and her heart more troubled than ever, instead of an affectionate hug, she grabbed her father's hand. Holding it tightly, as if it were her last salvation-anchor, she addressed him.

"How are you, Dad? Are you in pain?"

"I'm lucky to be here and to be alive. My only pain is to have caused you and your mom grief and unnecessary worries."

"You shouldn't feel sorry for us. Right now all that matters is you, only you. What's the doctor's diagnosis?"

"Thank you, darling. I'll be in a cast for a few months and if no complications occur, I'll be up and running."

"I'll keep you company until Mom arrives, and then I must return to my duties in Washington, D.C."

With unusual resolve, but in a polite manner, she told Brunilda and Brutus she wanted to be alone with her father.

Unconvinced, the two watchdogs looked into Mark's eyes. He nodded slightly. Their master, without using words, had spoken. They had no other option but to leave promptly, their tails between their legs.

Heloise, more confident and more confiding, asked her father.

"Dad, were you interviewed by the FBI and did you receive any preliminary report from them?"

"I was interviewed extensively. Honestly, I wasn't pleased with some of their questions."

"Why?"

"Because they gave me the impression they suspect something sinister, an inside job, or at least carried out with some help from the inside."

"Dad, I think that's a fairly routine approach. You must suspect everybody, with the exclusion of no one."

"But that bothers me immensely. The only ones who had knowledge of our schedule and itinerary were two of my most trusted people."

"Dad, let the FBI do their job. They'll realize soon enough if that is a cold trail."

Heloise had her own suspicions, running in the same direction as the FBI. She could not speculate or elaborate, for lack of solid evidence, but her gut feelings were pointing in one direction and one direction only.

She dared not share any of those feelings with her father, because she did not wish to hurt his pride since he thought of himself as a good judge of character.

That would have offended him deeply, making irreparable their estrangement and final their rift.

Inquisitive, and in this case justifiably so, she wanted to have a talk with one of the federal agents.

By profession, this agent, Luke Mayer, was primarily a profiler and not a field investigator. He was working on her father's alleged kidnapping among other cases.

When Heloise questioned him, he pulled out from a stack of folders, a brown one. It was not very thick. Only a few pages with handwritten observations by the three officers, present at the crime scene.

Those agents, after taking pictures and collecting evidence, cordoned off the entire area. Subsequently, they thoroughly inspected every inch of it.

They all agreed on some generic conclusions. First of all, it wasn't a casual drive-by shooting. Secondly, the criminal act was prepared well in advance. It was staged after meticulous planning and preparation, involving a good amount of money and quite a few experts in that type of assault.

Finally, it could not have taken place without the support of an insider. Otherwise why would the car transporting Brunilda and Brutus have not even a scratch while the others were bullet-riddled?

Luke Mayer, upon sharing these preliminary conclusions, promised Heloise that the agency would do the impossible to find the underlying cause of the senseless and vicious massacre.

Needless to say that the young lawyer left the meeting with a reinforced conviction of an accomplice nestled among her father's closest aides.

The two tragedies, Angie's mysterious death and her father's deadly assault, coming so close together, ended the age of innocence in Heloise's world outlook.

The widespread conviction that **everything happens for a reason and some good always comes from evil** no longer held true for the good-natured, trusting young woman.

There were sinister forces at work on the world stage, apparently unstoppable and unexplainable, pulling people and societies into deadly confrontations.

Any passive attitude was condemned to abuse and humiliation; any blind acceptance to extinction.

Heloise, under the heavy weight of these experiences, was ready to hold the reins of her life in her hands and choose the direction of her destiny.

Both tragedies had affected her differently, despite a deep emotional involvement present in both.

Angie's unexplained death had touched the most intimate fibers of her being, provoking a ravenous indignation, eating away her previous passivity and complacency.

The cowardly assault on her father brought about a lot of grief, without the resolve of springing into action. She felt paralyzed, but not totally disengaged, depressed but not vengeful.

This antithetical inner disposition did not surprise Heloise. On the contrary, she felt quite at peace with her contrasting emotional world.

She did not have to prioritize her investigations or choose one over the other. Her family had become her friend and her friend her family.

She was prepared to put her life on the line for Angie, while, for her father, she would stay vigilant but on the sidelines.

Still absorbed in similar considerations, Heloise was startled by Brunilda's abrupt interruption. Accompanied by Brutus, her senior co-worker apologized in a humble manner for intruding unannounced.

She asked Mark's permission to leave immediately for Washington, D.C., because something urgent had come up. She would explain the predicament with abundant details at a later date.

With the blessing of their boss, Centurion's top aides left the hospital room and the city of Los Angeles, en route for the capital city.

Brutus and Brunilda did not need to be geniuses to understand, from the FBI interrogations, that they were under a cloud of suspicion.

The only way to save themselves from further humiliation down the line was to act quickly and personally uncover the primary source of the leak.

The only other person who had access to Mark Centurion's itinerary was Brunilda's secretary, Rosita.

The solution to this unpleasant incident appeared very simple and straightforward, with no margin for error.

Regrettably, what at times seems easy, in the majority of cases, turns out to be extremely difficult.

In Rosita's case, any dirty, or even worse, criminal dealings, were completely out of character. She was the most honest, trustworthy employee anyone could have ever hoped for.

The poor young lady will never forget the crucial moment when her boss, Brunilda, stormed into the office and began addressing her in a menacing tone with rude words.

It was so disparaging and degrading that she began crying like a child scolded by a parent or teacher. She did not even pay attention to the unfounded accusations. As soon as she realized what it was all about, she tried to regain her composure and in between her sobs offered a plausible explanation.

She remembered tossing in the trash a few preliminary copies of Mark's itinerary, without shredding them. It was very possible that they fell into the wrong hands. At that stage, it was highly improbable they could catch the criminal, because the cleaning crew rotated not only every day, but also every morning and every night shift.

Not totally convinced, Brunilda requested a search warrant from a judge in order to check Rosita's bank accounts. The search was ineffectual. There was no evidence of any unusual transaction; in fact her checking account balance was so low anybody would have wondered how she could survive on that meager income.

Rosita remained disturbed and profoundly shaken by this chain of events. Consequently, she wanted to quit her job on the spot. Fortunately for her, Brunilda, who after all had a heart, did not accept her resignation; on the contrary, moved by Rosita's financial situation, she gave her a raise.

Still Brunilda had to deal with a relentless FBI investigation and suspicious accusations hanging over her head. The whole scenario did not look very promising.

Brutus, at that point, thought of himself as an unintended target and therefore off the hook.

Meanwhile, on the West Coast, Heloise came to the realization that Brunilda was not a simple corporate lawyer. She was her father's top aide, confidante and right arm. She yielded a lot of power. Behind a powerful man, there was a strong woman, unperceived by all and ignored by many.

Heloise had worked side-by-side with Brunilda for several years, yet perceptive and discerning as she was, up to that date she had not grasped the influence and secret power of that woman. How could that have happened?

Beneath Brunilda's refined manners and feminine attitude, was there anything abnormal or sinister?

Chapter III

Paul Marcikkus, an influential ecclesiastic within the ranks of the Catholic hierarchy, was a fervent admirer of Mark Centurion's project, the City of Mary.

When he eventually received the news of Mark's failed kidnapping and subsequent injuries, he contacted the immediate family and kindly presented his well wishes.

Mons. Marcikkus, thanks to his extensive dealings with powerful people, knew how to conduct himself in similar circumstances. Well-versed in the ways of the world, he was admired for his *savoir-faire*, so atypical among clergymen. People, inside and outside the church, respected him, paying homage to his distinguished accomplishments.

Surprisingly enough, in his humble origins, he was not like that at all.

Born from an immigrant Lithuanian family, he had to struggle during his childhood, as a result of WW2 food rationing and a shortage of basic necessities.

From early on, he came to the painful realization that there was no salvation outside the Catholic Church.

Imbued with religious principles and pious feelings, Paul generously answered God's call of becoming a priest. In his teens, he entered the seminary, and inconspicuously underwent rigorous years of training.

This average priest, where everything appeared common and ordinary, was anything but ordinary. His physical presence and muscular build consecrated him as the Pope's perfect bodyguard.

His savvy knowledge of banking, fiscal paradises and dirty money laundering facilitated his ascent to the highest echelons of the Vatican finances.

"The Gorilla," as he was jokingly nicknamed within the Curia's circles, did not have anything to envy among the most impressive men of the pro-wrestling world or the stunning specimens of the bodybuilder organizations.

Paul Marcikkus was a tower of strength. Huge with blonde hair, thick eyebrows and piercing blue eyes, he gave the impression of being a warrior from another century.

Athletic and agile, he excelled in sports. Several pictures hanging from the walls of his office depicted him in a baseball uniform holding a bat, or in a golf outfit in the act of hitting with elegance and precision.

Nobody could better represent the religious and sport world in a perfect symbiotic relationship.

Well into his priesthood, when his religious fervor had simmered down and the mundane reality kicked in, Paul became more concerned about his physical, rather than his spiritual, power.

He observed how people were impressed by his magnetic presence, while his Christian message of salvation seemed to fade into the background.

His body, endowed by nature with special gifts, would become, little by little, the true sacrament of salvation.

Ultimately, Paul would carry out his priestly mission through his physical ability and raw financial intuition.

His earthly aspirations found complete fulfillment when the Pope chose him as his trusted bodyguard.

On every important excursion or foreign trip, Marcikkus stood by the Vicar of Christ, ready to kill or be killed.

The first part of the last expression "ready to kill" could sound preposterous, but nothing is beyond the realm of reason or reality when it comes to "The Gorilla."

Once, during a trip abroad, when the Pope was greeting the many dignitaries before disembarking from the plane, something very awkward happened. A metal object slid from beneath Paul's black cassock, falling noisily on the laminate floor. It was a mini machine-gun, an Uzi of Israeli fabrication.

Very few people from the papal entourage took notice of that suspicious incident, and even less dared to make any immediate comment.

This was Mons. Marcikkus, brave, bold and fearless. He was just the man ready to put his body in front of a bullet or knife in order to save His Holiness.

While his faith in body strength and commanding personality grew, his reliance on God and sacraments was being replaced by a secular theology, where the Supreme Being was no longer the center of the universe, now replaced by man.

Our clergyman in a famous saying summarized this new theology: "You can't run the Church on *Hail Marys.*"

Concretely, he was referring to the management of the ecclesiastical institution, and specifically, to the Vatican banking system.

Without a specific preparation on finances, he became in a short time *God's Banker,* that is the Vatican's Finance Minister or President of the Pontifical Commission for the State of the Vatican City.

As *God's Banker* he was responsible for IOR (Istituto per le Opere di Religione), the Vatican Bank.

This bank, without windows, commanded an extraordinary financial power, even in the private sector.

With no supervision, Marcikkus had a free hand in managing huge amounts of money and entering into risky transactions with unscrupulous speculators.

The Pope trusted him blindly, and *God's Banker* swam like a shark in the murky water of financiers like Michele Sindona (with ties to the Mafia), Licio Gelli (venerable Master of P2, Masonic Lodge), Roberto Calvi (president of the Banco Ambrosiano), etc.

His highly risky ventures, disregarding the most basic moral principles, seemed to bring a lot of wealth into the Vatican coffers.

From money laundering to the creation of dummy financial companies, from ties to the Campania Mafia to supporting political parties and Masonic Lodges, from financing questionable products of international companies to fraternizing with drug traffickers (like Manuel Noriega), there was no limit or boundaries for our intrepid financial wizard.

"Bring in the riches, and I will be your friend and ally" appeared to be his motto.

It is necessary to point out that, with such ill-gotten money, Paul's boss, the polish Pope, provided a generous hand to the independent movements in his country, and to a large number of global political parties favorable to the church.

No wonder the Pontiff's admiration for Paul Marcikkus went through the roof. He was the real savior of the ailing Vatican finances, and the best promoter of Catholic organizations throughout the world.

Money was the best "Devil's manure" to fertilize and cultivate "God's garden" on earth, his Church.

Pennies from heaven or billions from hell? Hard-earned cash through sweat and labor, or easy money flowing from dubious transactions?

This was not even a dilemma for Paul and much less a moral scruple.

The memory of his father dying at the age of 60 without proper healthcare, for lack of insurance, was a painful lesson that he would never forget. The poor man had worked his whole life as a window-washer without reaping the financial benefits of what he had sowed.

On the contrary, he was repaid with a painful death and great desperation from his wife, who could not provide for medical assistance and a proper burial.

If his father, so honest and industrious, could have seen his son now, would he have been proud or would he have cursed him? Very likely the latter.

However, Mons. Marcikkus did not care in the least, because he had the Pope's blessing and the gates of Heaven open at his arrival.

Strange and ironic conclusions stemming from highly controversial religious premises often converts the intrinsically evil into a perfectly acceptable commodity.

Nothing more Machiavellian than this, where the end (spreading salvation through Christianity) justified the means (illegal and immoral financial transactions).

In the meantime, the extraordinary monsignor was riding high in the popularity wave, adding high-profile contacts to his long list of acquaintances. Among them, we can number the American millionaire John D. Rockefeller, the Sultan of Brunei, the president of Paraguay, Alfredo Stroessner, and finally the infamous Manuel Noriega of Panama.

No wonder that even the most critical among the curialists (like the super pious and spiritualist group, the Millenarianists) were silent, being gagged by his successes.

At the very peak of his glory and power, Paul Marcikkus felt omnipotent and acted like an Egyptian Pharaoh, surrounding himself with pomp and splendor.

People came from the four corners of the earth to pay him homage and ask for advice on the oddest subjects.

One request for a meeting caught his attention. It was Heloise Centurion, his friend Paul Centurion's daughter.

The funny thing was that she begged for anonymity. She did not want anybody to know about the encounter, not even her father.

The information she had about the monsignor was not from her father, but from a young priest, just returned from Rome, after graduating *summa cum laude* from the Lateran University.

If somebody within the Catholic Church knew anything about that mysterious card of hers, **Moral Phalanx**, it was certainly the maverick Marcikkus.

No need to look somewhere else, or diversify her search, when the biggest religious finance minister was right there for everybody to see and admire.

Paul did not hesitate to accommodate her, being so close to the rich family; nevertheless, he was anxious to find out the purpose of her visit.

Through his secretary, he sent her a polite letter, indicating a few possible dates and a place for the rendezvous.

Heloise, bursting with joy and full of hope, chose the first date, June 2.

After notifying her parents and the law firm of a brief vacation in Italy, she flew non-stop to the Eternal City.

For an American eye, the first impression of the Roman ruins is neither overwhelming nor earth-shattering. Used to grandiose and modern buildings in her home country, Heloise remained untouched and skeptical in the presence of the Roman forum and other ancient monuments.

Her accommodation near *Piazza di Spagna* without being luxurious was certainly comfortable and friendly. She quickly reminded herself of her mission. She was not there for pleasure, but uniquely for business and a very serious one, that could potentially change her entire life.

She waited in trepidation for her face-to-face meeting with the famous monsignor. She had met him before, during some close family gatherings and on special occasions.

However, this time it was something special, where all the weight of the encounter was on her shoulders.

Mons. Marcikkus arrived punctually at *Caffè di Spagna*. Much to her surprise, he wore a black suit and white shirt instead of the clerical collar and cassock. He walked with an assured gait, like a man in complete control of the situation.

He smiled at her, shook hands and sitting at a corner table of the *caffè*, he ordered some *panini*, a cappuccino for Heloise and a double espresso with a shot of grappa for himself.

Opening the casual conversation, he spoke in a deep voice: "Welcome to Rome! How is your family?"

Exchanging a smile suffused with a feeling of uncertainty, she answered, "Thanks. My family is doing fine. I appreciate you taking time out of your busy schedule to meet me."

"It is not very often," he replied, "that I have the opportunity to break my routine, and spend some informal time with a friend. I suppose you had a very cogent reason for calling this planned meeting."

Heloise briefly narrated the obscure circumstances of her friend's death and the horrible car accident of the young university professor, both in possession of a card called *Moral Phalanx*.

"My father," she continued, "gave me the same card after my Bar exam, with a stern warning of using it only to avoid bankruptcy or total destitution."

"I suspect something evil behind it. Upon serious reflection, I concluded that only a powerful organization of a religious nature and with abundant wealth could issue such a card. My father, questioned by me, did not offer any credible explanation. Consequently, here I am, asking for your assistance."

The monsignor, pausing for a moment that seemed like an eternity and staring at Heloise, sighed deeply. His hands were restless, trying to grasp something elusive.

Was he in possession of the truth, or was he gasping in astonishment for a salvation table? Was he the reincarnation of an ancient oracle, ready to proffer some sibylline words with hidden meaning, or a vulgar charlatan in the business of deceiving people?

Heloise found it impossible to decipher his cold and stern face, despite his polite attitude.

Finally, Paul opened his mouth and asked Heloise to show him the ominous card. She pulled it out from her wallet and handed it to him.

Again, another interminable pause, during which he scrutinized the card, flipping it over several times in search of a mysterious clue.

At the end of that look-alike cabalist ritual, he assumed a prophetic attitude and stressing every syllable, he gave his verdict. "I am not an expert in these kinds of things, and I hope not to disappoint you in your desperate search. However, I can assure you that such a plastic is not issued by any religious organization. Some powerful private group, whose objectives are ultimately patriotic, backs it. More than a credit card, it is an identification card. Its origin is indubitably American."

Paul Marcikkus, who had familiarity with Masonic Lodges, Mafia members, drug traffickers and notorious politicians in collusion with those movements, perhaps had some inside knowledge, not available to mere mortals like Heloise.

"If I have been of any assistance," he continued, "giving you some significant indication, I am glad. If the opposite is true, I beg your forgiveness. In any case, don't ever forget that it would be my pleasure to stand by you at any time, and to shield you from any danger in your endeavor to unearth the truth."

Heloise remained perplexed by his response and did not know how to react. Should she thank him, or just manifest her light displeasure? Perhaps both reactions could have been appropriate.

He was not taken aback by her hesitation and reassuring her with a gentle pat on her shoulder, he added, "I am sure you will do well in the future."

She courteously refused an invitation to a typical Roman dinner in a *Trastevere* tavern, and remained uncommitted to an unexpected proposition of lecturing a group of American seminarians studying Canon Law (the Church law).

She told the monsignor that she needed some time before deciding. She did not have anything prepared on the concrete subject of The American Justice System, and it could appear pretentious and conceited to address such a selected audience without a careful preparation.

"If you allow me," she explained modestly, "I will notify you tomorrow."

"As you wish," replied Paul, unmoved by her resoluteness. "Take your time, and keep me informed." After that, he slid some bills on the table, indicating that the meeting was over.

In so doing, he got up from his chair, shook hands with the young, attractive American lawyer, and left her pensive and more confused than ever.

At this point, to describe her internal turmoil is not easy, since all her hopes were dashed and the only things remaining were complete emptiness and disappointment.

Was it even sensible to have come all the way to Rome for such a Delphic utterance, meaningless to her intellect and impractical for her line of action?

This could not be any harder to swallow than the disastrous Roman defeat at the Caudine Forks.

Anyhow, Heloise harbored doubt as to the credibility of Mons. Paul Marcikkus despite hearing, until now, lavish praises about him. Was he all that great or was he hiding skeletons in his closet?

During their conversation, she picked up a few things, not exactly pertaining to the ecclesiastical world. They let transpire a mundane conduct, quite improper for a man of the cloth.

For starters, the way he looked at her could not be defined as modest and circumspect, but rather as impertinent and charged with sexual overtones.

His chain-smoking habit, disgusting to say the least, denoted a voracious appetite that could not be satisfied by religion alone.

His arrogance, camouflaged under pretenses of piousness and politeness, gave the impression of a man uncomfortable with his public image.

Not all this conformed to the representation made by his friends and admirers of a noble warrior, fighting the good fights of the Lord.

A voice inside Heloise told her to give heed to his indications, while some strange feeling was pushing her away from him.

But, as the saying goes "good advice can come even from the Devil," she genuinely thought better to take advantage of his guidelines and rethink the whole strategy.

This inner struggle left her exhausted and with no desire for anything. She returned to her hotel room and took a nap, restoring her body and mind.

The following day, almost oblivious of her previous fiasco, she called the American monsignor, letting him know of her decision. She would lecture the seminarians in appreciation for his help.

Paul was quite happy to hear from her, and even happier for the lecture. He would personally set the date and time, promising that he would not miss it for the world.

She felt better having something to chew on. Idleness, as a matter of fact, was her worst enemy.

With great enthusiasm, she began jotting down some ideas about justice in general. Behind her approach, there was a clear **ideological intonation**, not very conducive to a rigorous scientific exam, but highly gratifying in demolishing myths and opening up dogmatic minds.

Escorted by the trusted papal bodyguard and with a gentle smile on her lips, Heloise reached the podium. The conference room at the Lateran University was packed with young seminarians wearing their black cassocks and white collars. It was a spectacle never seen before, capable of intimidating the most experienced public speaker in the world.

Devoid of any theatrics and with a charming feminine voice, able to unchain untamed passions, she opened her arms and began.

"Thank you for having me here. A special acknowledgment to Mons. Marcikkus for his unexpected invitation. I am a trial lawyer from Washington, D.C., here in Rome on a brief vacation.

It is a real honor for me to address such a distinguished audience, and it is a great privilege to be in the city of Caesars and Popes, cradle of western civilization and mother of all jurisprudences.

Rome taught the world law and order. The empire, with its social organization, was the supreme model, to which everybody has to conform if he has any pretension of being civilized. Moreover, the Roman Empire was thought of as a reflection of the celestial order on earth. When it fell, the darkest desperation caught every living soul, thinking that the world was coming to an end. From there on, there is a constant and desperate attempt to rebuild it, from Charlemagne to the last Austro-Hungarian emperor, in order to assure the survival of humanity and avoid total chaos.

However, I did not come here to talk about the marvelous reality of the Roman Empire, but to say a few words about the *American Justice System*.

I will title my lecture **Justice Unfinished**.

As you know, Americans are very proud of their judicial system. They believe, in fact, that it is the best under the sun.

"You are innocent until you are proven guilty" and the "jury system" seem to be the benchmark and foundation of a similar belief.

Nobody on the planet comes even close to the marvelous judicial creation that makes a nation overconfident on its fairness and equality.

In all fairness (the expression sounds paradoxical), my compatriots seem to forget the many injustices and inequalities being perpetrated amongst them under the cover of the same system.

How could it be possible or even thinkable that a body of laws judged almost perfect might generate such enormous miscarriages of justice?

You do not have to go very far to stumble upon cases where justice was blatantly trampled on, despite a universal outcry and public condemnation.

How can you forget the O. J. Simpson case, where a brutal murderer was let free, by reason of his fame?

How can you sweep under the constitutional carpet the Supreme Court decision, during the 2000 presidential election, regarding the Florida vote recount?

On that historical occasion, the Supreme Court, the majority of which was Republican, agreed 7-2 that there were Equal Protection issues in using different standards of counting ballots in different counties. Subsequently, they voted 5-4 to ban further recounts using an alternate procedure. G. W. Bush was certified as the winner in Florida by a margin of 537 votes, thereby defeating Gore. It was only the third time in American history that a chosen candidate won the vote in the Electoral College without receiving a plurality of the popular vote.

These "celebrity cases," as we dare to define them, pale in comparison to the thousands of injustices perpetrated daily against blacks, minorities and immigrants. American soil is soaked with innocent blood spilt in the name of Justice.

How many alleged criminals condemned to the electric chair, or to spend their life in jail, are found innocent through a subsequent DNA test?

Is the *American Justice System* still a model to be offered with pride to the nations of the world?

Surely, we cannot deny its many positive aspects, neither can we look at it with naïve eyes.

The truth is that there is no perfect Justice on earth. Moreover, Justice, as such, does not exist, period. It is an abstract concept, a universal idea, invented by man.

Our ancestors, at the dawn of humankind, horrified by the crude reality of violence, abuses and deaths, could not accept unjust and unhappy endings, where individual existences were truncated prematurely and unfairly.

The lack of Justice, on this troubled planet of ours, pushed them to embrace a belief in a second life, where Justice would reign supreme. An impartial Judge would reestablish fairness and equality. The just man would be rewarded and the unjust punished.

For them, the impossibility of reaching any measurable Justice on earth convinced them of something better after death. If this would not hold true, our present life would be a mockery and a cheating. Moreover, humankind refused to accept such a tragic comedy, such a senseless existence.

This is not the right place to discuss the truthfulness of this popular philosophy, but it tells us something loud and clear—do not expect full Justice during this lifetime, because there is none.

The beautiful slogans written on the façades and walls of our majestic court buildings are mere myths.

"Justice is blind" and "Justice is equal for all" are blatant lies, because Justice is never blind and rarely equal.

Think for a moment about our specious departmentalization of Justice: military justice, civil justice, ecclesiastical justice...They are all deceptive because they strongly suggest different measurements for different classes of people.

On one occasion, Jesus said, "The poor you will always have with you." (Matthew 26:11). As a statement of fact, Jesus projects indirectly a perennial reality of inequalities and injustices.

Confronted with this bleak panorama, a double attitude is historically possible. Some people become skeptical and agnostic about Justice, repudiating everything and showing a defeatist attitude. Their conformism leads them to absolute acceptance and collusion.

On the other hand, some people exult and rejoice, because it is precisely from this filth where their commitment for equal rights and better treatment for the downtrodden of the world blossoms.

Since, by its very nature, Justice is imperfect, fallible and unfinished, these courageous human beings are spurred into action to perfect it and make it less fallible.

Justice unfinished is by far the greatest motivator and the highest reward for a man thirsty of Justice. "Blessed are they who hunger and thirst for Justice and righteousness, for they will be satisfied." (Matthew 5:6).

According to this beatitude, man will be satisfied only through the pursuit of Justice. It is a fact well established that accumulation of material goods, immoderate sex gratification and the pursuit of greater power, would leave man with a vast, aching emptiness.

The earnest pursuit of Justice is the noblest of missions. Man, actually, joins God in his unfinished work of reestablishing balance in the broken equilibrium of human relations.

Dear students, just picture for a moment a world where perfect Justice reigns and everything occupies its rightful place, without violence, usurpation or wrongdoing. It would be extremely boring, unattractive and depressing.

The reason for Justice's existence is the sad reality of Injustice. This is our beautiful and at the same time scary world, where the sharpest contrasts engender the most alluring opportunities for people of goodwill.

Dear seminarians, your generation, like any other in history, has a special calling—to work for Justice.

A burning desire must consume your heart and soul. We should not sit on our laurels. We must reject the stereotypical notion of perfect systems, of being better and superior to other people. We are not superior to anybody. We have a fundamental duty to roll up our sleeves and work for Justice. **Our Justice is imperfect, fallible and unfinished**.

Until a shred of Injustice takes root on our human soil, our mission will be incomplete. Until a vestige of wrongdoing will be found, our conscience should not be at peace.

Justice less imperfect, less fallible and less unfinished is our final frontier, our goal, our last breath of life.

Dear seminarians, society, church and humankind need you. Do not fail or betray them, otherwise, you will fail and betray yourselves.

I hope I have provided you with good ammunition for your difficult journey. God bless you and anyone working for Justice."

Visibly moved, the audience broke into rapturous applause. Nobody realized at that moment that Heloise's lecture was tailor-made for young students, trained in the use of a dogmatic mentality. To our chagrin, this flees from relativity, uncertainty and historicity, like the Devil from holy water.

Despite a marked ideological leaning, their comments were highly laudatory, and they were mesmerized by her familiarity with the Gospel. For a non-Christian, that was certainly remarkable.

Overall, it had been a great success for Heloise, but the most prodigious thing was her personal identification with what she had been proclaiming from the center of Christianity.

Now, more than ever, her life would be dedicated to carrying out a mission of Justice, as a lawyer and detective.

Irrespective of the sacrifices or risks, she would renew her efforts in uncovering her friend's cause of death, and she would work in the courtroom with integrity.

With this fierce determination and a gentle smile on her face, she took leave of her new friends, who promised to pray for her.

After all, although she did not get very much out of her meeting with Mons. Marcikkus, she got a renewed sense of purpose with this lecture, and that was more than enough for her peace of mind.

Still basking in the warm glow of a mission accomplished, she received a surprising phone call. It was not from home.

A mysterious voice, with a strong Italian accent, asked for a meeting in the lobby of the hotel where she was staying.

Since the tone was polite, almost imploring, and the request very reasonable, Heloise did not suspect any foul play. Even so, her heart remained unsettled and her mind was racing over the speed limit.

A wild flight of ideas began darkening her blue sky with an ominous premonition of a possible impending storm.

Against all odds, Heloise showed up before the designated time. The concierge introduced her to two people, a man in his thirties and a woman in her fifties.

Their appearance was ordinary, in striking contrast with their intense posture.

Nothing in the world had prepared the young American lawyer for what was going to happen next.

They shook hands. The man, presenting himself as a translator, revealed the name of the lady standing contiguous to him.

"Her name is Catherine Longhi," he said, "and she has something to show you."

"The name is not familiar," replied Heloise, "but I am curious to see what she has got."

The mystery lady, without uttering a word, pulled out from her purse an old-looking picture and deposited it with extreme care in Heloise's hand.

The young woman had the same sensation she had experienced a few times in a courtroom when officially presented with a smashing piece of evidence.

Bewildered, she stared at that picture, immediately recognizing her father as a young man.

"How did you get this picture?" she asked in astonishment.

Catherine did not answer the question, instead she made a clear statement, and said, "This is my father." Her voice was hesitant, her pronunciation bad, but the idea extremely clear.

Heloise, who had not yet connected the dots, because the reality was more far-fetched than any imagination, appeared overwhelmed by that sudden revelation. She remained speechless and totally lost. Time stood still, the world stopped spinning and everything in front of her vanished.

Afraid of fainting, she grabbed the chair contiguous to her and held it firmly. Was Catherine speaking the truth or was she an impostor?

At that very moment, she could not determine her sincerity and went on inquiring how that was possible.

The many details offered, so far back in time, could not be verified. There was no way for Heloise to recognize or remember anything of what was said. That real-life romance had taken place before she had been born. Obviously, her father had never mentioned his one-night-stand on foreign soil. Nevertheless, he was the only one holding the key to such an embarrassing puzzle.

There was a long pause in their conversation, in which nobody wanted to take the initiative. It was very awkward for both of them.

By reason of their sensibility, they seemed to agree tacitly on an overall strategy. Catherine, following her mother's example, would never try to contact her father. Her mother, Caterina, was convinced that if her lover had the intense desire to get in touch with her, he would have done so. He had her phone number, he knew where she lived, and he should not have harbored any doubt about her devotion and eternal love.

How could he or she forget that memorable night, when in their warm embrace, they promised each other total devotion? He kept calling her Catherine (instead of Caterina) and gave her the sweetest kisses on earth. When her baby girl was born, she could not think of any other name than the one her lover used repeatedly on that memorable night. Therefore, she named her newborn Catherine, as a perpetual remembrance of the magic moment in which their love and passion took human form.

The little girl, now a mature woman, since her early childhood, always wished to know her father. However, she assumed, what was the point of desiring him if he did not desire her?

Everything changed when through some powerful friends, she came to know of the existence of Heloise, her half-sister. She could not resist the impulse of meeting her, despite the strange feelings inside her heart.

Now she was face-to-face with her little sister. The urge to hug her was overwhelming. Nevertheless, Heloise's cool, detached attitude paralyzed her. The moment she dreamt of was there, but ineffectual and almost prosaic.

Finally, Catherine dared to step forward and holding her half-sister's hands said, "I don't want to impose anything on you. Do not mention this encounter to our father. I do not wish any embarrassment or problem. My mother died, and I never married. You are my only family left. I just want to love you, and if it is possible to be reciprocated. Allow me to hug you and kiss you."

She began to cry. Heloise, touched by her honesty and simplicity, could not resist. Without realizing it, they found themselves in each other's arms, shedding abundant tears and savoring the moment.

Strangely enough, Heloise felt her sister's love, so genuine and so deep that her outlook on life took a different turn.

She had lost a very close friend yet by a miracle, she found a precious sister. What could be better than that?

She had somebody in whom to confide, whom to trust and, most important of all, whom to love. The atmosphere mutated into warm from icy and the attitude from distrustful into familiar and loving.

Afraid of being obtrusive, Catherine did not want to ask Heloise to visit her native village, but with a sisterly persuasion implored her for a second meeting.

She was dying to know more about her sister's life, the same way Heloise was curious to find out more about her new family member.

Being perfectly in tune with each other's thoughts on the subject, they immediately convened a meeting for the following day.

Over a marvelous dinner, they had the opportunity of chatting to their heart's content. Catherine, through the translator, narrated the most relevant moments of her existence.

She did not get married, although she wished to do so from the bottom of her heart, because she feared that marriage would have interfered with the other two big loves in her life.

She was an elementary school teacher and adored her students, lavishing most of her affection on them. Also her mother, always frail and sickly, required her constant attention and assistance.

She dedicated the best years of her youth to this dual mission. When her mother passed away, it was too late for her to change radically.

If happiness can be measured in acts of egoistic satisfaction, Catherine was surely unhappy. However, if happiness springs from a life of selfless service to others, Catherine was the happiest woman of her community.

A special bond united these two souls, deeper than any family connection.

Heloise was a champion of justice, spending every single instant in correcting wrongdoings in the courtroom and outside. Catherine was burning her candle on the altar of education, consuming all her energy day and night in favor of her students.

More than blood sisters, they were mission sisters. Their commitment to others consecrated them "sisters," on a superior level, unknown to common folks.

They felt a strange communion between them, that no evil in the world would be capable of destroying.

This magic atmosphere did not stop Heloise from requesting a DNA test. She did not doubt Catherine's sincerity, but she needed some tangible proof to present to her father, if unforeseen circumstances led to that.

Obviously, she was not planning to reveal this family secret to anybody, as she had promised to her half-sister.

As an American lawyer, practicing in Washington, D.C., she was well grounded and knew how the justice system worked. Her father was quite realistic too and would not accept anything, unless backed by incontrovertible evidence.

She collected the sample herself and sent it by certified mail to a lab in Maryland, confident she would find the results on her return home.

The crucial time had come to wrap up her stay in the Eternal City in some meaningful way.

In Catherine's company, she visited some churches of particular significance, a few catacombs, and the magnificent Vatican Museum.

However, the place that affected her most was a little orphanage run by the Sisters of Charity near the *Città Leonina*.

Those small faces, exuding pangs of nostalgia and pain, awoke in her motherly feelings like never before. She wished she had someone to care for, to protect and to cherish.

A significant monetary donation relieved somewhat her sense of inadequacy and impotence.

Departing from that place, she knew that half of her heart would stay there for eternity. Catherine, always so sensitive, shared the same emotional turmoil, without reaching her sister's breaking point.

Two days later, Catherine accompanied Heloise to Fiumicino Airport. After exchanging phone numbers, they hugged each other with an embrace that seemed to last forever. They looked into each other's eyes. Some moisture clouded their vision, and from that moment on, things no longer looked the same.

The serenity, the clarity and the security experienced during the previous days were gone and with it their peace of mind.

Unwillingly, they had put in motion something new in their ordinary lives, whose consequences could not be foreseen.

Chapter IV

Unpredictability in life is a sure thing. Heloise was not accustomed to knowingly applying such a rule to her activities. Nevertheless, this was the most fitting definition for her trip to Italy.

Back in Washington, D.C. when thinking about her disguised mission, she could not make any sense of what happened.

Despite her valiant effort to find a clue to her friend's untimely death, Heloise came up empty-handed.

Conversely, the unexpected discovery of Catherine filled her heart with tender feelings but, at the same time, cluttered her mind with disturbing questions about her father's moral standing.

Struggling through such a maze of doubts, dithering and irrationality propelled Heloise into an unstable state of mind, where moments of desperation followed periods of exaltation, without seeming causes.

Her demure and low-key attitude contributed in some measurable amount to that shaky psychological profile.

A dark period ensued. Was it a cosmic conspiracy or just a normal sequence of events? She felt alone in an ocean of emotional instability and spiritual abandonment.

To confide in somebody meant to open up to betrayal and treachery. The overall picture was neither pretty nor arresting.

Heloise was not a religious person, but in such a dire situation, she felt the fundamental need for a Superior Being, able to rescue her from that fearful precipice.

Was that wishful thinking or a primeval instinct of survival? Whatever it was, it was a scary stage needing some sort of practical solution, long-term or short-term it didn't matter. What mattered was an exit strategy from that tunnel without light.

She tried to rally her spiritual, emotional and psychological energies in a desperate attempt. Unfortunately, the demiurge she counted on never showed up, instead a bizarre turn of events forced its entrance into Heloise's tormenting muddle, sweeping away any prediction and submerging any expectation.

Lost in her thoughts, the young lawyer was walking absentmindedly down Pennsylvania Avenue. She had difficulty concentrating on anything, and finding a new plan of action as a private investigator.

Nowhere could she find a logical connection, nowhere a sensible explanation in sight. Everything was confused, murky and in a perpetual limbo.

It was June 18, 1982. A perfect morning in the capital city, with an intense sunlight. The heavy traffic and the multitude of different individuals helped maintain anonymity, feeling a miniscule being in an ocean of life and movement.

Suddenly, Heloise's vagabond eyes were attracted by a small title on the *Wall Street Journal* sitting on a nearby newsstand.

"Roberto Calvi's body found hanging from a scaffolding beneath Blackfriars Bridge in London's financial district."

She had heard of the collapse of Banco Ambrosiano, the second largest private bank in Italy, and the disappearance of its chairman, Roberto Calvi. She knew too about the association between Banco Ambrosiano and the Vatican Bank (Istituto per le Opere di Religione), its major shareholder.

Prominent political and religious figures were involved in the schemes of those two financial institutions, with ramifications at home and overseas.

The collapse of the bank and the death of its chairman sent shockwaves through the entire fabric of Italian society.

A huge conspiracy theory took shape, where players like the Vatican with its figurehead Paul Marcikkus, the Naples Mafia (Camorra), and the Propaganda Due or P2 Masonic Lodge concurred to Calvi's elimination.

These, afraid that Calvi, a fairly honest man, in an act of contrition and sincerity, could reveal many compromising secrets, pronounced his death sentence to be carried out by some ruthless mafia henchman.

For somebody that is not a connoisseur of Italian society and its lifestyle, it is difficult to understand these forces in collusion with one another. However, connivance, complicity and intrigue have for centuries been the main ingredients of Italian politics.

Through this tragic happening, Heloise came to know something sinister about her family friend, Paul Marcikkus.

Directly or indirectly, nobody ever knew, he was involved in that exemplary execution. It had all the appearances of a severe warning for anybody ready to cross over to the enemy camp.

The man, who treated her royally in Rome showing great interest and concern for her well-being, belonged to a gang of powerful and extremely dangerous people.

Reading specialized publications, she came across some disquieting rumors circulating in high places about Mons. Paul Marcikkus.

According to some well-qualified sources, the Machiavellian Marcikkus had a hand in Pope Luciani's death (September 28, 1978).

The lack of autopsy and the embalmment of the papal corpse the same day of death sparked the popular imagination, which mushroomed in theories of murder and cover-ups.

Motives for this radical kind of action were plenty. Excess of reformist zeal in the new elected, who looked upon the Vatican finance dealings as scandalous and people in command as corrupt. His fainthearted posture with strong feelings of inadequacy and ineptitude tipped the balance, offering his enemies an enviable flank for a deadly attack.

Obviously, for a court of law, these and other rumors lack solid evidence for any proper indictment or conviction, but tell plenty about the character and morals of our protagonist, Mons. Marcikkus.

Grave suspicions about his actions do not end here. His involvement in Emanuela Orlandi's unexplained disappearance appears not only possible but also credible.

Heloise, looking at this somber panorama in front of her eyes, could not conceal her embarrassment and shame for her family connection with this shadowy ecclesiastical figure and with her recent interview in Rome.

Her conscience would never allow her to entertain any kind of relations with similar personages.

Later on, when news of Marcikkus' indictment by the Italian Justice reached her ears, she remained astonished and dumbfounded.

It was no longer a question of rumors; Paul was a wanted man. Claiming immunity, for being a Vatican State's citizen, he was never extradited and never faced an Italian judge. A fugitive from justice, the clergyman made a mockery of the judicial system. In disgrace and impenitent, he spent the last years of his life in a parish church, in Arizona.

Indeed, he was partly responsible for the collapse of Banco Ambrosiano for swindling millions of dollars. Subsequently, the Vatican had to settle its acrimonious dispute with the Italian Government by paying a huge indemnification to the many creditors affected by the bank's crack.

The giant had fallen from his pedestal, crashing noisily and leaving behind inconvenient debris of abuse of power, religion and humanity.

Heloise, as a trained lawyer with plenty of sensibility, could not easily close an eye on this frustrated justice, where class and privileges had the upper hand on the above-mentioned scandalous posture. It was against all her principles and convictions; it was a real slap in the face.

For the dynamic young lawyer **Justice unfinished** was disheartening and distressing, but it was also a powerful motivator.

This was not the only storm she had to openly face upon her return from Italy. On the domestic front, several developments had taken place, which demanded her immediate attention.

Her father, Mark Centurion, had recovered fairly well from the leg wound received during the failed kidnapping on his trip to San Diego.

Even if he had to walk on crutches for a few months, he kept his spirits up and his workload unabated.

As it had been during his whole life, he behaved like a fighter, with courage and determination.

It was precisely for this reason that Heloise was tormented by dreadful thoughts. Due to his enormous economic power and his well-established prestige, was he a guileless captain of industry, or a cunning and dishonest man, the same way his friend Marcikkus turned out to be?

It is fair to say that no acceptable instrument or reasonable standard existed to measure such an imponderable reality.

This rendered Heloise's judgment impractical, making her unhappy and fearful. While her mother greeted her warmly and affectionately, upon her return from Rome, her father exhibited some cordiality accompanied by aloofness and distance.

Overall, the suspicious daughter experienced the same uncomfortable feelings she had in Marcikkus' presence. As odd as it might seem, she did not possess any appropriate word to describe such an emotion.

She would not easily dismiss her intuitions. In the past, she had seldom been proven wrong in following her gut feelings.

The second reality bothering her was Karina's behavior. In her grandmother's words, the little girl seemed to have lost her mental balance.

During the night, she was screaming in her sleep, waking up frightened. During the day, she appeared insecure, resentful and many times insubordinate.

She would reject her father's instructions and answer back in a rebellious manner. The previous sweet girl had vanished, giving way to an unmanageable and difficult child.

Did she require the expert treatment of a child psychologist and a change of custody, or was this just a temporary phase that would be cured over time?

Her father, Brutus Barker, did not have any qualitative time to spend with her, on account of his overwhelming and oppressive work schedule.

This appeared to be the acceptable explanation that everybody would expect from a businessperson like Brutus. The reality was that he had bigger fish to fry.

As he had before with his wife, Angie, ignoring her pleading for affection and attention, he did now with his daughter, who was going through a delicate stage.

Evidently, this prompted the grandmother to seek custody of the grandchild in a family court. The situation, actually, was becoming unsustainable and Karina's emotional stability seemed to deteriorate with the passing of time.

Brutus' mother-in-law, properly coached by Heloise, dragged him in front of a judge and to everyone's surprise obtained permanent custody of her grandchild.

The besieged father did not oppose any resistance in the battle to retain his daughter, giving in easily to the demands of Karina's grandmother and looking almost happy to be relieved from the obligation of his fatherhood.

He gave the clear impression that his priorities lay somewhere else. Dark clouds of an impending storm loomed large on the distant horizon.

The FBI agents had indicted, for the failed kidnapping of his boss, one of his aides. However, they could not establish any direct connection between the two. Whether he was in any way involved in that crime or not remained a mystery.

His position as the most trusted man in Centurion's organization had been seriously compromised and his future jeopardized.

Heloise was not surprised by this ominous development. What shocked her most was Brutus' reaction. For a man, who in a very short time, had lost a wife, a daughter and his own reputation, to remain cool, almost philosophical, was a real shocker.

To understand this mysterious personage, we must step back in time.

Brutus Barker had not been born with a silver spoon in his mouth. Quite the contrary, he grew up on a small farm in North Dakota, where the cold in winter numbed his extremities. He became insensitive to nature and to humankind. Frostbite and parental scolding left him unscathed.

As things and animals camouflage themselves in order to conform to their environment, the same way the young Brutus made himself adaptable and versatile, like a spineless jellyfish.

If things did not turn out the way he wanted, he assumed their shape, adapting himself to the new surroundings.

During his military service, he passed unnoticed, trying to please everybody from the sergeant in command to the last recruit.

After this uneventful period, by pure chance Brutus met Mark Centurion. It was instant infatuation. Mark captured immediately and almost by instinct the essence of that youngster: adaptable, trustworthy and dependable. That was the son he never had, and always wanted.

Brutus was glad to join the new entrepreneur and put his life on the line for the cause. Mark had great plans for the eager learner. Furthermore, Brutus had much to show his boss. Along the way, the journey together became easier and more pleasant. They trusted and confided in each other.

However, in the rough and tumble world of business does not exist a match made in heaven. The initial perfect symbiosis of the seasoned Mark Centurion and the rookie Brutus Barker, over time transformed itself into an obligated partnership.

While Brunilda Pusher rightfully assumed the reins of the public relations division, becoming lawyer and spokesperson for the company, Brutus was Centurion's right hand, his confidant and the only one sharing the deepest secrets of the prosperous organization. The mutual admiration and devotion simmered down and the splendor of the promising dawn never materialized.

In the last couple of years, tensions and frictions had marked their rapport. Some close associates had noticed this distancing of minds and hearts, but none of the causes transpired outside the inner circle.

Unfortunately, at this juncture, neither of the two could dream of taking drastic action. Neither dismissal nor resignation was thinkable or possible.

The separation from the company of either one would have meant the dissemination of secrets highly detrimental to both.

For better or for worse they were tied together for life. Only death could have put an end to that painful breaking up and away.

Would the cool, spineless Brutus wait for natural causes to terminate Mark's existence, or would he collaborate with them in that mission of mercy?

Heloise had sensed something abnormal in that alleged intimate partnership, but she could not put her finger on it.

Perhaps it was time to switch direction in her investigative search. Instead of the credit card trail, she should put Brutus' conduct under the microscope.

That seemed an innovative and brilliant idea. According to an old principle, when every clue dries up outside the family, start suspecting family members.

While Heloise was reaching these astonishing conclusions, that would reverse the particular course of her investigation, she received the official results of the DNA test.

There was no doubt; Catherine was a blood relative and her half-sister. Centurion had a lot of explaining to do, if it ever came to that. However, the younger daughter was not in any hurry for confrontations or cheap explanations.

She had more pressing matters at hand that required her immediate attention.

Karina's emotional and psychological well-being was at the center of her worries. As soon as she could find a little spare time, she rushed to the grandmother, who had the child's custody.

The short conversation with Karina benefited both. The girl received a tremendous morale boost and Heloise valuable hints regarding the family drama.

As soon as they saw each other, they hugged like mother and daughter.

"Hey, Karina, what's up?" was Heloise's opening line.

"Not much," answered Karina, as she smiled faintly at her.

"How are you doing in school?"

"I'm trying hard to raise my grades and improve my conduct."

"Great, I'm sure you'll do better gradually. The important thing is one step at a time. Do you like your new arrangement?"

"Yes, I like staying with Grandma, but I miss my mom. I wish she could be alive and with me."

"That's very normal. Those feelings will stay with you for quite a long time."

While they were talking, a sudden change in Karina's facial expression struck Heloise.

"What's bothering you?" she asked immediately.

The girl assumed a pensive look, and remained hesitant, almost afraid.

"You can tell me anything. I won't say a word to anybody," Heloise insisted gently.

There was a feeling of restlessness and anger deep in Karina's soul, ready to burst out with vehemence.

Like a good therapist, Heloise managed to coax the girl to open up and relieve her heart from a burden too heavy for her age.

Karina clenched her fists and shedding a silent tear, in an outburst of emotions, said, "I hate my father! He was so mean to Mom, and I couldn't do anything. I feel really bad."

"Don't feel bad. You couldn't have done anything. Your dad was under a lot of stress and maybe unconsciously he was taking out his frustration on Mom. You shouldn't be too harsh on your dad, even if meanness is never justifiable. Cheer up, and if your Grandma allows me, I will take you to a nice movie."

Karina, still agitated and distressed, looked up at Heloise, and holding her hand, thanked her profusely.

Her eyes brightened. Her soul appeared cleansed of hatred and anger.

Nobody had ever talked to her like that, and nobody ever touched and understood her so deeply.

A light breeze was blowing, gently kissing their cheeks, during their walk to the movie theater. They chatted like old friends and returned home with warm feelings in their hearts.

That short companionship restored their faith in humankind, always threatened by disappointments and failures.

Heloise did not fail to apply her reflection on Karina's few remarks. The superimposed image of Angie's happy family was just that, a façade hiding abuse, neglect and violence.

Brutus, the cool man from North Dakota, able to adapt to people and circumstances, could not conform to Angie's lifestyle and points of view.

Was this enough to suspect him in her death? Motives appeared solid but the absence of tangible proof was more overwhelming.

On a slightly different note and expanding the reflection, was it legitimate to ask whether—since Brutus had fooled so many people on the family front—could he be deceiving even more in Centurion's close-knit organization?

Given his character and antecedents, this did not appear an academic question.

Heloise was at a painful crossroads. The credit card "**Moral Phalanx**" or **Brutus Barker** was the excruciating dilemma. Which could foster her investigation or kill it completely? The choice was neither easy nor simple.

The first did not deliver any promising discovery, and the second was more nebulous and slippery than an eel in a muddy pond.

She thought of taking some time off and letting things settle down. Maybe new developments could shed more light on that inextricable affair; maybe some previously unnoticed clues might resurface.

Hurry and rush never favored a good investigation. A cool-off period might be the best medicine.

If she imposed a moratorium on her investigation, she could not put a stoppage on her overflowing imagination that was working overtime, presenting unimaginable scenarios and conflicting theories.

The more she appeared to come close to some viable option, the further the harsh reality hit her, pushing her back to the starting point.

Chapter V

Nothing in life is sweeter than waking up in the morning full of hope and expectation. Inversely, nothing is more depressing and disquieting than to find yourself on a dead end with no exit.

Heloise was trapped in a labyrinth, from which she was unable to extricate herself. The night after the encounter with Karina had been miserable, with sudden jerks, frightening dreams and cold sweats.

It was a Herculean task to get up in the morning and put on a normal face, pretending to be worry-free and plenty of smiles. She did not even try, preferring a somber mood and an uninviting look.

She was on her way to work, when she heard on the radio about the mysterious death of a U.S. Naval Academy cadet in Annapolis, Maryland.

It was not the usual case of severe injuries caused by hazing, or the result of a genetic malfunction in some part of the body.

The forensic doctor fell short of reaching any conclusion and left the diagnosis open. For the first time, he found something medical science could not explain.

The most bizarre detail given by the journalist, present at the scene, was that the young student, together with his military dog tag, was wearing a plastic credit card, unknown to his superiors, his schoolmates, and to the general public.

"The name of the plastic, **Moral Phalanx**, is quite unusual for this day and age," was the comment of the newscaster, who ended saying: "Is it a real credit card, an amulet, a fetish, a lucky charm, or some sort of identification? Nobody seems to know, not even the boy's parents."

When Heloise heard those two magic words "Moral Phalanx," she jumped up in her seat and instinctively steered to the right, stopping for a strong cup of coffee. She really needed a potent stimulant. A double espresso with a shot of grappa did the trick. She had acquired the taste for such a drink during her recent stay in Italy. Her mood improved considerably, but her mind remained foggy.

Was that a heavenly warning to follow in the direction of the credit card, or a mere banal coincidence to be disregarded?

Despite the espresso, that moment was anything but sweet and uplifting for Heloise. More perplexed and puzzled than ever, she reached her office and began organizing her day.

The more she tried to concentrate, the less concentration she could achieve. Miraculously, the day went on without a hitch, and she could formulate a new plan of action, in the calm of her apartment.

She would make a last attempt to trace the origin of the "Moral Phalanx." In case of failure, she would not hesitate to follow the second clue, Brutus Barker or BB for short.

She was quite aware of the ineluctable law of investigation. The more time passes, the colder the trail becomes.

Yet, a certain peace of mind returned to Heloise's tormented soul, and night fell on her still unsolved investigation.

In the ensuing days, Heloise gathered as much information as she could on the mysterious death of the naval cadet. The clear purpose was to uncover connections, if any, among the cardholders.

On the surface, the three cases appeared totally unrelated. Angie Barker, a regular homemaker, with no strong political leaning or ideology; Icarus Proctor, a university professor, on the extreme left of the academic creed; Titus Potamous, a navel cadet, full of ambitions and dreams of glory.

In total honesty, she added herself to that short list, coming to the conclusion that no possible link existed among all of them.

Nevertheless, an external connection, the credit card, was there, for everybody to see.

This strengthened her motivation to pursue, almost blindly, the evasive clue.

Still holding on to the old parameters of some religious organization with the power of money, she threw herself into the numerous cults, proliferating all over the continents.

Who can ever forget James Warren "Jim" Jones, founder of the People's Temple, who became synonymous with group suicide in Jonestown, Guyana?

How can anybody fail to remember David Koresh, leader of the Branch Davidians religious sect, believing himself to be the final prophet? Raided by the U.S. Bureau of Alcohol, Tobacco, Firearms and Explosives and subsequently under siege by the FBI, all ended with the burning of the Branch Davidian ranch. Koresh, 53 adults and 21 children died in the fire.

Finally, the Heaven's Gate cult, led by Marshall Applewhite and Bonnie Nettles. The cult's end coincided with the appearance of Comet Hale-Bopp. In the upscale San Diego community of Rancho Santa Fe, Applewhite convinced 38 followers to commit suicide so their souls could take a ride in a spaceship that they believed was hiding behind the comet carrying Jesus.

These and other gruesome episodes, which impacted the popular imagination, constituted negative examples for larger movements with messianic aspirations.

Heloise, after thorough research, believed she had found the right religious movement. It was called "Creciendo en Gracia" or "Growing in Grace" and was founded by the televangelist Jesús Moranda (not to be confused with the historical figure José Luis de Jesús Miranda).

A charismatic man, a growing religious phenomenon, an extraordinary accumulation of wealth, and blind devotion are all the signs of a possible source of the "Moral Phalanx."

In Heloise's conviction, Jesús Moranda could turn out to be the clue she was looking for.

An extensive reading of all the material at her disposal gave her the impression of a histrionic manipulator of the deepest human feelings, capable of breaking any theological barrier, and imposing with charm on his followers the most tyrannical spiritual servitude.

The road to this final destination had been long and not without obstacles for the smooth preacher.

Born in Puerto Rico immediately after WWII, he suffered the sting of poverty and the lack of a nurturing family. Uprooted from his native land, he began learning the street life in Miami, Florida.

Alcohol, drugs and petty crime became his faithful companions, until he landed in jail. During this period, he had an epiphany, where an Angel of God revealed himself to him and commanded him to become his Supreme Messenger to humankind.

He compares himself to the apostle Paul, who was thrown from his horse and blindly abandoned his Judaic ways to convert to Christianity.

His journey from the bosom of the Catholic Church, through the different Protestant denominations, up to his total self-proclamation as the second Christ, sees a slow transformation of his religious ideas and a progressive organization of his movement.

Self-taught in the interpretation of the Bible, he picks and chooses the passages that might foster his new vision of an appealing religion that offers secure salvation for a small price.

First, he establishes himself as the second Christ, or as he calls himself erroneously the Antichrist. In his peculiar reading, the Antichrist is not the Supreme Villain, or Devil, challenging Christ to a final mortal combat, but the real new Christ, in his second coming.

After assuming this powerful role, he appropriates the symbol of the Beast, 666, tattooing it proudly on his arm. The other arm is emblazoned with an astonishing tattoo, SSS, which summarizes his simplified theology. "Salvado, siempre salvado." "Once saved, always saved."

Jesús Moranda is the vendor of salvation for a small monetary price. His motto could appropriately be "Salvation comes one dollar at a time." Once you bought his salvation, this salvation belongs to you forever; it is your belonging, your personal property. As a reward, you are marked on your arm with 666, the sign of the Beast. It constitutes your new baptism, which separates you from the condemned masses. Now you are the chosen one, the perpetually saved, the beatific one.

Moranda teaches that the lies and falsehood of Peter, James and John have been successful throughout our history, and that the Roman Catholic Church along with all the other Christian denominations are perpetuating this mendacity and deception.

He is the new Jesus Christ sent by God to remove the veil of hypocrisy from the people's eyes and make them victorious against all God's enemies.

The new kingdom of God is one of complete grace, where people are above sin. Regardless of what they do, they are above sin, since they are the Predestined and the Elect.

Moranda is freeing all mankind from the bondage of the old Byzantine theology. Now, they can act as they please if they harm none. Finally, they are free to indulge in any conduct they choose to follow.

The old Ten Commandments are irrelevant.

Hell no longer exists.

The Devil has been destroyed.

Sin is a myth.

Moranda is greater than Jesus.

This simplified theology, absurd and essentially contradictory, is not only appealing; it fills an enormous vacuum and an urgent need in the hearts of countless people.

It gives simpleminded and unsophisticated people a sense of security never dreamt before, and a freedom of action that only God can claim.

Moranda, in his absurdities and contradictions, is an unparalleled genius, satisfying the necessities of our modern society, deeply religious and at the same time looking for security, simplicity and freedom.

All of this can be found in Moranda's theological concoction, which generously distributes salvation and receives in return a surprising amount of material wealth.

Not bad for a poor Puerto Rican boy, trapped in a vicious spiral of alcohol, drugs and crime. The Christian religion became for him the ultimate deadly drug, making him and his followers somnolent, despondent and zombie-like to the cries of common sense and reason.

Heloise was not interested in Moranda's theology, unsettling and extravagant even for non-professional eyes. She was searching desperately for any financial connection with the mysterious credit card "Moral Phalanx."

The self-appointed modern-day Messiah was anything but naïve and a simpleton when it came to organization, control and money. This terrain made Heloise curious and suspicious at the same time.

If Moranda was quick in sweeping away the intrusive moral restrictions and cumbersome Christian regulations, he certainly did not do away with one basic prescription—the tithe.

He understood that his movement must pretend to survive and prosper from the only piece of legislation necessary from the old regime—this tax to support the church.

Every member had to pay one-tenth of his income in order to belong to the new Kingdom of God on earth.

None of his Christian critics, from the most indulgent to the fiercest, ever mentioned or criticized this aspect, because every single one of them was deeply attached to this scandalous moneymaking machine.

Yet, this should be the only meter or standard used in measuring the authenticity and veracity of each religious movement, whether it is Christian or not.

Which confession, cult or sect could survive without any monetary support from its members? Unfortunately, when money becomes an end in itself, any spiritual message is lost.

The more attached one becomes to material wealth, the more he distances himself from God.

Any modern preacher or religious representative should never forget those harsh words uttered by Jesus: "For it is easier for a camel to pass through the eye of a needle than for a rich person to enter the Kingdom of God." (Luke 18:25)

The biggest obstacle to salvation, in Jesus' message, is money, while for Moranda the only necessary thing to open the Gates of Heaven is monetary contribution.

We are not here to criticize Moranda, or to point out his evangelical contradictions. We consider and ponder how beautifully he sets himself up in this so-called Christian tradition.

We should admire his ingenious intuition as Jesus praised the dishonest steward: "And the master commended that dishonest steward for acting prudently. For the children of this world are more prudent in dealing with their own generation than are the children of light." (Luke 16:8)

The lack of serious theological principles and moral values is made up with an extraordinary organization and a tight control.

It is precisely in this area where Moranda's skills supersede any traditional cult leadership.

The structure of the new Kingdom of God resembles the power of the U.S. presidential apparatus. Starting with the emblematic seal that reads "Creciendo en Gracia. Gobierno de Dios en la tierra. 666. The Antichrist has appeared" (a complete imitation of the American seal), up to the nine bodyguards that follow Moranda everywhere, and the impressive display of luxury cars, all speak loud and clear of might and grandeur.

The delusions from which the poor Puerto Rican boy suffers do not end there. His thirst for more power, sex and money—the three most powerful human drives—propel him into unusual forms of exploitation and domination that would put ordinary people to shame.

His sexual escapades, so blatant, led him to divorce his first two wives. Unable to control his voracious appetite, he cannot confine himself to a monogamous life.

The brainwashing indoctrination of his members excels in methods of repression and persecution, when some of the members nurture foolish ambitions of autonomy and originality.

The theological principle of "Once saved, always saved" also applies strictly to members—"Once a member, always a member."

This total slavery, for some extremely valuable because it generates certainty and security, for others becomes an unbearable, suffocating bondage.

Unfortunately, members do not realize they are falling into a deadly trap, and if they are smart enough to grasp the contradictions, it will be too late.

The thirst for money, disguised under the pious forms of donations, collections and contributions, inspires and guides the whole of Moranda's ministry.

His finance administrator, free from government taxation for being a religious institution, imposes with an iron hand on his members the tithe, a source of incredible wealth.

Moranda's charismatic personality, combined with his lavish lifestyle and licentious conduct, bear witness not to a biblical prophet, but to the real Antichrist, to the Supreme Evil that leads the Good Shepherd's sheep astray.

The pick-and-choose Bible guru should open the Gospel and read Jesus' admonitory words: "See that no one deceives you. For many will come in my name, saying, 'I am the Messiah,' and they will deceive many." (Matthew 24:4-5)

In an act of humility and contrition, he should confess his deception and hypocrisy and ask for forgiveness, giving back his ill-gotten riches to their rightful owners.

However, this will never happen, because it would contradict the very nature of the false prophet, whose DNA is deception and fallacy.

Heloise, in her reading of this captivating religious figure, would never reach a similar conclusion, and therefore she does not shy away from his dangerous tentacles.

On the contrary, she sets up a meeting with his second-in-command, convinced that this original cult might be the issuer of the credit card "Moral Phalanx."

Was that too much of a stretch, or a legitimate clue in her investigation?

The young lawyer was impatient to meet with Jude Falcon, nicknamed Piranha by his parents. Obviously, as a small child, he had a prodigious appetite, devouring any food in sight and leaving his siblings starving.

Growing up in Miami, he went through difficult times, being expelled from a couple of schools. Thanks to his father's toughness, he got his college diploma, majoring in Business and Administration.

No longer under parental supervision, he began wandering aimlessly, like many youngsters at that age. By pure accident, one day he fell under Moranda's magic spell.

That preacher, delivering a spiritual sermon with fiery passion, ably responded to all his questions. What was more fundamental, he approved of his disorderly conduct and way of life.

The bond of those two souls was instantaneous and from that moment on their destiny became closely intertwined.

The preacher, with histrionic gestures, attracted more sheep to his congregation, while Jude did not hesitate to shear them. The same voracity used when he was small was carefully applied now in collecting the tithe. Same instinct, different direction.

Apparently, Heloise was in the dark about Jude's personality, and did not know what to expect from their encounter.

Yet, her expectations were surpassed only by her curiosity about the new cult. A strange world, with which she did not have any familiarity, was opening up in front of her very eyes.

She arranged a meeting with Falcon, establishing a time and place. The man seemed friendly on the phone, asking only if she would be accompanied by anyone.

The answer was negative. She was traveling alone, and did not have any personal interest in their religious movement. She needed only some financial advice in regard to a credit card.

The arrangement was for the following weekend. In this manner, she would not interfere with her work, and would eliminate suspicions from friends and relatives.

The days in between appeared long and tedious and her brief interactions with people were devoid of any human interest.

Heloise was focused on one vital goal, and all the rest held little appeal for her.

Finally, the day she had longed for arrived. She took an early flight from Washington, D.C. to Miami. When she eventually reached her destination, a torrential rain was pouring down, complicating any movement.

Without difficulty she rented a car and with the help of a map, she tried to navigate safely though the pounding downpour.

Several times Heloise missed the freeway exit, but after a few hours of fighting with the adverse weather, she reached the huge warehouse, headquarters of the cult "Creciendo en Gracia," founded by Jesús Moranda.

She breathed a sigh of relief and, with satisfaction for her extraordinary accomplishment, parked her rented car. Quite a few people were mingling around, chatting among themselves with a curious facial expression that was hard to define.

She approached several young women and asked politely for Jude Falcon's office. Following their indications, she walked straight through the first door, and not far away, inside that enormous building, she spotted a large receptacle bearing Falcon's official name.

Nervous, she looked at her watch. It was two-thirty in the afternoon. She was half an hour early. Despite that and faking exuding confidence, she knocked on the door. No response from inside, and no significant movement in that vicinity.

Her nervousness transformed rapidly into impatience and soon after into irritation. Like the weather outside, her mood was a rollercoaster.

The time seemed immobile, almost eternal. Did Falcon stand her up, or was her imagination running wild?

She was in no mood to take a tour of the vast warehouse. The exterior look was not appealing at all, yet the interior appeared impressive. Moranda's picture, hanging from strategic places, reminded people of his omnipresence.

How could anyone miss the dictatorship mentality behind that vainglorious display of the leader?

If that was not enough to create a sense of loss in the observer, the up-to-date equipment for radio and television broadcasting would have left anybody in awe.

Heloise did not grasp the concept of that place. Was it a modern TV station, an ideological museum, a prayer sanctuary, or a stock exchange? Maybe it was the City of God transformed into the city of man. Hybrid dwellings for hybrid men.

The young Washington lawyer had just landed on a different planet, with no possible reference to a familiar habitat.

While pondering the meaning of her presence among those walls, a screeching voice called her name.

Startled, Heloise spun around. A robust man, dressed in a Versace suit, with an imposing demeanor and inquisitive eyes, addressed her.

"Are you Heloise Centurion?"

"Yes, sir."

"How was your flight and did you have problems with the rain?"

"The flight was uneventful and the rain was certainly a disturbance. Anyway, I made it here without any incident."

"Let us go to my office, where we can have some privacy. By the way, is there any relationship between you and Mark Centurion?"

"Mark is my father."

Jude Falcon could not hide the surprise on his face. He was not dealing with an ordinary woman, but the daughter of a famous and successful entrepreneur.

Unconsciously, he tried to adjust his attitude. Nothing inappropriate should transpire from his manners and conversation.

With a nonchalant air, he continued his conversation, "Can I be of service?" he asked.

"I hope so, very much," replied Heloise. "I came all this way to inquire about a credit card. As a criminal attorney, I dealt with a few clients in possession of such a plastic. Every single one of them expressed to me the intense desire to know the terms, conditions and the issuer of the card, in order to avoid legal implications, in case of a possible wrong use of it.

After briefly investigating several possibilities, I came up empty-handed. You are my last resort."

"Which credit card are you talking about?" asked Jude, with inquisitive eyes.

"Our voluntary organization issues third-level members (the highest level of participation) a special credit card. I wonder if perhaps you are referring to this."

Heloise, for a second, genuinely thought she had reached her final destination and discovered the origin of "Moral Phalanx." However, when Falcon began describing it, she physically felt like she was falling from a high-rise.

The initial trepidation gave way to disappointment and desperation. Hiding her feelings as well as possible, she listened attentively.

"The card's name is ACTUS, Greek initials for Antichrist Son of God, Savior. This acronym should not be confused with the most popular one, called ICTUS, inside a stylized fish, signifying Jesus Christ, Son of God, Savior. I'm sure you've seen this sign on the back of some cars. However, these two symbols, despite their similarities, plainly express a radically different membership.

The first, ACTUS, belongs to the followers of Jesús Moranda, the Antichrist, or the reincarnation of the new Christ, superior and more powerful than the historical one.

The second, ICTUS, proclaims its faith in Jesus Christ, and has been used by Jesus' followers since the introduction of Christianity.

Besides, the first and last three digits of our credit card are always 666.

Finally, our credit card is easily recognizable by the logo ACTUS inside a shield and the numbers. If you wish to see a brochure with terms and conditions, I would be happy to provide it."

"That would be excellent," replied Heloise, showing a simulated interest in something she did not have any use for.

Jude promptly extracted a copy from a drawer of his desk, and handed it to her with a look of satisfaction.

In conclusion, he added, "It was a real pleasure talking to you. Anything else I can do for you?"

"That was more than enough," she replied, "as a token of my appreciation for your invaluable assistance, I am pleased to leave with you this envelope, containing a small donation for your organization."

In saying, they shook hands and she took her leave from the man that could have been her savior. Instead, he had resulted in a senseless diversion on the bumpy road to solving the mystery of her friend's death.

All of a sudden, she came to the sad conclusion that anybody could play the detective role on a TV series, but not everybody could do it successfully in real life.

Finding the solution to her puzzle immediately, and there of all places, would have been true serendipity.

Maybe her pretensions exceeded her expertise and capabilities, and her lively passion and goodwill were insufficient for such a demanding task.

Gloomy inside and out, a perfect reflection of the meteorological conditions, she left that alien territory, moving steadfastly toward her car.

Pushing her way among the throng, mingling around, she observed a woman who exactly resembled Brunilda's secretary.

Was that a perverse trick played on her by some evil genius, or was somebody following her on her frantic quest for the truth?

She observed more keenly, but the look-alike woman had disappeared. Probably her imagination was overheated.

High temperature can cause hallucinations, but neither excessive heat, nor extraordinary personal conditions could justify such a deception.

Everything seemed normal yet Heloise was deeply convinced that Brunilda's secretary, Emily Schultz, was tailing her, who knows for what perverse reason.

Chapter VI

Emily Schultz, the third child of a large family, was born on a Nebraska farm, where fields of maize, with their golden sweetcorn cobs, dominated the vast spaces, graciously reaching the horizon.

Until the age of eighteen, when she left her rural existence for college, she was seeing the world divided into enormous parcels of land, populated by animals, domestic and otherwise, and enriched by life occurrences, like births and deaths, marriages and funerals, school and hard work.

The cyclical alternating of seasons and the daily succession of sunrises and sunsets regulated her childhood years.

Nature, with its gentle and occasionally rough hand, constituted the supreme regulator of activities and emotions. The farm experience molded and colored every creature's breath, leaving in them an indelible sign of a rustic authenticity and a raw honesty.

Her college years, in a medium-sized city, changed all that. In the beginning, the impressionable Emily missed her open spaces, and nature's alternating changes. She found it difficult to adjust to the artificial city lifestyle. It was all so upside down that she thought she could not come to terms with those modern aberrations.

No counselor could give her the peace of mind and clarity of convictions of her adolescence, and no one could bring back the sweetness and comfort of her beloved farmland.

However, time has its way of taking care of problems and healing sour wounds.

Imperceptibly, the city nightlife substituted the farm day life, the occasional college attachments replaced the long-lasting friendship of the cornfields, and the innocent soul of the country subsided in the presence of a more sophisticated academic conscience.

The two opposite life experiences neither engaged in mortal combat, nor cohabited in harmony.

One juxtaposed the other, taking turns in dominance, like Roman wrestlers of equal physical strength.

Emily was growing under the neon light, unaware of this atypical dual personality. It was not bipolar or schizophrenic; it was rural and urban, simple and complex.

She did not reject bucolic habits of her past. She absorbed instead the social trends of the new environment.

The unexpected outcomes of this gradual transformation were there for all to see. A new Emily, attractive but reserved, flexible but determined, unpredictable but fundamentally faithful emerged.

In order to pay for law school, she applied for a secretarial job at Brunilda's firm. Not only did she obtain the desired position over many applicants, she also became in a very short time her superior's confidante.

To mitigate the hardships of her heavy schedule, Brunilda gave her stress-free assignments. To go to a concert and keep an eye on some lawyer's associates, to collect gossip and report to her, to detect any blooming romance among employees, etc.

Social spying comes naturally to certain characters. Emily felt comfortable in that unofficial capacity, and did not have any scruples about spying on her co-workers.

When Brunilda told her to follow Heloise unnoticed to Florida and carefully interrogate her contacts, she did not hesitate for a second and embraced that specific task as a sacred mission.

Obviously, she was kept as much in the dark as everyone else about the reasons for putting a tail on Heloise. Emily did not care less. She was happy to serve her master and win points.

With dark sunglasses, a large hat and a trench coat, she boarded the same plane as Heloise.

She followed her to the "Growing in Grace" center. After the meeting with Jude Falcon, Emily had a brief personal exchange with him.

Finally, in a torrential downpour, she left after Heloise, in the direction of the international airport.

For Emily, the whole experience had been surreal. She was chasing a ghost, being a ghost herself.

Heloise was too distraught to think clearly and act rationally. The heavy rain was impeding her visibility, and the squeaky noise on the windshield did not help.

She managed to reduce her speed, but motorists coming from behind were recklessly overtaking her, causing a psychological chain reaction even in the most cautious people.

Instinctively, she pushed herself to keep up with the flow, playing a dangerous game. The increasing velocity, surpassing at times the legal speed limit, the scarce visibility, and the psychological frustration for the failed mission, created the perfect conditions for what was certainly going to happen.

Unhappy with that dangerous situation, Heloise was about to take the first exit, in order to avoid that insane deadly spiral. Unfortunately, she did not realize that a fairly good sized piece of debris lay in front of her.

In a daring attempt to avoid it, she steered excessively to the right. As a result, she slid on the wet pavement and hit the embankment of the highway, crashing head-on.

The impact was tremendous. She lost consciousness instantly, bleeding profusely and remaining trapped between the contorted metal of her totaled car.

The scene horrified Emily, who was traveling a few cars behind. She parked her vehicle in the appropriate area and immediately dialed 911. Other people had already stopped and were trying to extricate the poor victim from the tangled front panel and driver's seat.

Every effort was in vain. The common perception was that Heloise's life could slip through their fingers at any moment.

They had to wait for the paramedics and a special police unit. In the meantime, Emily called Mark Centurion and Brunilda Pusher, informing them of the accident.

It took more than an hour to get Heloise out of that deadly wreckage. She had a pulse and her breathing was barely audible. Paramedics did their best to stop the blood loss.

Heloise was transported to the nearest trauma center, for an immediate intervention.

So many serious injuries covered her body that even the skilled physicians had difficulty in establishing priorities. With maximum urgency, they initiated the rebuilding of that broken-up doll. The comatose state spoke loudly of Heloise's delicate situation, leaving no doubt that the surgeons were working against all odds.

Even if they could repair broken limbs or severely damaged organs, there was no complete assurance that she would regain consciousness, much less function normally again.

It was not a pretty picture for a dispassionate observer. For family and friends, the sight of the young woman in a vegetative state was disheartening enough to cry their eyes out.

Heloise was not gone, but she was not there either. Where was she?

Her loving mother, Magdalene, arrived from Washington, D.C. in the company of her husband, Mark Centurion. He held her hand as she sobbed uncontrollably. She was whispering, as only an affectionate mother can do, "Heloise, my girl, come back to us! Listen to your mother's pleas. I love you more than anything in the world. I beg you not to leave us. My angel, if you hear my voice, open your eyes. I'll stay by your side day and night until you provide me with some clear indication that you are alive."

After a dramatic pause, full of pain, Magdalene in total desperation addressed a few incoherent words to the Almighty, "Oh, my God, if you need a human sacrifice, take me instead of my daughter. I am ready to leave this temporary dwelling. Please, allow my girl to live. She is a good person, and surely she will help many needy people."

Would anybody listen to the sorrowful prayer of a desperate mother?

Certainly, the doctors were doing the impossible to save Heloise's life. Her blood pressure and pulse were stabilized, her breathing healthy and almost normal. She was still being fed artificially. Any internal bleeding was surprisingly detected and stopped. The broken limbs in a cast and the punctured lung sutured.

The broken doll was back in one piece, the blood was flowing through her veins, but any movement was absent from that immovable body.

Would it take a miracle to bring her back to consciousness? On the other hand, would time silently perform the marvelous work that only nature is capable of doing?

Mark Centurion, the powerful man, in the presence of his almost lifeless daughter, could not express his loving feelings or shed a tear of compassion or sorrow. His eyes and mouth were dry, like a well cursed by drought.

Impotent in the presence of such an irremediable tragedy, he could not formulate a plea, utter a prayer, or make a wish. His wife's ramblings did not even touch him, because, spiritually and emotionally, he was not there.

His existence had been transferred mysteriously to another level, where emotions were banned and personal desires prohibited.

Mutated into a human statue, he had to be literally carried away, together with his wife, by the nurses. Their company, actually, was not helping anybody, neither the patient, nor the medical staff.

The inconsolable Magdalene put up a strong resistance, but to no avail. Not in a million years could she have ever imagined seeing her daughter in such a desperate condition. It was the worst possible nightmare for a mother or any human being.

Life can be cruel, even ruthless. However, hope is the last thing to die in a mother's heart. Magdalene would hope against hope and fight with every means at her disposal.

Heloise, before leaving Washington, D.C. for Florida, had given the phone number of her half-sister, Catherine, to a trusted friend, Marjorie.

Did she have a premonition of some impending disaster, or was it just a routine precaution? Whatever the reason behind it, she told Marjorie, "If anything happens to me, please call this lady in Italy and let her know about my condition. She is a very close friend of mine."

Marjorie, smiling, promised that everything would be executed by a nod and a wink.

When the news of the tragic accident eventually reached her, her first reaction was to fly to Miami and be at Heloise's side. Nevertheless, mindful of her pledge, she immediately contacted Catherine.

Not without difficulties, as a result of the language barrier, Marjorie conveyed the devastating news.

Catherine, as well as she could, assured the solicitous caller that she would catch the first available flight out of Fiumicino, Rome.

She begged Marjorie to be so kind as to pick her up at the airport, and subsequently accompany her to Miami. Catherine was aware of imposing a lot on that nice woman. She explained, in broken English, that she could not accomplish very much without her help.

The understanding Marjorie put her mind at rest saying that it was no imposition; on the contrary, she was very happy to be of service to a friend of a friend.

Reassured by those kind words, Catherine thanked her repeatedly, and said goodbye. By reason of the unexpected call, she did not have time to process the crucial information. No sooner had she hung up than a flood of emotions created in her a mental and emotional turmoil.

Catherine feared the worst. Would she have enough time to arrive? If yes, would Heloise recognize her?

Unfortunately, this was not a good time for speculations or indulging in sentimentality.

She immediately contacted her travel agent and booked a flight to Washington, D.C.

The following morning she stepped for the first time on American soil. Coming from a small Italian village, everything in the nation's capital looked imposing to her.

Marjorie, carrying a huge sign with her name on it, was waiting for her.

She could not miss it. A warm, cordial handshake sealed their first encounter. The young, bubbly Marjorie, within the restrictions imposed by the somber occasion, showed an extraordinary gentility.

Speaking slowly and with pauses, in addition to some universal signs, and thanks to an adult English course taken by Catherine, their communication, if not easy and articulate, was certainly effective.

During their commute to the apartment, Marjorie informed her guest of the latest developments on Heloise's health condition.

Still in a deep coma, she was alternating between periods of stable vital signs and unforeseen complications caused by dangerous infections in the liver. The overall picture was discouraging.

In the apartment, Catherine took a shower and in the company of her new friend, consumed a frugal meal.

The atmosphere was unusual for the foreigner just landed. The tranquility and relaxed pace of life had given way to a fast, almost hectic lifestyle. Everything was *now* and *here*, not *later* or *tomorrow*.

Marjorie made a few phone calls, one to reserve the flight, another to Magdalene to announce their arrival, and finally to her parents to let them know of her absence for an undisclosed number of days.

After that, they were back in a taxi to the airport. The city at that time of the day was magnificent in its entire splendor. Spacious avenues, massive buildings and world-famous monuments were the crown jewel of that princess of power.

Nobody, dweller or stranger, could remain indifferent in the presence of such a display of grandeur.

Catherine watched in awed silence the beauty and majesty of Washington, D.C. whose international renown was well deserved.

While passing in front of historic or panoramic sites, Marjorie offered some brief explanations, respectful at the same time of Catherine's personal reflections.

Not even a dream could be more enchanting than that. She was cruising ecstatically through Pennsylvania Avenue, passing in front of Capitol Hill, and admiring in the distance Jefferson Memorial. It was all real, and all overpowering.

Oblivious for a second of her main objective, Catherine was impersonating the part of a tourist, lost in a fantasy island of incredible attractions and marvelous sights.

It was only a matter of a few fleeting minutes, and all of a sudden, she found herself surrounded by people at the airport.

Marjorie did the necessary practices for boarding the booked flight. Everything went smoothly.

On the plane, Marjorie explained to Catherine how great Heloise's family was. The father, Mark Centurion, was famous, rich and powerful. Half of the American girls would have died to have Mark as their father. He was the embodiment of the successful businessman and the epitome of the rags-to-riches street boy.

Magdalene, on the other hand, was the perfect mother, humble, attentive, and always ready to put others before herself. Her life was based on self-denial and sacrifice. She was not a Mother Teresa, but in the humility and abnegation of her little world, she came quite close to that famous model.

Finally, Heloise was a great lawyer, not because of her eloquence and astounding legal tricks in the courtroom, but for the passion and fervor of a thousand crusaders. Justice was always the final pursuit, the north star of her career.

Marjorie knew so many things about the Centurion family, but she ignored a basic one. Catherine was a blood member of that elite nucleus. She was Mark's daughter and Heloise's half-sister.

That secret would remain as such for everybody. Catherine and Heloise had vowed never to reveal that bond, which could have potentially destroyed the unity of their family.

Certainly, it would not have been easy for both of them to keep up appearances. However, it was imperative for their survival. If the image was substantially tarnished, could it remain hidden to curious outsiders?

At that point in time, Catherine's major fear was her sister's comatose condition, and the scary consequences in the event of an indefinite duration of that unconscious state.

Her second biggest worry was meeting, for the first time, her own father. Could she keep cool and unemotional, or would she betray herself and break down, overpowered by uncontrollable emotions?

She was not sure of anything. Too many variables could change the outcome of that historical encounter.

In the meantime, her fellow traveler was also preoccupied by Heloise's state, but without reaching Catherine's anxiety level. She was more concerned about logistics than unwanted outbursts of feelings.

Their arrival at Miami airport signaled the boiling point of their unspoken agitation. Still a short taxiing period and then the difficult, feared meeting would take place.

The trauma center where Heloise was being treated was a state-of-the-art facility. The building was modern and functional, the equipment beyond expectation, the surgeons world known, and the staff attentive and caring.

Marjorie and Catherine, as soon as they approached the information desk and asked for Heloise Centurion, were promptly escorted to Room 303.

On their way, they observed the cleanliness of the place, and the subdued behavior of visitors. The silence was interrupted only by intermittent announcements over the intercom.

The surroundings and general atmosphere gave the impression of a sanctuary, where the only divinity on display was suffering and misery.

At their soft knock on the door, Magdalene appeared. From her gentle face emanated grief and sadness, a far cry from the usual confidence and self-assurance.

As she gathered her breath, with a dreamy voice and a slight nod of the head, she invited them in.

Chapter VII

Brutus Barker, the vitriolic man from North Dakota, and Mark Centurion's right arm, breathed a huge sigh of relief when he heard of Heloise's car accident.

Finally, that loose cannon snooping around, trying to dig up dirt about his family, and not believing in the natural causes of his wife's death, was put to temporary rest by some welcome mysterious hand.

Brutus had never liked Heloise. In his opinion, she monopolized Angie's attention, and stole her from him. In that strange relationship made of love-hatred, she constituted his chief rival, his worst enemy.

Everything about Heloise irritated him, from her voice, deceitfully sweet, to her smile, Mona Lisa cold and impersonal.

His eyes could not rescue any positive aspect in that attorney, so admired by many.

It was a well-deserved break to see the two major threats, hanging ominous over his head, disappear almost instantaneously: the distrustful and suspicious lawyer, and the FBI agents investigating his involvement in Mark Centurion's failed kidnapping.

Now, he could go about his business as usual, and have a free hand in whatever venture his boss assigned him.

At the beginning of his ascent to power, everything came to him graciously and abundantly. The same way, now, all doors would be open for him. No fears, no impediments and no restrictions.

Business, in order to prosper, needed unrestricted action of movements, and unlimited access to any upcoming opportunity.

Prohibitions and restrictions would strangle any progress, and choke any initiative. This was Brutus' unbridled economic philosophy.

Nothing and nobody would stop him from freely pursuing his master's imperial design of dominating global markets, reshaping men, and creating a new and improved world.

Just when he was feeling free from shackles and hurdles, a phone call from the local police brought him back to the crude reality.

At the first ring, he picked it up. "Hello, who is this?"

"Hello, this is Officer Tim Trinket, from the local police. May I speak to Mr. Brutus Barker?"

"Speaking, officer."

"Would you be available for a routine questioning, in order to complete our investigation on a fatal car accident that occurred more than a month ago?"

"Sure, officer, although I doubt I can provide any relevant information."

"Let me be the judge of that," Officer Trinket answered sharply.

"Of course," Brutus replied somewhat sheepishly.

The conversation, short and to the point, provoked a real tizzy in Brutus' sharp mind.

Honestly, he did not have a clue or a probable cause. Who was the victim anyway?

After carefully pondering all the possibilities in any kind of involvement, as a participant or spectator, he came up empty-handed. He could not even remember a car accident in the past few months, let alone a probable connection with one.

However, all of a sudden, his memory seemed to bring back something unpleasant. With an unconscious gesture, he cleared his front with his right hand. Was he trying to sweep under the carpet an inconvenient and disturbing recollection?

The truth was that his previous peace of mind had vanished, leaving him in great uncertainty.

He did not have much time to recover his composure. The doorbell rang, announcing the untimely presence of the police officer.

With a polite but nervous nod of his head, Brutus let Mr. Trinket in. They did not shake hands. Brutus showed the agent a sofa, where he sat. Skipping the usual preliminaries, Tim came straight to the point.

"Mr. Barker, we are concluding an extensive investigation on Icarus Proctor's accidental death. We still have a few loose ends that we would like to tie up. Your name appears on the list of phone calls made, the day before the accident, to Carreras' Garage."

"Mr. Carreras," interrupted Brutus, "is my mechanic. No surprise there, if my name is among the many callers."

Disregarding the snappy remark, the investigating officer continued: "We have reason to believe Proctor's car was tampered with, while it was serviced there. We do not have any clues yet as to the motives of such a criminal action, but we are following the money trail. Some significant sums, in fact, were deposited into Carreras' account around that crucial time.

Around the same period, you made several phone calls. So, I would appreciate it if you tell me candidly the nature of those communications, and whether or not you knew Mr. Proctor."

"If you had enough time," responded Barker, "to control those sensitive areas, you surely did not fail to check the list of customers serviced on those days. If you did, you certainly found my name and my car, a new BMW. It was there more than a week for a costly repair of the engine, which was not up to smog standards.

As to the victim, Icarus Proctor, I flatly deny any knowledge, even remote, of that person. Moreover, the first time I heard that unusual name was the day of the accident, when it was reported by all the local media, for the massive pile-up of cars and the huge delays of the main thoroughfare."

Officer Tim Trinket, a good judge of character and an excellent reader of body language, observed Brutus' guarded, defensive posture neatly choreographed by a certain ironic tone of voice. Besides, how could he miss his well-formulated explanation, which did not leave any room for doubt or suspicion?

The whole scenario, so impeccably presented by Brutus, appeared too good to be true.

With a not-so-subtle warning, the qualified officer concluded his questioning by saying, "I hope you have been totally forthcoming and sincere with me. If, through Carreras, we happen to stumble upon some incriminating evidence, I assure you that I will come down on you as hard as I can and with the full force of the law. In the meantime, Mr. Barker, I wish you a great day."

Without any hesitation and with a firm gait he walked out the door, leaving Brutus holding his breath.

This man, apparently unmoved and impenetrable by external intimidation, had just experienced the worst jolt of his life.

A trail of suspicion, like an invisible trap, was slowly taking shape, leaving him snared in a web of intrigue.

First, Heloise cast serious doubts on Angie's alleged natural death. Second, the FBI investigated him in Mark Centurion's failed kidnapping. Finally, the local police suspected an active involvement in Icarus Proctor's deadly car accident.

What was the world coming to? The untouchable man, above suspicions, had all of a sudden become a uxoricide, a kidnapper, and a terrorist.

Was there any grain of truth in those nasty rumors? From Barker's nervous reaction, the seed of mistrust and skepticism was planted.

Future developments would reveal the consistency, or not, of those veiled accusations.

While justice will work indefatigably in its endless search for the truth, Brutus would not cease in his risky pursuit of power and fame.

Would he be intoxicated by those powerful, high-octane human stimulants, turning himself into a despicable creature, or would he be victorious and triumphant, reaching the unreachable, and performing the impossible?

From this moment onwards, he would incessantly attempt to escalate the costly peaks of fame. However, at the same time, he would be under the microscope of the law enforcement agents, his boss, and his lover.

Yes, indeed, Brutus Barker had among his many conquests, a stable sweetheart to fill the complete emptiness and dissatisfaction left by his frigid departed wife.

This might come as a surprise, but it could not be totally unexpected, knowing our worldly man. What is certainly surprising is the identity of this secret lover.

Emily Schultz, the golden girl from Nebraska, with the complicity of her employer, Brunilda Pusher, had found Brutus' good graces and favor.

It was the perfect liaison of convenience for the unlikely human trinity. Each benefited greatly.

Barker finally enjoyed the pleasures of a close relationship with a female with the good qualities of a sexual partner: passionate and unpretentious, country simple and city slick, understanding and modestly reserved, submissive but not succubus, in command but not domineering.

Emily entered the inner circle of power and money, ensuring a future of stability and reasonable comfort. Despite the age gap or maybe thanks to it, she felt honestly attracted to the man of few words, discovering in him a much-needed father figure.

Brunilda, the prude woman, keenly concerned with people's morality, took pleasure, in a twisted way, in carefully putting a mole in her archrival's quarters.

It is difficult to establish who was the major repository of advantages from this web of intrigue. The only thing certain was that the mishmash of human relations was a time bomb, ready to explode at any time.

A slight misstep from any of those players could trigger a deadly explosion with innumerable consequences.

When we come down to human interactions, you cannot exclude any type of reaction, from the most bizarre and unexpected to the most calculated and predictable.

Mark Centurion and Emily Schultz, slightly acquainted with one another, were back in town from their trip to Miami.

The first was compelled to fly there not by fatherly devotion and attachment, but solely by parental duty, which Mark exercised very sparingly.

The disconsolate and dolorous act he put on in the presence of his daughter's prolonged vegetative state was just that: an act. The master of manipulation in transactions and business dealings, this time exceeded himself in exuding feelings and sentiments that were not there.

Anyhow, he was extremely believable, leaving a superb impression of a perfect grieving father.

Emily, on the other hand, was ordered by Brunilda to go to Miami, on a spy mission. However, the real promoter of this original idea was none other than Mark Centurion, so loving on the surface yet so ruthless deep down.

Amazingly enough, the tragic circumstances converted the spy girl into a truly convinced rescuer, making out of her a Good Samaritan.

Brutus, aware of their return to the capital city, was expecting a phone call from both. Who would be first, the businessperson or the secret lover?

Obviously, he would be pleased and exceedingly satisfied only with the second one. A romantic encounter with his dream girl would have been a soothing balm on his still bleeding wounds, inflicted by the police's harassment.

If the whole world was crumbling around him, only her presence and the touch of her soft skin very likely would have meant survival among the rubble, and flourishing in a desolate landscape. She represented so much to his thirsty heart that just one drop of honey from her lips could revive his dying soul.

He was pacing nervously up and down inside his room, his mind set on the pleasurable side of his expectations, when his cellular rang.

The mere sound of that magic instrument put in motion a cavalcade of gut feelings, short lived. In fact, an unwelcome masculine voice came through, creating total discomfort.

"Hello, it's me, Carlos."

"Hi, Carlos, I apologize. I was expecting somebody else. What can I do for you?"

"Is this a bad time? I can call back later."

"Oh no," said Brutus, stumbling over each word coming from his mouth, "I'm listening."

Carlos had the distinct impression that his lucrative customer was in the middle of something unpleasant. Without the previous confidence and spontaneity, he resumed his conversation.

"This morning, the local police showed up again. Dissimulating their action under false pretenses, they requested to have a brief word with the mechanic who repaired Proctor's car. Since he was not on duty, they had to wait. After a long hour, Pedro Almendarez, the mechanic, appeared in a roaring Corvette. Unmoved by the police presence, he followed them into my office. Behind closed doors, the questioning went on forever. Finally, the officials came out and left with a self-satisfied smirk on their faces.

I am sure they will be back if any inconsistency emerges between my statements and Pedro's interrogation. What am I supposed to do?"

Brutus answered, "Keep as cool as possible. Play along. Never give the impression that you are correct in your assertions. Always use the words: maybe, possibly, I do not remember well. For the rest, I will take care of everything. Trust me, you will not be in trouble anytime soon. Have a good day."

Brutus, certainly, did not belong to the category of people having a good day. Until now, all had been crappy. What else was in store for him?

He was still brooding over what he had heard from Carreras, when a knock on the door startled him. Who could be visiting him unannounced?

Was it Emily, the blonde girl from Nebraska? In such a case, she would be the only redeeming feature of that forgettable day.

Incredulous, he opened the front door. The strong desire to see a feminine presence was frustrated once more. Instead his boss was standing there, a very enigmatic look on his face.

That was the last person he wished to meet. Their relationship had gone from cold to icy after the attempted kidnapping. The son he believed he had found in Brutus, was justifying, day after day, his historical name with a strange behavior of detachment.

Suspicion concerning his conduct wasn't a police prerogative only. This negative sentiment was also widespread among relatives, friends and coworkers, including his great mentor and generous benefactor: Mark Centurion.

His sudden presence, on the threshold of his front door, brought back resentment and hostility. However, Brutus greeted him with a forced smile and a superimposed affectation, so natural it could deceive any trained psychologist.

Mark, with a peremptory wave of his hand, dismissed his bodyguard, who waited outside.

All seemed so formal and perfunctory that the words, which came out of their mouths, at the very beginning, didn't mean a thing.

Now, the two men, the old Caesar and the young Brutus, were sitting, in the spacious living room, face-to-face, like two Roman gladiators, ready to battle for their survival.

If this was the overall atmosphere surrounding our protagonists, the outcome of their verbal duel was a total washout.

Centurion wanted to be reliably informed about the latest business moves, and the developments on the police investigations. Brutus painted an accurate picture of the company's financial situation, and a less believable description of the law enforcement activities.

The boss, with a rare clarity and lucidity of mind, listened attentively to his subordinate's narration of events, screening every single statement. Brutus' description was punctuated by a few pertinent questions.

The second-in-command did not mind those brief interruptions; he feared only hidden warnings, and subliminal messages.

Obviously, at this stage of the game, neither of the two was interested in pulling the strings excessively, as it could result in a rupture, detrimental to both.

The dreaded meeting ended with a handshake and a pat on the back by the boss. The underlying hostility did not surface; on the contrary, the prevailing atmosphere was just informational.

Centurion walked out of that mansion holding his head high, reassured that his protégé would not go astray anytime soon.

Brutus, keeping his end of the bargain (close partnership with his superior), would go on, enjoying a powerful protection and a respectful position within the community.

People with authority should pay attention to the unspoken messages of their subordinates, and through plain communication, diffuse the potentially explosive bad moods and the always-present misunderstandings.

Strangely enough, Brutus felt relaxed, almost reinvigorated, after that talk. He totally forgot about his sweetheart Emily, and the many petty things in his ordinary life. He was more than ready to carry on the battle in unison with his boss.

In the very beginning, he had signed on his master's agenda with an admirable enthusiasm, now without much conviction, but with great determination, he was set on reaching the ultimate goal.

The quixotic adventure of creating a completely new man was not only becoming believable for the North Dakota man, but feasible.

Intrepidly, he would dedicate the best of his energies to pursuing that fleeting chimera, toning down his amorous escapades, and keeping in check his unbridled dreams of power and riches.

Would those genuine resolutions have a long life? Or would they be the first victims of a sudden change of circumstances?

In this day and age of disposable relationships, cybernetic speed and instant gratification, nothing should come as a surprise.

There is undoubtedly a tacit indulgence, moreover a widespread acceptance of behavioral forms, unthinkable a few years back.

New technology and new ways of communicating are accelerating this questionable transformation, leaving people gasping in astonishment for what will be next.

Brutus was not an exception. His responses to altering circumstances would conform amazingly to new social trends.

Still immersed in a profound meditation of far-reaching consequences, he heard the distinct noise of an approaching car. It stopped at his doorstep with a familiar blaring of the horn.

It was Emily Shultz, the never-forgotten siren, whose very voice could have melted a stone heart. Bursting with trepidation and joy, Brutus opened the front door and could not resist that attractive smile, alluring him into her car.

That feminine presence was more than sufficient to throw the poor man into total disarray, not only emotionally, but mentally as well.

Oblivious to his previous resolutions, his firm commitment to his boss' noble mission, he found himself at her complete mercy.

As a fierce bull, blowing steam from his nostrils and looking around in a menacing way, can be transformed instantly into a meek and docile ox, ready to perform any job required by his master, in the same way, Brutus was sitting in the car next to Emily, looking for her slightest sign to engage in the dance of his lifetime.

He struggled to regain mastery over his emotions, but it was pointless and futile.

To say that Emily was savoring the moment would be a gross understatement. Fully conscious of her feminine power, she did not hesitate to use it to her own advantage.

Planted as a mole, by Brunilda, she took full advantage of her double role of spy and lover.

Would the most innocent and pleasurable encounter of that memorable day turn out to be the deadliest ever? Or would it go down in his personal history as an innocuous divertissement?

Completely insensitive to the potential damage, he was more than willing to sleep with the enemy under the illusion of a playful partner.

He had never before mixed business with pleasure; he was well aware of the disastrous consequences. His lips were always sealed in the presence of sexual partners. However, he had never before had an undercover agent, so enjoyable and so deceptive at the same time.

Liquor in excess could tip the scale of his guarded posture and make him sing like a canary. In addition, "*he that sings once, weeps all his life after*" as the saying goes.

Away with all the inhibitions and restraints! Brutus was finally alone with his Emily, and nobody would stop him from enjoying a moment of pure ecstasy.

Chapter VIII

Magdalene, the emaciated mother, unable to close her eyes and rest for any length of time, looked at the new arrivals as dispassionate observers.

Catherine and Marjorie, plummeted into a new dimension where normal feelings and reactions were increased exponentially, experienced a strange sensation of inadequacy and weakness.

Overcoming certain awkwardness, Marjorie introduced Catherine to Magdalene. She had heard her daughter talking about this friend from Italy. Moreover, she understood how close they were. However, she never imagined coming face-to-face with her so soon.

However, Catherine was there, next to her, waiting for some sign of acknowledgment and acceptance.

Magdalene reluctantly came back from her self-imposed banishment from the human race. She leaned forward to scrutinize Catherine's face and overall appearance. Finally, extending her arm, she shook hands, and imperceptibly said, "Welcome!"

For Catherine, afraid of intruding in somebody's life, that opening, while certainly not warm, was nevertheless reassuring.

She never dreamt of being greeted with open arms or any type of celebration. After all, she was a perfect stranger with no claims or demands.

After that timid gesture, in an impulsive act of affection, Catherine tenderly hugged the grieving mother.

Magdalene, deeply touched by that spontaneous outpouring of love, shed some silent tears. An involuntary witness to a deeply moving scene, Marjorie could hardly refrain her emotions.

Another magic moment followed, when Catherine gently shifted her attention from the mother to her motionless half-sister.

Without paying any attention to Mark, with a delicate gesture, she removed some hair from Heloise's eyes. After, bending over, she kissed her and whispered, "Heloise, it's me, Catherine. I'm here, next to you."

Nobody could have ever captured the mysterious connection between those two human creatures. Nobody could have ever understood the secret bond that united those two fraternal souls.

No indication of any movement or acknowledgment on Heloise's part, just a motionless body, kept alive by artificial means.

Where were those gracious gestures, that captivating smile, that enchanting composure? Where was that melodious voice and that vibrant life, dedicated to justice and righteousness?

Catherine remained silent, expecting something miraculous to happen. Nevertheless, the skies did not open bringing back the vivifying energies, and the earth did not rumble announcing the rescuing knight.

All seemed irremediably lost, all seemed gone forever. A veil of sadness and desperation covered Catherine's face. Still holding her sister's hand, she stood erect, like a solitary column of an ancient temple, and wept and wept.

Neither Marjorie nor Magdalene could grasp the intensity and depth of that attachment.

An interminable pause ensued, broken only by sporadic hospital announcements.

Finally, the arrival of a nurse interrupted the inaction of that silent gathering. Asked to abandon the room, they obeyed without the slightest resistance or objection.

The medical specialist would conduct a thorough examination to determine the patient's condition.

Everybody was anxious to hear some comforting news, even if all appearances led in the opposite direction.

The doctor, a Harvard graduate and a luminary in the field of head trauma, greeted the visitors with some words of encouragement. Immediately, he entered the room and began performing his examination with an empathetic accuracy.

Doctors, an amazing breed of miracle workers, are considered all-powerful and almighty when they come to determine the physical conditions of a mortal.

Their orders are commands and their diagnoses Words of God. Rarely does the patient have a say in his treatment. He must follow to the letter what he is told to do.

In Heloise's case, the contrast between the reality of a physician, as a human being, and his perceived persona, with a halo of untouchability, could not be more striking.

In fact, he could measure the least of progresses in those broken bones, assess with preciseness the healing process of the wounds and get a perfect reading of the vitals: temperature, blood pressure, pulse and respiration.

However, he was very impotent in predicting, even with a minimum of certainty, when Heloise's consciousness, the only vital thing that would make her alive, would come back to that motionless body.

Would the improving physical conditions be a forerunner of her regained consciousness, or just a deceptive sign of her total demise?

The doctor could convey to the relatives a huge amount of relevant information, leaving them awestruck, but he could not give them the only assurance they were waiting for: their beloved one recognizing them and talking again.

They were unaware of this physician's limitations, and like any credulous beings were hoping against hope, and believing in the impossible.

The wait outside the door was becoming agonizing for every single one of them, especially Magdalene.

She was praying to the invisible God with the fervor of a novice and the intensity of a mystic.

Catherine and Marjorie could feel their hearts pounding in their chests, ready to jump out of their bodies. Mark had already left for an undisclosed location.

Finally, the agonizing wait was over, and the doctor, holding Heloise's medical chart under his arm, exited the room.

From his look, if something indicative had transpired, was the total absence of any meaningful indication. Was he at a loss with his diagnosis? If so, his appearance would be deceptive.

The three women stared at him as they would probably stare at a mythological oracle, and waited for some kind of sibylline response.

Relying on the general presumption that the doctor knows best, they listened to his every word, evaluating the inflection of his voice and the professional demeanor of his body.

"Heloise's vital signs," he began, "are stable. The healing of her wounds and broken bones is proceeding slowly, as expected. Some infection might still occur. With a few more analyses, x-rays and MRIs we shall have a more complete picture. Then and only then, will I be able to formulate something definite."

Magdalene, not in the least reassured by those expressions, scientifically sound, but completely devoid of any human significance, dared to ask, "Is my daughter going to regain consciousness, and will she ever be able to move again?"

The doctor, assuming a prophetic posture, and without looking straight into the eyes of his interlocutor, answered, "I can't promise you anything. Only God and Nature could give you a more qualifying response. I wish you a good day."

With that, he left the three poor women with fundamental questions unanswered. The big man, with the awesome power of giving back life to terminally ill people, failed to give peace of mind to three defenseless females.

Would God or Nature ever heed their desperate pleas for mercy? Would Heloise be capable of walking again on this earth, and carry out her noble mission of establishing some justice in the broken relations of our quarrelsome and litigious society?

Too many unanswered questions floated in the simple minds of concerned relatives and friends. The prevailing feelings were a mix of hope and desperation, very difficult to express or put into words.

For Marjorie the mission was over. Her family and job demanded her immediate presence. It was with great regret that she had to leave the private clinic, wishing all the best to Magdalene and Catherine, true guardian angels.

She made it clear before saying goodbye that she wanted to be promptly informed of any development on Heloise's health condition.

Catherine thanked Marjorie from the bottom of her heart, for the invaluable assistance she had warmly received since her arrival from Italy.

A warm hug to both of them sealed Marjorie's departure for Washington, D.C.

The two remaining women, so distant among themselves but so close to the patient, looked silently into each other's eyes. Too many barriers existed in their personal lives to establish a cordial rapport.

The uneasiness was patent in their facial expressions and body movements. Slowly overcoming the emotional divide, Magdalene suggested, in a caring way, that they take turns monitoring Heloise.

Catherine, being younger, gladly chose the night shift, while Magdalene would be in charge during the daytime. For their period of rest, they booked individual rooms in a hotel, just across the street.

Upon agreeing on this mutual arrangement, very acceptable to both, they went their separate ways. Committed to providing their best assistance, they favorably experienced a sense of relief, a sweet peace, unthinkable a few minutes earlier.

They had no idea what the future had in store for them, neither were they eager to know, afraid of some unwelcome development. They were living one hour at a time, praying for God to spare them from the worst.

Would their round-the-clock vigil at Heloise's bedside be an interminable one? Or would the dawn of a new glorious day shine sooner than expected, bringing immeasurable happiness?

Being late in the afternoon, Magdalene would stay, while Catherine would go back to the hotel and rest. Her shift would start at dusk and she would spend the night in the company of her half-sister.

She could not recall remaining up at night for any indefinite period of time. It was certainly a new experience, completely unusual and original.

The strange word "shift" did not have any resonance in her subconscious, while "vigil" instantly took her back to medieval times, when monks spent many night hours in prayer, and aspiring knights kept vigilant all night before being knighted in a pompous ceremony.

Still major Christian festivities were celebrated with a solemn vigil, where confessions and special dishes would speak to the faithful of purification and abstinence.

Obviously, as a teacher, she was more in tune with this European tradition than with the American working experience.

All wrapped up in this historical past, Catherine, refreshed and restored, showed up on time for her duty.

Magdalene, understandably worrisome, made a couple of recommendations and left the Italian woman to fend for herself. To be completely truthful, she did not have the slightest idea how to deal with that unexpected help.

Catherine, on the other hand, was fearful of not fulfilling the expectations implicitly bestowed on her. Anyhow, life is a cornucopia of constant surprises, and there is no point shying away from them.

The unconscious Heloise, lying motionless on the bed, brought back memories of her mother, Caterina, suffering from an incurable illness. How could she ever forget or be oblivious of her beloved mom's long and painful journey toward her final destination?

She was not sure whether it was Heloise's compulsory walk toward death, or just a necessary stage on her way to recovery.

However, she was quite certain of one thing. She would do anything in her power to prevent her sister from leaving her alone on this earth.

She was sitting all alone, intently observing her sister's facial expressions, when her cellular rang. It was Magdalene, the solicitous and attentive mother, inquiring about Heloise.

To every single question, Catherine responded, "All fine, all fine." Somehow reassured by that foreign voice, Magdalene hung up. Soon after that, she called her husband in Washington, D.C., wishing him goodnight. Finally, she went to bed, closing her eyes on a difficult day.

With every passing hour, Catherine was becoming sleepier. She tried to fight back that somnolent state, but she could not prevent dozing off for short intervals.

During those moments of light sleep and drowsiness, scary images populated her mind, feeling lost in a vast prairie with no path or direction.

Was that a true reflection of her deep sentiments? Far and away from her country and native village, immersed in a new culture and surrounded by unknown faces, it would not be surprising to feel at a loss.

In between a guilty conscience, remorse and tiredness Catherine saw the pale light of dawn filtering through the glass windows. Her first vigil was coming to a close without incident.

The nurses checking the patient every hour on the hour left her undisturbed, whether she was awake or not. She apologized to one of them for falling asleep on and off. With an understanding smile the nurse told her not to worry. Apparently, that was a common practice among the night shift personnel and Catherine was fitting quite well into the new environment.

When Magdalene arrived at eight o'clock, the comment from Catherine was, "All fine, no change." There was no good news, but there was no bad news either. Probably, another anxious day, and another uneventful shift awaited both of them.

Very parsimoniously raising her hand in greeting, Catherine left the ward and the hospital.

Her sleep during the day was interrupted numerous times. Her body refused a prolonged rest, as artificial and unnatural.

During those interruptions, her imagination was galloping through a myriad of possibilities of what to do during the night.

She came up with a dubious plan. She would picture herself in her native village, dictating class to her little students. In order to capture their attention and stimulate their creativity, she would start narrating some inspiring stories.

Maybe Heloise, in her apparently unconscious state, would connect emotively to the sound of that voice, even completely ignoring the meaning of that yarn.

Would it work, or would it be merely a childish foolishness, as ineffective as useless?

Catherine was neither a medical doctor nor a psychiatrist, but she surely possessed some feminine intuition. What science could not do perhaps her ingenuity could obtain in some miraculous way.

Anyhow, all that mattered was to hope and to try. If it wasn't beneficial for Heloise, at least it would be advantageous for Catherine, keeping her alert and vigilant.

Satisfied with her simple ploy, she appeased her spirit and put her mind to rest. A few more hours of sleep, and she would awake totally renewed.

With a boosted morale, she marched toward the hospital, ready to engage Heloise's hidden monsters and her own secret fears.

This time, Magdalene saw her in a different light. Catherine appeared to transude confidence. The sense of being lost had vanished, and the conviction of a mission brightened her eyes.

In her ill-concealed desperation, Magdalene herself felt more animated and hopeful. Perhaps not all was lost. Some little ray of hope would filter through the thick clouds of that menacing sky.

In an unusual move, the poor mother hugged Catherine, with affection foreign to her personality.

The second night was not so bad for Catherine. Around eleven o'clock, when everything was becoming quieter inside and outside the building, she put in motion her plan.

With a gentle and persuasive tone of voice, she began narrating a beautiful Italian tale of yesteryear. Embellishing it along the way, by adding details that were not in the original, she was not only entertaining herself but also keeping her sister company.

Would any of those sounds reach Heloise's living soul, or would they be just a strange vocal resonance among those mute walls?

Time passed slowly, almost imperceptibly, while Heloise was not sending any signal through her motionless body.

Wasn't she receiving Catherine's communication, or was she just waiting for the right time?

The tale lasted a few hours and at the end of it Catherine, overcome by fatigue, was falling asleep. She was holding Heloise's hand, when all of a sudden, in her drowsiness, she perceived a slight movement.

Was her sister trying to convey some mysterious message, or was it just her sleepy imagination making up sensations that were not real?

Totally awake now, and with her eyes wide open, she scrutinized her sister from head to toe. Nothing unusual came across her observation. Everything was as before. No movement and no sign of any kind.

Maybe her imagination was playing a sadistic trick on her. Any hope of something good was dashed in the blink of an eye.

She promised herself to be more vigilant, and not to doze off shamelessly as she had done before. How could she forgive herself, if for any reason she missed her sister's return from that comatose state?

Another night and another day. Every day when the daylight faded imperceptibly into the night, Catherine came back to the hospital. Every morning when the dawn became brighter and warmer, Magdalene showed up with unflinching determination.

Like two warriors, ready to engage in mortal combat, they faced an invisible enemy, sneaky and cowardly, unwilling to confront them face-to-face.

One week had passed and nothing had changed. Only one thing was deteriorating progressively: their determination to stand firm, holding their position without withdrawal or retreat.

Time, with its wearing action, was becoming the worst opponent. Any strategy, physical or psychological, was crashing against its pervasive omnipresence.

Catherine was battling an even more damaging element. Her dwindling finances would not allow her to stay much longer in a hotel. Prostrated with grief and on her knees with pain and fear, she summoned up her courage and made a last attempt.

At this stage, when everything seemed ineffective or even ridiculous, she did not mind looking foolish.

Her love for Heloise and her compassion for Magdalene, to whom she felt greatly attached, moved her in one direction.

Going back to her experience as a teacher, she remembered something very clearly. When everything had failed with her students, she would turn infallibly to the narration of a heartbreaking story from the book *Cuore* by Edmondo De Amicis. The result was always miraculous. Even the most insubordinate boys would abandon their defiant attitude and rebellious posture.

Therefore, on the fifteenth day of her vigil, after being handed over the shift duties by Magdalene, she decided to fight her last monstrous battle.

With all the passion she could master, she would narrate the story "*From the Apennines to the Andes.*"

With that moving tale, she would hope to bring back Heloise's wandering soul and put an end to this intolerable situation.

In case of failure, she would pack her bags, and return inconsolably to Italy, unless some Good Samaritan came to her financial rescue.

When everything quieted down around her, Catherine realized that her heart was pumping with excitement and, with her heavy breathing, that was all she could hear.

Holding, as she had the previous nights, Heloise's right hand, and kissing it with deep affection, she called upon her sister in a ceremonious way: "My dear Heloise, listen to your Catherine. I've tried my best so far, but all my efforts were in vain. My dearest one, this will be my last attempt. Do not disappoint me, but mainly have pity on your mother. Do not dash her hopes.

Wherever you are, come back to us. I saved my best story for last. This is so moving that nobody ever could refrain from shedding abundant tears.

Once upon a time, in Genoa, Italy, there was a poor family. The parents had a very hard time feeding the hungry mouths of their numerous children. The affectionate mother, faced with the tragic alternative of letting them starve to death or abandoning them in search of a job, reluctantly but valiantly chose the second one.

With a stoic attitude, she crossed the Atlantic Ocean in an enormous ship, and after a long and troubled navigation, disembarked in Buenos Aires, Argentina.

Employed as a domestic by an engineer family, every month she sent back money and news to Italy.

Embarrassed but not ashamed by her new condition, she changed her name.

One year had barely expired, when every communication stopped. Imagine the grief and pain of the poor family in Italy. They did not mind the lack of money, but the unexplained silence of their mother and wife was killing them.

The smallest of the children, Marco, still unable to contribute to the family finances because of his tender age, in a supreme act of love for his mom, decided to leave everything behind, and go in search of his beloved mother."

After this introduction, Catherine, taking her time and using the best of her storytelling abilities, began describing Marco's unbelievable decision and his consequent endless ordeal.

The family's strong opposition did not prevent him from sailing across the Atlantic, overcoming mountains of troubles and oceans of pain.

His long, perilous journey from Genoa to Buenos Aires, from Rosario to Córdoba and Tucumán constitutes a real odyssey, where courage, bravery, suffering and humiliation are the backbones of this unusual human experience.

Along the journey, he found helping hands from compatriots, but also physical and mental abuse from unscrupulous profiteers and cruel exploiters.

The success of this incredible search had been seriously compromised many times by hunger, disease and total exhaustion.

Against all odds, the resilient young boy, born and reborn in the crucible of a burning love, reached his final destination.

At this point of her narration, Catherine realized that many hours had passed. Her mouth was dry and her voice hoarse and raspy. Soon would be dawn and the end of her shift.

At any cost, she would finish her story and make her final and desperate appeal to her sister. Taking her courage in both hands, she called upon Heloise to listen attentively.

"Marco, starving and exhausted, walked a few more miles outside the city of Tucumán. Not very far away, he could see a ranch, where his mother was supposed to work. Thinking of that place as his Promised Land, he accelerated his steps, despite his body's refusal to obey.

Unfortunately, his mother had fallen gravely ill, and had declined any medical intervention. Having lost all hope in her strength and future, she was determined to die.

Mother and son were fighting their final battle: the first refusing to live, the second struggling to survive.

Finally, a knock at the door, hesitant and uncertain. The lady of the house, surprised, opened and what a moving scene. Marco was about to collapse on her doorstep. He had only enough strength to pronounce his mother's name. Shedding his last tear, he begged to see her.

From her bed the ill mother could hear the movements, the whispering and the unusual confusion. All of a sudden, in the chiaroscuro of her room, a familiar face appeared to her. Was it a dream, a hallucination, a visual memory of times past?

No, it was her son, Marco, in the flesh. He ran to her with the passion and longing of a child. Smiling and crying, sighing and whimpering, they hugged each other in an eternal embrace of love.

In that very moment, the ailing woman miraculously recovered the will to live. Immediately, she asked the doctor to perform the delicate operation.

The courageous boy, the loving son, with his arrival, had brought his mom back from the tomb."

"Heloise! Heloise!" exclaimed Catherine, in her final plea, "don't you see that unconditional love is stronger than death? Heloise, Heloise, come back to us! Your mother and I are waiting for you. We love you from the bottom of our hearts."

Exhausted and almost without a voice, Catherine looked at her sister. No response whatsoever from that angelic face and statuary body.

Still holding her right hand, in desperation, she let herself go on her chair. Love worked miracles in stories and tales, but apparently not in real life.

With a bitter taste of disappointment and desperation, she would wait for Magdalene to come and substitute her. Was she at the end of the line? Was it time to go back to her country?

The first sign of daylight filtered through the French windows, the hustle and bustle of the city, waking up, reached her ears. Tired and despondent as she was, she noticed neither light nor noise.

What she noticed instead was something else. She felt a slight grasp gripping her hand. Was it another cruel deception of her superheated imagination?

Incredulous and skeptical, she observed the hand that was being held by hers, and immediately after, she inspected Heloise's eyes.

Those beautiful blue eyes were wide open and intent on her, while the feeble attempt of that right hand seemed to convey an unmistakable message: "I'm back, and I'm here, look at me."

Catherine, in an unprecedented move, nearly jumped out of her skin. Oblivious to any composure and restraint, she began screaming at the top of her voice something totally unintelligible.

Fearing a sure tragedy, pandemonium broke out. Nurses, doctors, visitors ran precipitously to the place where the commotion originated.

It was an incredible sight. The comatose young lady, unable to move or communicate for more than two weeks, was awake and alert, observing what was happening. Catherine, next to her, was shedding tears of joy and uttering incomprehensible sounds.

The good news, like lightning on a stormy summer's day, reached the four corners of the hospital. Magdalene, the inconsolable mother, was notified, and the other relatives and friends as well.

No one was able to comprehend the prodigious event in all its implications. Only Catherine could make some sense out of that miracle. All her efforts had finally paid off!

Love, indeed, is stronger than death. Love can overcome and vanquish what medicine and doctors cannot.

The first person Heloise recognized was her half-sister, Catherine, and the only one she reconnected to her near-death experience, as she would recount later on.

It was not a simple recognition by Heloise; it was an affectionate and moving acceptance, a joyful reunion, a rediscovery of her secret sister.

As soon as she heard the news, Magdalene ran to the hospital, holding her breath. She kissed Heloise so many times that she forgot all past sufferings and misery.

However, the marvelous bond uniting Catherine and Heloise, when unconsciously perceived by Magdalene, made her jealous and uncomfortable.

That stranger, to whom she felt emotionally attached, threatened her supremacy in Heloise's heart.

This tainted perception did not prevent the envious mother from celebrating with the rest. Her daughter's comeback from the underworld was the most joyous occasion of her entire existence, as if she had been born for the second time.

Whatever was the reason for her rebirth, nothing, not even her displaced role as mother, would spoil it.

Gradually, with the passing of days, Heloise was recovering and remembering her fatal accident and her subliminal and extrasensory experience.

Her feelings were numbed, her mind foggy, her conscience in wait. Suspended outside time and space, total silence and absolute oblivion surrounded her.

No past, no future, just a meaningless present pervaded her comatose subsistence. She was like a blank sheet of paper, detached from a spiral notebook, and floating in a motionless vacuum.

From time to time, she could sense or imagine, she was not sure which one, a familiar voice pronouncing her name.

Where was that calling coming from, in case it was real? There was no direction, no path, and no exit. Could she move, reach the siren voice, alluring her to abandon that suspended state?

That pleasant voice was becoming more insistent and persuasive, like an immaterial beacon of hope, sucking her into its rays of life.

Unable to resist that powerful magnet, Heloise found herself immersed again into the familiar categories of geographical space and chronological time.

As soon as she opened her eyes, she recognized immediately the source of her energizing power, the seductive and irresistible siren, calling her back from the bowels of the earth. It was the sweet Catherine, her loving and caring sister.

A mother's love, so celebrated and idolized through the centuries by humankind, had proven ineffective. Instead, the tender affection of a humble foreigner came out triumphant to everybody's utter amazement.

This open acknowledgment by Heloise, brutal in nature but innocuous in wording, made Magdalene green with envy.

That insidious stranger, from her daughter's savior had become, all of a sudden, an opponent to be feared.

Even miracles at times can bring out the worst in people, creating incurable wounds and irreparable rifts.

Chapter IX

Brutus' rendezvous with Emily was pure ecstasy, indeed. The ancestral inhibitions were thrown out of the window and the prudent and cautious postures, learned in his training with Master Centurion, were drowned in a bacchanalia of liquor and sex.

The night was neither too intense nor long enough for a man starving for sex, and thirsty for affection. While the stars illuminated the skies above, Emily brightened up the obscure landscape of the somber executive.

The improvised orgy reached its climax in the wee hours of the morning. After that, the frantic haste for enjoyment and satisfaction flowed unconsciously into a light somnolence, followed by a heavy sleep.

When Brutus opened his eyes, the sun was already high, above the horizon, and Emily, smiley and complacent, was bringing a cup of freshly brewed coffee.

A terrible headache and a desire to vomit, clear signs of a monstrous hangover, greeted the waking hero.

He had not felt that bad since his college years. In the meantime, his chatty lover, in a skimpy camisole, offered him the hot beverage, and asked softly, "How do you feel?"

"Terrible!" he answered. "How about you?"

"Splendid!" she said, "it was a night to remember."

She was dead right. He would never forget that night, but for reasons that he would never have suspected.

Emily, like a classic spy, with her sensual games and refined female seduction, had extorted some compromising secrets.

In fact, in his inebriated state, he had loosened his tongue. Taking full advantage of the situation, Emily grabbed the powerful bull by the horns. Artfully, she asked him about his health, fears and problems. Without him realizing, she prodded the poor intoxicated man into forbidden territory.

It was then that key words came out of his mouth.

His rambling on disconnected topics did not make much sense at first, but on further examination something very sinister appeared to be happening, which constituted the core of his apprehensions.

Emily did not need to understand or unearth the company's skeletons in the rubble of the fallen giant. Only, by memorizing a few words and referring them to Brunilda, she would carry out an important spy mission, for which she would be largely gratified.

To a night of immense pleasure, she would add a generous bonus and a promotion. Not bad for a Nebraska girl, grown among corn and hogs.

Brutus' position was already compromised in Centurion's eyes, let alone with the police investigation. This new imprudent and reckless conduct would lead inevitably to a reassessment and likely a downgrade of his functions and duties.

As soon as his head cleared from the toxic effects of his inebriation, one thing emerged from the muddy waters of his conscience.

Caught by an unusual agitation, while sipping his coffee, he started moving his lips, and repeating in an obsessive mood, "Did I talk too much? Did, from my conversation, anything indiscreet transpire?"

Emily, who could easily detect fear in animals' behavior, whispered in Brutus' ear as she gently caressed his forehead and cheeks, "No need to torment yourself. Your secrets, no matter how big they are, are safe with me. Cheer up. With me at your side, you shouldn't fear a thing."

On subsequent examination of this reassurance, instead of calming down, he became more agitated and uncomfortable.

If she said, "Your secrets are safe with me," there was no doubt he had strayed into forbidden territory. Therefore, he begged her to disclose the main content of his dialogue.

Diverting his attention from the key words uttered in his confession, she reassured him again, "You talked about Hawaii, and how enchanting Kaanapali was. You revealed also that you had a secret crush on a local girl. She was so gorgeous that her beauty blinded you totally. Shame on you! I will ignore that and forgive you."

Emily's deception was perfect, because the credulous executive immediately stopped his self-destructive impulses of fear and panic. A gentle smile reappeared on his face, and a strong hug sealed their sensual friendship.

How simple-minded and foolish a man can be in the presence of an enchanting but deceitful woman!

The damaging words, still resonating in Emily's ears, were in complete contrast with her oral version. No love story, no little amorous games, but risky programs of manipulation and destruction.

Somehow, Brutus had let transpire the existence of an underground laboratory in Kaanapali, where delicate experimentations were carried out, with the creation of new pharmacological products, capable of altering human behavior. The word "assassination" came up several times, without any proper name attached to it.

It seemed that the second-in-command had a heavy load on his shoulders, maybe too bothersome even for his callous conscience.

After reinforcing their common bond, sexual in nature, the two lovers left for work, each with a different agenda on their minds.

Emily, in a closed-door meeting, conferred with her boss, Brunilda, about Brutus' alleged revelations. The existence of such a laboratory came as a big surprise to the company's lawyer. Who could have ever imagined that the great philanthropist Mark Centurion would engage in criminal activity, so close to the Nazi ideology and praxis?

She found herself at a real crossroads. To disclose the dark secret to her boss, as she was assigned to do, or to keep it under wraps for the time being, afraid of indisposing him. To be betrayed, in fact, by his closest associate, would not be an easy pill to swallow for the old man.

By sparing her boss from the ultimate deception, she would indirectly save Brutus' neck from the guillotine; on the other hand, by harboring the traitor's reckless conduct, she would inflict a severe blow to her boss' loyalty.

It would not be the content that would provoke Centurion's fury, but Brutus' impudence in revealing the company's top secrets to a cheap tramp.

As a master tactician, Brunilda proceeded with extreme caution, avoiding unnecessary casualties. That was a real ace up her sleeve, that could be used in due time.

She felt stronger and more powerful guarding the company's dirty secrets, but, at the same time, diminished and belittled for not being an integral part of the inner circle.

In possession of that damaging information, one day she could possibly topple her arch-rival, Brutus, and assume the regalia of Vice President.

That had been her dream since the very beginning of her career.

Born and raised in New York, Brunilda was a very smart girl and a super liberal teenager. At age twenty, she had experimented with all that was available, from sex to drugs.

Intolerant of any parental control, she left home at age eighteen. With a rough couple of years in a demeaning job, she could save enough money to begin college. Part-time working and evening classes allowed her to enter law school and graduate, eight years later, *summa cum laude*.

Extremely proud of her achievements, she answered an ad, joining a prestigious law firm, in Washington, D.C.

She was fascinated by politics, intrigue and scandals of all kinds. What better place than Washington, D.C. to satisfy her voracious appetite for thrills and spills!

Politics and finances were her strong suit. In a few short years, she had built up quite a reputation, being known as the shark lawyer and the Amazon counselor. Her killer instinct, going straight for the jugular, left the courtrooms of the capital scattered with corpses.

Her instant success attracted Mark Centurion's interest. Money talks, and big money talks louder. He made her an offer she could not refuse.

Flapping her wings outside the law firm, she became a real star. Her dreams and ambitions were supported by a few incredible beliefs, not acquired in school.

According to Brunilda, people are either born to rule or be ruled. There is no middle ground. The perfect explanation can be found in nature. Like in a beehive there is only a queen bee, the same way in every human organization, there is one master, and one master only. The rest must follow his lead and obey.

She was born to be a leader and to subject others to her commands. Fierce and fearless, she conducted her business as a supreme commander-in-chief, with no hesitation or second thought.

Another curious belief, related to her femininity, was the following. Some women are born to procreate, some to educate. She belonged to the second group. Procreation was not for her. She was destined to mold innumerable minds. As a potter gives shape to formless clay, so would she put an expressive face on countless living bodies.

That face would conform to the law of the land. Under her inflexible hand, lawless citizens would become law-abiding subjects, criminals turn into respected human beings, and careless people into caring souls.

That was her mission in its pure and primordial stage. However, as frequently happens with inspired reformers and exalted visionaries, time and circumstances work their way into the human heart, subverting priorities and corrupting intentions.

Brunilda was no exception to this historical nemesis. If she believed strongly in nature, she could have unmistakably predicted such a turn of events. It was unavoidable, because it was in the nature of things.

Her irrepressible search for justice, accompanied by a strong desire for a just punishment, slowly subsided in the presence of a surging subservient urge for power and prestige.

A flirtatious necessity to please her boss added a peculiar flavor to the new emerging personality. Brunilda, the consecrated unmarried woman, reverted to the use, under the perverse impulses of her youth, of her dormant sexual allure, in order to further her unrestrainable ambition.

Blinded by those mundane undercurrents, she did not realize that Mark Centurion was well past his roaring years of amorous escapades and forbidden romances.

Even if he enjoyed subtle advances with undertones of maternal protection and feminine caring, springing up, at times, from Brunilda's well of inexhaustible energies, Mark didn't need to satisfy his sexual drive, because there was none left.

To engage in any promiscuous intercourse would have been too much of a burden for the old man, solid as an oak but sapped of his burning virile passion.

The acclaimed lawyer so penetrative in the courtroom had lost her touch and understanding of the different stages of human life.

That did not prevent Brunilda from trying repeatedly, but always unsuccessfully and with a sense of disappointment.

Now the tables had turned on her. To reach the top and convince the boss of her undisputed loyalty, she possessed a formidable weapon—Brutus' unwise indiscretions.

All her dreams were within easy reach. It was only a question of time and opportunity.

Brutus, on the other hand, had the sword of Damocles hanging by a single hair above his head. Completely unaware of his perilous position, and ignoring how quickly happiness can be lost, he left Emily's cozy bedroom.

He drove to his luxury apartment. While humming a cheerful tune softly to himself, he put on a designer suit. A pleasant day was unfolding in front of his eyes.

At the office, he greeted everyone, even the janitor, with a broad smile. His orders were not harsh and irritated, but persuasive and soothing.

It was obvious to everyone that something had happened, and its nature should not be a mystery to anybody.

Observing him walking and interacting as if he were on cloud nine, employees whispered strange comments in each other's ears.

Slowly, that honeymoon-like posture subsided and a creeping nervousness obscured his radiant facial expression.

What was happening inside that man, made of steel and forged in coldness?

He was convinced that Emily would call him, showing gratitude and appreciation for the marvelous night spent together, or at least some joyful expression of satisfaction.

To his chagrin, the hours passed inexorably, and no sign from his idolized lover. Lunchtime came and went, and still no communication from Emily.

Unable to put up with that intolerable situation, Brutus grabbed the phone, and from a florist around the corner, he ordered a beautiful bouquet of red carnations to be sent to Emily's office.

The flowers were delivered within the hour, but there was no apparent attempt by Emily to contact him. A few more hours, and the intolerant Brutus had to resign himself to his miserable fate.

The fact of not knowing what was behind that silence was consuming him. Was it a rejection or a simple negligence? Was it a lover's cruel game, or a bloody betrayal?

The sly businessman, so shrewd in his material dealings, didn't have a clue on the slippery road of romance.

The many disappointments of his past life did not teach him one iota about women.

The following day a distracted Emily called him. Keeping aloof and distant, she asked how he was doing.

Such coolness was hardly conceivable by Brutus, let alone acceptable. In retaliation, he answered using the same strategy. The exchange of words was short and to the point.

He had never been rude to her, but this time it was different. She had to understand that she was playing with fire.

After hanging up, he was more confused than ever, not knowing where he was stood and whether their romance had any future.

At the opposite end of the spectrum, Emily was enjoying a rare mental clarity, and an indubitable certainty of her future.

For her, Brutus was a means to an end. The end had been achieved, so the need for the means no longer existed. She could dispose of him coldheartedly, at any time.

If a scorned woman is dangerous, a scorned man might become a time bomb.

Considering Brutus was under investigation by the police, under suspicion in the eyes of his boss, and now under undue pressure from Emily, the epithet of "time bomb" might sound mild and inoffensive.

Under such pressure, fatal mistakes are bound to happen, and Brutus was no exception.

To complicate matters further, the police were getting to the bottom of the car accident in which Icarus Proctor lost his life.

The mechanic, Pedro Almendarez, had confessed to tampering with the brakes. The prospect of a big payoff from his boss, Carlos Carreras, did not prevent him from talking.

It was only a matter of time until Carlos gave in, under the relentless police tactics. That would be the end for Brutus. It was imperative to stop, once and for all, the leakage.

He came up with a plan, brilliant in his opinion. He would pay Carlos handsomely, forcing him to take a well-deserved trip to Jamaica. Once there, he would arrange for his assassination by a local thug.

What could go wrong? No money trail, no papers of any kind, no phone calls, just an anonymous third party connecting the dots of the killer spider web.

If successful, after the implementation, this would be the first known skeleton in Brutus' closet. However, his readiness to take away, in cold blood, a human life might induce the reader to believe in a pattern of previous unscrupulous crimes.

At this point, the only certainty is his callous disregard for human life, and his heartless determination to play this cerebral chess game, sacrificing anything in his path, until the final victory.

So far, he had managed to keep a step ahead of the police. Would blind fate protect him in the future, or would he stumble and fall flat on his face?

All signs of an impending disaster loomed large on the horizon—fury of a scorned man, a formidable opponent in Brunilda, and founded suspicions from all the authorities around him.

While Brutus was in the planning stages of his assassination plot, he got the incredible news of Carreras' shooting.

An enraged motorist had gotten into an altercation with Carlos, for unknown reasons. Without a second thought, he executed the gas station owner with a single shot in the head, mafia style.

It was hard for Brutus to believe his luck, just when everything else was crashing down around him. However, his state of euphoria did not last long, because a phone call from the local police brought back his fears and insecurities.

He had to surrender voluntarily into police custody, being the prime suspect in Carreras' murder. If this turn of events was really twisted in nature, what followed was even more twisted and ludicrous.

Brunilda was appointed by Mark Centurion to defend him. It was like the classic tale of the fox guarding the hen house.

Finally, the acclaimed lawyer had total control over her chief rival. In possession of his amorous indiscretions, and in charge of his criminal defense, she could easily turn the tables on him.

However, the good name of her company and boss were of paramount importance to Brunilda. Disregarding petty squabbles and personal animosities, she would look at the big picture and mount a formidable defense.

Not even her own son, if she had one, could have received better legal assistance.

During the two weeks before Brutus' appearance in front of a local judge, Brunilda left no stone unturned, uncovering a total lack of evidence, rush to judgment and plain prejudice in the police investigation.

The day of the arraignment turned out to be Brunilda's biggest epiphany ever. Instead of Brutus being charged with murder, the police had to face the music. Astoundingly, the officers in charge of the original investigation were brought up on charges of gross negligence and misconduct.

Unable to halt Brunilda's barrage of heavy artillery, the police retreated in confusion and disgrace. The judge dismissed the case against Brutus for lack of evidence, and he was totally exonerated of all charges.

The triumph could not have been more impressive and the victory sweeter. Brunilda proved again to be a brilliant lawyer and an unbeatable litigator.

Mark Centurion was extremely proud of her. She was the biggest asset the company ever had. On the other hand, the shadow of suspicion that had fallen on Brutus had darkened his career prospects, jeopardized his future and his survival as Centurion's number two.

His immediate job, now, was to collect the pieces of his reputation, so damaged and tarnished, and try to compose an image palatable to the public in general and the authorities in particular.

He had never experienced a similar rude awakening in the past. He had to swim against a strong current, and fight against all odds.

Among the uncertainties, there was one sure thing. The police, after that public humiliation, solemnly vowed to seek revenge. That brassy lawyer and that weasel of an executive would pay dearly for their impudent attack on the police force.

If Brutus was under suspicion before, now he would be under constant threat. Monitored twenty-four hours a day, every little indiscretion, every tiny misstep would weigh heavily in the eyes of law enforcement.

Obviously, our exonerated hero, while reconstructing his image, shall try to keep a low profile, but without abandoning his previous lifestyle.

Unfortunately, he was completely unaware that the nail that sticks out is the one being hammered first.

The police compiled a long list of friends and foes, phone numbers and places, routine actions and extraordinary moves. Their tight surveillance was unrelenting.

Not even an international terrorist would command such a painstaking operation. However, when dealing with the significant issue of defending the honor and life of a single police officer, nothing is ever excessive or unjustified.

On Centurion's recommendation, and to diffuse some bad publicity, Brutus booked a flight to Maui. The luxury hotel in Kaanapali would be his hideaway for some time. This would not come as a surprise to anybody, since every other month he would officially visit it in his supervisory capacity.

Everything was ready, when his only niece, Chelsea, from North Dakota, showed up unexpectedly. She was a delightful young woman, studying at Miami University. As soon as she heard of her uncle's troubles, she flew into Washington, D.C.

She hugged him warmly and with a big smile, she protested her unconditional support. This scene, so moving in many ways, did not provoke the same reaction.

Brutus did not reciprocate with the same amount of passion and affection. He felt like his sister's daughter, under those circumstances, was not helping at all.

Despite his lack of enthusiasm, he put up a great performance:

"I am delighted to see you, dear Chelsea, after such a long time. I would have never expected such a visit. You look absolutely stunning. By the way, how is your mom?"

"I'm glad to be here," she answered, "in these trying times for your career. I hope I'm not imposing on you, knowing your hectic schedule and your great responsibilities. My mom is doing fine, and she loves you very much."

"You are more than welcome, dear. Nothing would please me more, at this very moment, than your supportive presence."

Uttering those words, he was lying through his teeth. In fact, he would rather be with that traitor Emily, or any cheap slut, than with his niece.

Unfortunately, for her, and fortunately for him, Chelsea could not read minds and uncover the real Brutus. However, sagacious as she was, she could sense some stretching of the truth.

Graciously, she accepted those unnatural protestations of affection and appreciation, thanking him from the bottom of her heart.

A master in converting awkward situations into positive ones, his first thought was to improve his tarnished image of a family man utilizing his niece's presence.

In the battle for custody of his daughter, Karina, he gave up too easily. Now, it was time to gain back some of his lost reputation.

He immediately cancelled his flight to Maui, instead scheduling some social events, where he would put his niece on display.

The police did not believe any of that crap, and kept a vigilant eye on the man, so versatile and resourceful in his diabolic plans.

Mark Centurion, through Brunilda's emissaries, was following him too, ready to cut him loose from his association, as soon as the occasion arose.

The FBI investigators worked sedulously on Centurion's unsuccessful kidnapping attempt. Apparently, at one point, after arresting a couple of the kidnappers, they came into possession of some significant leads.

Their connection with Brutus Barker appeared more solid than they genuinely thought at the very beginning. In order not to blow their chances of a conviction, as in Carlos Carreras' case, they evaluated every little shred of evidence, and waited patiently until they could extract some more valuable information from the two men in custody.

News of their gradual progress was made purposely available to Brutus' acquaintants. In this particular instance, the federal investigators believed that the dissemination of relevant information would serve better than the proverbial tight lips posture.

At one of those social events where Chelsea was expected to shine, something very unusual happened.

Kegs of German beer were rolling in from a supplier, overflowing pints were being passed around, and people's tongues were getting looser. The merriment was reaching its apex, when suddenly an eerie silence took hold of the noisy audience.

Only a feminine voice could be heard. It was Chelsea, the young revelation of the evening, arguing bitterly. Everybody was dumbfounded at her extemporaneous outburst, when she angrily tried to stop the rumors circulating about her uncle.

The gossip that Brutus was about to be indicted in Mark Centurion's kidnapping pushed her into overdrive, spinning her out of control.

She would allow nobody to soil her uncle's reputation, and much less to equiparate him to a criminal.

Very emotional and with bitter tears in her eyes she left the gathering. The social event that was expected to be a joyous one, with the presence of a rising star, making everyone comfortable and at ease, ended up a near disaster.

The FBI's subtle stratagem could not have been more successful, to Brutus' sheer embarrassment. For the young and naive Chelsea, it was a rude awakening.

Apparently, her uncle wasn't a knight in shining amour, a spotless and immaculate cavalier, a gentleman and gallant baron of industry.

No soothing words or protests of innocence from the embattled uncle dissipated the dark cloud hanging ominously over his reputation.

Chea (Chelsea's nickname because of her thick, curly hair reminiscent of the product invariably advertised every Christmas season), the adorable pet able to perform sheer magic, had totally lost her halo of enchantment.

Reduced to a common mortal, and deprived of sensitive attributes, she would never regain confidence and trust in herself, or her adored uncle.

The unfortunate episode, like a blood baptism, signaled the end of her innocence. It indicated also the cancellation of any other social event, pushing her back into her cherished anonymity.

From now on, she would rather go skinny dipping in some frigid lake in Alaska, than take part in any social happening in Washington, D.C.

Still a sense of something unresolved troubled her delicate conscience. She had been completely sincere in her actions and reactions. Could she say the same in Brutus' case?

She had to wait patiently for some time before finding the underlying cause of that confusing matter. In the meantime, with nothing left to look forward to, in the capital city, she retreated to her university campus in Miami.

Her departure was neither emotional nor touching. For both of them, it came as liberation from an unintended bondage.

Brutus, always under police surveillance, did not waste any time. The rumors, circulating about his involvement in Centurion's failed kidnapping, accelerated his frantic escape. The strategic planner, successfully tested and approved in his business transactions, gave place to a retrieving general.

He had learned an important lesson during his childhood in the North Dakota wilderness—hide in a burrow when a predator is chasing.

A second important lesson he should have picked up in a hurry during his niece's incident, was certainly total devotion and attachment to family. Chea showed him that blood truly is thicker than water.

Unfortunately, Brutus never put family in the center of his universe. Egotist as he was, he was the universe, and everything else had to revolve around him.

Honesty and forthrightness were not his strong suit, the same way filial affection and tender devotion toward the members of his family did not exist in his barren world.

He had been and would always be a loner. The father figure he found in Mark Centurion was just that, a mere figure.

Feeling no regrets for his past upbringing, he put the pieces of his crumbling existence on an imaginary table, making a valiant effort to piece them together.

However, fruitless and incongruent as it was, he faced an impossible task. Nobody could bring back his wife, and no judge was ready to revoke his daughter's custody. Cleared in Carlos Carreras' murder, he was still being actively investigated in Centurion's attempted kidnapping.

His alleged friends, Brunilda and Emily, were secretly conspiring against him. His boss kept a safe distance from him. In this way, his best backing had vanished, leaving him unprotected and an easy target for any voracious predator.

Betrayal and abandonment created in him a fundamental need for revenge. Before they destroyed him, he would destroy them.

Was the classic tragedy of Brutus murdering Caesar being reenacted in this modern drama of intrigue, manipulation and treachery?

Was Barker's first name a dreadful presage of his bloodthirsty nature?

From a black present, one could expect only a stormy future. In addition, a huge storm was gathering strength, threatening any living creature in its path.

Brutus was reading the handwriting on the wall. Without being a superstitious man, he felt his heart pounding in his chest and his courage slipping away.

CHAPTER X

Heloise's miraculous comeback from her coma left a bitter taste in Magdalene's mouth. An imperceptible tension emerged between her and Catherine.

For this reason, the celebration, instead of being exuberant and uninhibited, turned out restrained and subdued.

That subtle aversion became outright hostility as soon as Heloise made known her decision to retain her half-sister at her side, and leaving her in charge of the daily operations of her rehabilitation.

Catherine's vigilant supervision, in her new role, was creating a serious rift between mother and daughter. Being very sensitive, she had no stomach for this kind of family squabble, and courageously decided to return to her homeland.

Heloise, obviously, would not have any of it. In her judgment, it was better to somehow indispose her mother than to lose Catherine.

It was difficult for relatives and friends to understand that odd decision. However, if they knew the sacred bond that united those two souls, probably the whole situation would have not become so incomprehensible.

Revealing that burdensome secret would undoubtedly create more damage in Magdalene than good. It was preferable the lesser evil of a disgruntled mother than the knowledge of her husband's infidelity.

A well-balanced program of physical therapy was restoring the natural movement of Heloise's limbs, and the strength of her muscles.

Her mind, however, was trapped in a serious dilemma and no psychological counseling was able to put order and clarity into her ideas.

Once back to her usual self, would she freely pursue her amateurish investigation of the infamous credit card (probably connected to several murders), or would she give up that wild goose chase, and renounce shedding some light on her friend's mysterious death?

Unless her recovery proved to be complete and permanent, no definite resolution could be taken. This could be protracted for weeks or, more likely, months, leaving everything hanging by a thread.

For Heloise, always active and on the run, this forced idleness was far worse than a coma. How could she picture herself fiddling around, while severe injustices were being perpetrated at all levels, and murderers were terrorizing poor neighborhoods?

Every season in nature has its meaning and function, likewise every stage of her life should have a reason and a purpose. It was up to her to discover that secret mission.

During the two weeks following her prodigious awakening, she discovered something else, very important and meaningful.

Her family ties, especially with her father, had been loose, almost detached. Since she had not been naturally inclined to form her own family, she established a close friendship with Angie.

After her sudden demise, a great emptiness was left in Heloise's heart. Now, Catherine was filling it in abundance, overflowing with enthusiasm and confidence.

That was the closest she ever came to a real family. She did not need other amorous connections or liaisons. That was more than sufficient to satisfy all her desires of belonging. Catherine became her Rock of Gibraltar, her lifeline in the tumultuous ocean of life.

For that reason, she wanted Catherine at her side, purposely displacing her mother to a secondary role. There were no hard feelings toward the woman that gave her life, just a necessary readjustment to the new reality.

This newfound balance in her existence propelled Heloise into a different stage. Catherine would guide her masterfully through her rehabilitation, and probably, later on, could play some meaningful role.

Life is full of surprises, and this was true for Heloise, for her mother, and for anybody involved in her remarkable story.

Two weeks of intense counseling and physical therapy allowed Heloise to be discharged from the hospital and live in her apartment, under Catherine's care and vigilant eyes.

Mark Centurion was glad, but not jubilant, that his daughter was out of danger. He wanted to celebrate her return home with a special dinner.

No one could ever imagine his surprise when he saw for the first time (the brief encounter in Miami did not count) Heloise's faithful companion and assistant. Catherine made quite an impression on the old man. That name and nationality brought back some vivid memories, that he was determined to take undisclosed to his grave.

Shaking her hand, a strange sensation pervaded his entire body. Looking straight into her eyes, he noticed a peculiar resemblance to a nice lady he once loved in a foreign land. Was that an incubus, fruit of his old age, or remorse of a repressed memory, ready to jump out of hiding?

Whatever it was, Catherine made a lasting impression on Mark. She knew quite well that he was her biological father. Instantly, an irrational impulse of hugging him invaded her subconscious. Paralyzed by that strong instinct, she tried to contain herself. Afraid of any damaging indiscretion, she smiled at him in such a way that only a daughter can do in the presence of her father.

Just Heloise, and no one else, captured that magic moment, so full of filial devotion in Catherine, and so intriguing and disturbing for Mark.

Modest and discreet as she was, the mysterious Italian woman, a real living ghost from the past, did not raise any suspicion in those participants.

The dinner atmosphere appeared relaxed and enjoyable. The conversation was smooth, even if somewhat contained.

The contrasting feelings in Mark and Magdalene did not prevent that family gathering from being successful. The reason that united all of them was far greater than some personal animosities, conveniently disguised under a patina of civility.

Heloise was obviously the center of attention, and everybody was all ears, listening to the mesmerizing recount of her unbelievable experience.

A near-death experience is not an everyday occurrence. To survive and tell the story is a rare privilege. What made this experience unique wasn't the fact in itself, so compelling, but the auditory stimulus that reincorporated Heloise into the human race.

Any normal person and far more any media people would be willing to exploit and sensationalize this distinctive feature; not so Heloise, aware of her mother's outrageous reaction.

To provoke the anger of her mother would have been an unpardonable mistake, and Heloise was wise enough to tone down all what appeared to be Catherine's merit in her prodigious awakening.

She expanded, with abundance of significant annotations, on the suspended state of her existence, where time and place had disappeared, and a blinding luminescent light, so often described in these types of extra-sensorial experiences, was completely absent.

No silent people walking around in white robes, no melodious music caressing her ears, no winged supernatural creatures whispering cryptic orders. Everything was unfamiliar, unusual and intimidating.

Her ubiquitous presence in that cavernous vacuum wrapped in an age-old unspeakable silence, made her unmovable, yet present everywhere, mute, yet desperately expressive.

Unaware of pain or joy, and apparently hermetic and impenetrable to outside interferences, she resigned herself to her undeserved fate of being a living dead.

However, that was not meant to be her final destination, nor an indefinite prolongation of her suspended animation. Inside her motionless heart resided a mysterious power able to connect to a distant galaxy, where human feelings, like love and hatred, had a powerful grip on any kind of life vicissitudes.

She had to find that distant connection, sufficiently strong to amalgamate the two separate poles, establishing a powerful current. When the connection occurred, the impenetrable barriers broke down, the immobile isolation ceased, and the completely impalpable world of vacuity and silence evaporated.

As soon as the sensorial perception of the three-dimensional reality reasserted its roots, everything became functional and operational. Life was back with unusual prepotence and an indescribable nightmare was over for good.

A spontaneous and generous applause saluted Heloise's esoteric narration. That was the stuff the famous thrillers were made of. That was a superb depiction of the most disheartening event.

Any expert in paranormal phenomena would be proud of such a description, and would find some of those unheard aspects worth an in-depth investigation.

Magdalene greatly appreciated Heloise's discreet approach to the saving connection, and Catherine was beaming with satisfaction for a job well done.

Everybody, consciously or unconsciously, had something to celebrate.

Mark Centurion, the aloof father, kept himself above the crowd's pleasing attitude, observing every single movement. In his family life, he had never before experienced such a unity of intents.

In a gesture of gratitude to the infinite powers of nature, in which he firmly believed, he wanted to make a toast, paying tribute to his daughter's courage and determination.

After that, a surprising gift. For her physical therapy and for her full recovery, Heloise could use all the facilities at the Centurion Hotel in Kaanapali, Maui, with all expenses paid and for as long as she needed to.

This would not be anything out of the ordinary for a father loving his daughter, but considering the bad blood between the two, the offer was certainly magnanimous.

Nobody was happier than Heloise. At that point and with that offer, she was convinced that her feud with her father was a thing of the past.

The joyous family gathering ended on this happy note, leaving a sweet taste in everybody's mouth.

However, this moment of happiness was just a fleeting instant for the feeble convalescent girl.

In fact, a new phase was beginning in her troubled existence. A terrible earthquake had leveled her priorities, turning her life upside-down and changing her soul inside out.

She had enormous difficulty figuring herself in her new role of patient. All commitments were suspended indefinitely, because her full recovery was in doubt, despite the doctors' cautious optimism.

Would she ever be able to go back to her distinguished profession? More importantly, could she ever walk normally? Her right knee, badly damaged in the car accident, required a difficult operation to replace a delicate part. Could the skilled physicians succeed, where many before had failed?

Reconstructive surgery had made giant steps in giving back normal appearances to broken limbs and ribs, and seriously disfigured faces. However, no one could take for granted every single operation.

Each time the potential risks involved were greater than the inflated results. Heloise was well informed of the scientific progress, as well as of tragic failures in that particular branch of medicine.

There were possibilities, quite reasonable in nature, that her recovery could be only partial, and that she would never be able to resume her normal activities.

Her secret mission of finding Angie's murderer, probably thrown into the wastebasket. Her passion for carrying out justice in the courtroom totally frustrated by her physical inabilities.

All this constituted Heloise's worst nightmare. She could put up with some kind of disability, but she could never reconcile herself to the prospect of an existence stripped of her profession.

Maybe on the sandy beaches of Kaanapali, cradled by the gentle breeze of the ocean, her outlook on life would become less dramatic.

In the meantime, the prospects of a normal life were slim and her impatience was bursting out of her skin.

A note of serenity came from Catherine, the well-grounded teacher from Italy. Reading her inner thoughts and her soul's torment, she told her with a persuasive smile, "Heloise, cheer up! Nothing lasts forever. Don't put the cart before the horse. Take one day at a time. Leave the rest to God and nature."

With her typical American upbringing, not for the world would she ever assume a submissive attitude, acquiescent to some impenetrable God or to a capricious nature.

With respect to her life, she would always be in charge and nothing would be left to chance. She could partially agree with Catherine, in relaxing somewhat, in taking it easy for a while, but she would never abandon completely the stewardship of her vessel.

On one hand, she was grateful to her father for his offer; on the other, she was unhappy to leave Washington, D.C., where all the action was. Kaanapali looked to her like total inaction, where she would be powerless and helpless.

Nobody could blame her for those natural feelings. That was her nature, and that was how she was forged through education.

In the two days of preparation before leaving the mainland, she had ample time to reflect on her life and the direction she was taking.

While watching TV, she stumbled upon a piece of news that made her stomach churn. A famous host was presenting two examples of people, cruelly fooled by nature.

A young lad, anatomically born as a boy, felt and behaved as a girl. He was convinced of being trapped in the wrong body.

Conversely, a young lady, anatomically born as a girl, felt and behaved as a boy. She was convinced of being trapped in the wrong body.

As soon as they reached the statuary age of decision, they underwent a corrective surgery, matching their overall feelings and convictions with the right anatomical gender.

The host, without much philosophizing on that bizarre fact, stressed the parents' bewilderment and confusion before the operation, and the two young people's happiness and satisfaction after the successful intervention. The medical procedure had finally reestablished the proper harmony between psychological perception and anatomical reality.

Looking deep into her soul, Heloise once again came violently face-to-face with her **frigidity**. Had she too been fooled by nature, depriving her, in a twisted way, of her sexual feminine drives, or was that a mere product of her upbringing? Could it be a strange manipulation of her DNA by some deranged researcher, or some random chromosome injected by a reincarnated Angel of Death, Josef Mengele?

Had she been set apart by destiny to be a virgin, unmarried and childless, or was that a personal choice, sacrificing her potential family life with a professional mission of pursuing justice?

She could not really answer this twofold question, nor could she stop torturing herself about her personal identity.

Apparently, nature was not working in a straight line, like a machine. Overcoming its own boundaries, it was producing a myriad of varieties within species and groups. Nothing was off limits. Every single product in nature is unique, and cannot be repeated. Normality becomes a synonym for abnormality and irregularity.

Would Heloise accept her frigidity as an essential part of her uniqueness, or should she keep brooding over her alleged abnormality?

Culture and education would lead her toward a painful irregularity; common sense and nature would point in the opposite direction.

These rare moments of introspection would become more frequent, especially now with so much time on her hands.

At this stage, Heloise had more important issues to worry about. Her identity as a woman was bound to subside, even if it would probably be in the back burner of her mind, as long as she lived.

The two days of preparation did not pass without a hitch. Heloise's mother insisted, with certain vehemence, on accompanying and assisting her during her Maui stay.

The daughter, without locking horns with her mother, was adamant in her determination, and refused the offer. From now on, only Catherine would be her faithful companion, her sole associate.

Her father assembled an impressive medical team made up of a physical therapist by the name of Christopher Todd, a doctor, John Wertmüller, specialized in reconstructive surgery, and his personal physician, Charles Kent, renowned in the field of experimental drugs. Charles had a young assistant who felt an immediate attraction to Heloise.

This magnetic Adonis, originally from Switzerland, was following a post-doctoral program under Charles Kent's supervisory guidance. His name was Ercole Bitossi. His dream was to replace his esteemed professor and mentor, Charles, in the direction of his experimental laboratory.

His array of qualities and abilities, topped by a brilliant mind, was stunning. However, there was a serious drawback in his extensive résumé. This disadvantage did not bear any relation to his qualifications and experiences. It had something to do with his private life and more specifically with his sexual preferences.

To nobody's surprise, as he was all embracing in the knowledge department, he was all-inclusive in the sexual sphere as well. In simple terms, he was bisexual, swinging both ways.

As soon as Ercole laid his eyes on Heloise, he experimented a great turbulence that clouded his judgment and altered his behavior.

Unable to keep cool and professional in her presence, at every step, he betrayed himself, either by stumbling over his words, or by exaggerating his attentions.

Unfortunately, the object of his passion could not reciprocate, because she was standing on the opposite end of that sexual spectrum. She was all-exclusive. She did not feel a thing for his gender, or for any other gender.

When Heloise realized that bizarre, almost comic turn of events, she felt compelled to have an unambiguous talk with the young researcher.

The revelation of her total frigidity did not shock Ercole, nor disappoint him. He did not go into a furious rage, neither, blinded by the rejection, turned into a crazy stalker. On the contrary, he mellowed down a great deal and became a solicitous and caring friend.

Trained in science to expect the unexpected, and to accept infinite possibilities, he was happy to discover in real life another way to credibly relate to people. Sex was important and essential to most people, not so to Ercole Bitossi, whose interests spanned beyond any normal range.

His first language was Italian, besides mastering German, French and English. It would be superfluous to add that this was a real asset for Heloise and mainly for her assistant, Catherine. The three became close friends and confidants.

Catherine was able to use her mother tongue, expressing herself in depth, and conveying the subtle nuances of meaning of each word, with immense personal satisfaction.

Heloise, on the other hand, in her never-abandoned undercover mission, would attempt to penetrate the meanders of her father's projects, in the field of secret drugs, where research and experimentation were paramount.

For similar purpose, Ercole could be of great value, discounting his amiable nature.

The circle of solitude and despondency had been broken around Heloise, and despite her restricted mobility, and her uncertain future, she could take wing and fly into forbidden territories.

Her father, as usual, provided her and her little entourage with his private jet for her trip to Maui. She could hardly believe this stroke of luck, and with all those attentions and services, she felt as if she were living in the lap of luxury.

Everything was ready for this incredible journey. Nobody could have expected anything better for a physical rehabilitation. The tragic car accident had been extremely trying and nearly deadly. The recovery phase could be foretold as rewarding and invigorating.

A few nostalgic feelings notwithstanding, the separation from her Washingtonian world was nearly as joyous as a high school field trip.

Heloise was dressed in white and blue. An immaculate white shirt and a navy blue jacket covered her top, while a pair of blue pants with a pair of black leather shoes completed her elegant outfit.

She looked very gracious and attractive even in a wheelchair. From her faint smile and her positive attitude, nobody could have guessed the seriousness of her physical condition.

Showing some emotion in her eyes and voice, she took leave of her mother and father. She promised to keep in touch with them. Magdalene was visibly shaken. Fighting back the tears, she hugged her daughter tenderly. Mark kissed his girl, wishing her all the best.

Assisted by Catherine and monitored by Ercole, she boarded a black limousine.

The flight to the Hawaiian island of Maui registered only one stop in Los Angeles for refueling. During the crossing of the Pacific, Heloise let all her fears go, and like a baby rocked by an invisible hand, fell asleep.

Upon her arrival, would a new dawn shine on her? Would it be bright and warm?

Chapter XI

The wheels of justice are famous not only for moving slowly, but also for failing to produce, as in Tinseltown, the right results. A few illustrious examples come to mind: O.J. Simpson, Robert Blake, Michael Jackson, and Phil Spector.

These celebrities, instead of being condemned for murder or pedophilia, were set free. With their trial, they made a complete mockery of justice. Justice has been brutally murdered under the lights of TV cameras and the flashes of paparazzi.

Nothing is more sarcastic and bitter than to hear, on one hand, lavish praises for the American legal system, and, on the other, to assist impotently in its public assassination.

On other occasions, as in the case of Martha Stewart and Paris Hilton, justice came out seriously tarnished.

Would the same occur in Brutus Barker's case?

Actively investigated by federal and local police, as was written previously, Brutus was suspected of kidnapping and murder. Would the investigators collect enough evidence to bring him to trial? If yes, would he hire a celebrity lawyer, capable of getting him off the hook, using every trick in the book?

It would not be surprising at all, given his position of undeniable influence and the huge amount of money at his disposal. Even without clout and influence, his chances would not be negligible.

In fact, how many obscure cases had been closed and buried under tons of documents, with zero possibility of being reopened and reexamined?

For those thousands of unsolved crimes, where the perpetrators remain free, a powerful cry for justice is heard daily in our cities.

On the other hand, for those thousands of solved crimes, where an innocent person is sent to jail, tears of desperation are shed daily, with little hope of being stopped by an opposite verdict.

A similar desperate outcry will resonate in mankind's conscience until the end of time. Unfortunately, our justice will stay **unfinished**, unserved and gagged.

Who will ever make the wrong, right; the unjust, just; the improper, proper?

Only valiant men and courageous women can narrow the overall gap between the mounting injustices and the little justice served in our courts.

Regrettably, human justice, carried out under any legal system, anywhere in the world, will always be partial and incomplete. Many injustices and crimes will remain unpunished. Many victims will cry out uselessly, while others will never have the chance to be heard once.

This humbling reality should make people reflect on the weakness of our legal systems, and the partiality and corruptibility of our judges and lawyers.

Justice will always be a work in progress, a human product, and an **unfinished** business.

Returning to our subject at hand, after this short digression, the FBI left no stone unturned regarding Mark Centurion's failed kidnapping.

The first peace of credible evidence, tying Brutus to that particular crime, seemed to be one of his assistants. His name was Atticus Bitter, originally from the Los Angeles Metropolitan area. His niece, by the name of Ephemeris, was a suspected gang member, with close ties to the criminal world.

One of the kidnappers, who managed to escape from the awful massacre, was subsequently arrested. During the endless interrogation by federal agents, quite a few interesting details came to light. One of them was his romantic involvement, at one time, with Ephemeris.

If the FBI could establish, either through confession or cash transactions, some connection between Bitter and the kidnapper, they could hit the jackpot.

According to their profilers, they possessed all the elements to uncover the truth. The trail they were actively pursuing wasn't so cold any more.

Adding to this the amount of relevant information acquired on the soured relationship between Centurion and Barker, they could have in their hands a powerful motive.

On the matters of Icarus Proctor's car accident and the subsequent death of the garage owner, Carlos Carreras, the local police were also making significant progress.

Pedro Almendarez, the assistant mechanic, after the disappearance of his boss, cut himself loose from previous ties, and started his own business.

During the police interrogations, he had only one intense desire: to come clean. With no pressure or fear, and out of the woods, he volunteered additional details.

He remembered some unusual phone conversations between his boss and Barker during the time when he was fixing Proctor's car. Moreover, he was surprised to see Carlos Carreras providing him with the part of the brake system to be replaced.

That same day, Brutus Barker had a lengthy conversation with Carlos. This was very uncommon too, because Carlos rarely sat in his office with a customer. With this information, the police investigators had a couple of steps left: look into Carreras' bank accounts hoping to find the ultimate convincing proof and discover the underlying motive behind that atypical killing.

The first step would not be that difficult. It would require only patience and time. His accounts, in fact, after his death, had been frozen and much paperwork was needed in order to gain access to them.

The underlying motive would surely present a real challenge, being that the alleged victim and perpetrator were two worlds apart.

In view of this, would the police investigation come to a grinding halt, and would Icarus Proctor's case sit in a police station basement, inside a box labeled "unsolved case"?

That was a possibility, and Brutus was quite aware of it. However, if human justice could not nail him down, sudden pangs of conscience would never cease to torment him, as long as he lived.

How could he sleep peacefully at night with such a burden? How could he smile during the day, as if nothing had ever happened?

If he planned to eliminate Carreras, in order to silence an inconvenient witness, there could be no room for doubting his involvement.

Was he following orders, or was he a cold-blooded killer pursuing chimerical world domination?

Only Brutus could answer these and other questions.

Maybe federal and local investigators could shed some light on this mysterious man and his organization.

In the meantime, all was conjecture, fed by indiscretions, rumors and flimsy clues.

Brutus, through an informer within the police force, was kept abreast of the latest developments. He did not have to snoop around himself, raising further suspicions.

His insecurities and fears stemmed from the FBI investigation. He couldn't infiltrate their rank and file, in spite of his multiple attempts.

One flank of his armor was open to his adversaries, whose maneuvers he couldn't monitor, thus leaving him vulnerable.

With the mentality of a hunted man, it was difficult to blend in, and keep a low profile. Nevertheless, since that was his very nature, absorbed in the gelid winters of North Dakota, Brutus was riding on his metamorphosis abilities, reinventing himself at every turn of his twisted life.

All this effort of camouflaging came to a screeching halt when his assistant, Atticus Bitter, was detained for questioning.

Federal agents from Los Angeles flew into Washington, D.C. with some damaging evidence and stunning revelations.

The arrested kidnapper, called Rambo, admitted to a short-lived love affair with Bitter's niece, and on top of that, he revealed that his gang leader, who was shot during the failed kidnapping, had phone conversations with Brutus' assistant a week before the fatal event.

Confronted with the phone records, Atticus Bitter could not deny having some conversations with Rigoberto Gómez, nicknamed "*El Cholo.*"

He was ready to swear that the content of those phone exchanges did not have anything to do with the kidnapping; they concerned Ephemeris, his sister's daughter. She had been straying badly since her connection with Rambo, and her single mother was extremely preoccupied.

At her instigation, Atticus tried to put some sense into Ephemeris, and poured some money into the gang's pockets.

It was impossible for the federal agents to verify this plausible explanation, since "*El Cholo*" was dead. They needed more tangible proof to establish Brutus' true involvement, through his assistant Atticus, in that sordid affair.

Rambo, kept incommunicado, under constant pressure by the FBI, cracked up, and disclosed the real essence of the plan.

The kidnapping was just a simulation to cover up the actual killing of Mark Centurion. During the struggle to drag him away from his bodyguards, while bullets were flying in all directions, one assailant, in a simulated effort to defend himself, would fatally wound Mark.

Falling on the ground, they would leave him there, and make good their escape.

Startled by this revelation, the investigators saw something more sinister behind that criminal action. It wasn't a question of extorting money from a rich man, but a diabolic plan of getting rid of him in a barbaric fashion.

Who would benefit most from this killing? All fingers were pointed at Brutus Barker, Mark Centurion's lieutenant and right arm.

If the conclusion seemed logical and inescapable, not so the path to prove it. Still the serious lack of evidence would make the FBI sweat blood before having something more tangible to present in a court of law.

While the noose was getting tighter around Barker's neck, his lifestyle and daily routine remained unaltered.

Everybody should be under the impression that he had nothing to fear, despite the constant mudslinging at his reputation.

The chameleon man could fool anybody and everybody. It was in his nature to be deceptive. Would his enthralling performance succeed in making the local authorities turn a blind eye to his activities?

All of a sudden, he became a solicitous father, a submissive company man, a polite lover.

The detached posture in relation to his daughter, Karina, gave place to an affectionate concern, his sneaky business-style management was substituted by a transparent day-to-day operation, and his aggressive and possessive interaction with women was transformed into an attentive and caring one.

When Karina became ill, and was taken to a private clinic, Brutus was the first to visit her. He couldn't refrain himself from crying profusely as soon as he heard that Karina was affected by a degenerative disease. The poor child was diagnosed with Amyotrophic lateral sclerosis (ALS, sometimes called Lou Gehrig's Disease). This is a progressive, fatal, neurodegenerative disease caused by the degeneration of motor neurons, the nerve cells in the central nervous system that control voluntary muscle movement.

For Brutus, it was a real shock to come face-to-face with such a reality, especially since it was unheard of for a child to have this illness.

The early symptoms (twitching, cramping, or stiffness of muscles; muscle weakness affecting an arm or a leg; and/or slurred and nasal speech) were scary, but more terrifying was that no cure had been found yet.

The very unfortunate girl was condemned to a progressive and undignified extinction, under the watchful eyes of her father and grandmother.

Confronted with this tragic fate, even the most virtuous man could collapse and rebel against God and nature.

What was Brutus' reaction? On the surface, he appeared unchanged. Nevertheless, beneath his icy and impenetrable exterior there was a violent storm of unidentified proportions rocking his boat.

A frightening situation was gradually developing in the darkest meanders of his soul. Deep down, in that muddy chasm of his feelings, there was still a cord vibrating genuinely for that innocent girl.

Nobody before had touched him so deeply, reaching a small particle of his true humanity. A powerful lightning bolt had struck him, leaving him almost paralyzed.

The intense light, instead of blinding him, revealed the only relation that possessed a magic and redeeming force. All the rest were lies and deceptions.

Power, money, women had led him to the edge of a precipice. Could his little girl save him from eternal damnation?

Karina was kept in the dark about the gravity of her illness, while Heloise was promptly informed. She immediately suspended her immediate departure to Maui and arranged to be transported to the hospital.

If anybody knew anything about near-death experience, intense suffering and excruciating pain, it was certainly the daughter of Mark Centurion.

Heloise hugged Karina tenderly and gave her a little present, a small teddy bear and a box of chocolates.

Upon the preliminaries, a brief conversation followed in grandmother's presence. The father was present too, in body only, because his mind and heart were lost in a desolate space.

Heloise, with a comforting smile, said, "Don't be afraid of anything. You will be perfectly okay in no time at all. People at your age are amazingly resilient. When I come back from Maui, I want to see you in perfect form."

"Don't worry," replied Karina, "I might come to Hawaii for a brief visit. By that time, you'll be able to walk normally, and take me around."

"I hope so too. Be good and listen to the doctors, Grandma and Dad. I love you."

"I love you a lot too," said Karina.

Heloise kissed the charming little lady, and left with tears in her heart, knowing it was only a matter of time.

A worrisome thought that would resurface repeatedly during her convalescent days crossed Heloise's mind.

How could life be so cruel and unfair to a poor, innocent child? What kind of world do we live in? Who is behind all the monstrosities that take place daily?

Is there any reasonable answer to these fundamental questions that have tormented and anguished humankind forever?

Heloise's bewilderment was negligible in comparison to Brutus' destructive cyclone, disseminating desperation in his heart and total derangement of his mind.

No questions about fairness and justice torturing his soul, just irrepressible surges of anger, vengeance and destruction.

His only true connection to life was being severed away inexorably and permanently. He had been bad, calculated and brutal in his life. However, in all his heinous actions there was always some alleged good reason, some apparent justification.

His daughter's degenerative disease had broken all the parameters of logic, installing chaos as a supreme denominator. There was no order, no harmony in the world. Nothing made sense any longer.

To an impartial observer, Brutus' demeanor appeared menacing and on the verge of explosion.

Almost irrationally, without saying goodbye to anybody, not even to his precious Karina, he left the clinic and wandered aimlessly for hours around the streets adjacent to the medical facility.

Finally, a policeman patrolling the area, observing his erratic conduct, asked whether he was lost.

"I am lost, indeed," he answered, "but not in the way you think. My daughter is going to die, and I can't do a thing for her. There is nothing for me out there any more."

The policeman felt compassion for this pained, troubled man, and said, "Can I accompany you to your residence?"

"I would appreciate it," was the answer. Without exchanging another word the officer escorted him home.

He dropped him quickly at his address, because he had to answer an emergency call received through the radio dispatcher.

Before leaving, he made sure that he could manage on his own, and he told Brutus that in the morning he would be back to check on him.

The distraught man did not have enough time to say anything before the officer was on his way. Like a robot, he entered his apartment and went straight to his bedroom. Without undressing and taking off only his shoes, he lay flat on his bed, shut his eyes, and fell asleep immediately.

A loud knock on the front door awoke him in the morning. As he had promised, the officer was back inquiring on his overall condition.

Yawning and rubbing his eyes, with a distracted air, he assured the officer that he was fine. Unconvinced the officer left the man stewing in his own juice.

That day, Brutus didn't show up for work, didn't answer any phone calls and didn't leave his apartment.

Without putting any food or drink in his stomach, he was sitting in the living room, staring at the white ceiling.

He appeared numbed by an intense pain, unable to move or change position. All he did was swing his head back and forth. Was a bell tolling inside, inviting him to his final destination?

Was he answering "yes" with his head movement, and getting ready to make right all his lifelong wrongdoings?

Nobody will ever know what was going on, inside his mind, during those crucial moments of his existence.

The truth is that after many hours of immobility, he stood up. With some determination, he got a camping rope, hidden in a closet, and a stool.

He walked steadily to the front entrance. There was a sturdy hook hanging from the ceiling. Apparently, he did not care whether it was strong enough. With frightening precision, he put the rope through it, and made a solid knot.

He stepped on the stool, put the noose around his neck, kicked the stool, and left himself hanging. It was noon on a cool Friday the thirteenth.

The man who dodged perfect storms, who transformed himself in the face of changing circumstances, couldn't accept the premature demise of his daughter.

He had given up her custody, but he couldn't give up his unconditional love for her. That tiny spark of true affection left at the bottom of his heart killed him.

Everything had gone sour in his life. His business life was in shambles. His love life, if it ever existed, was treacherous and deceptive. His family life had been destroyed by his own hands.

The only tenuous thread keeping him grounded was his abandoned Karina. When that was scythed down by a cruel destiny, nothing made sense any longer, not money, not power, not family, not women.

On top of all that, a creeping guilt, always absent before, was clamoring for a self-inflicted justice. Even if he had come clean in court for his alleged crimes, his conscience would never be silenced or suppressed.

Eternally trapped between the Devil and the deep blue sea, the only sensible solution was to put an end to all his miseries.

That was precisely what Brutus did, that cool Friday the thirteenth.

Two full days passed before anybody discovered the immense tragedy.

When the police officers, notified by Mark Centurion's office, broke into Brutus' apartment, they were met with a horrific scene.

The man, suspected in a couple of murders, was hanging in front of their very eyes. The *rigor mortis* had already set in. His body was stiff and cold, his tongue dangling, eyes bulging, lips dark purple, fingers black, and neck badly bruised.

The coroner would establish the exact time of death and its causes. In the meantime, suicide would appear the most logical explanation.

When the news reached the local media and the interested parties, a sense of consternation and horror spread like wildfire.

The unsuspected outcome of this rags-to-riches story sparked the imagination of many and touched the hearts of few.

Chapter XII

Heloise didn't even have time to settle down in her luxury accommodation at the Centurion Hotel in Kaanapali, Maui, when the terrible news of Brutus' suicide reached her.

Badly shaken, she felt that little corner of paradise on earth mutating into an unpleasant experience.

The man, believed responsible for the death of his wife, and which caused her to take a new direction in her life—starting a private undercover investigation—was gone forever.

Her noble quest for justice had lost its motive and inspiration. All her chase after a mysterious credit card, called "*Moral Phalanx*" had been seemingly in vain. Her car accident was a direct result of that improvised and extemporaneous investigation.

Had her fertile imagination played a cruel trick, ruining her existence and throwing her into a state of disarray?

That was a very high price to pay for a burning desire for justice. It would take a long time and a serious reflection to recover from such a crippling blow.

On top of her lengthy and painful rehabilitation, with a partial knee replacement, a broken rib to be repaired and a facial reconstruction, she had to reinvent herself with new priorities, and a new mission.

It seemed that her previous world had collapsed, in more ways than one, and the fragments of that beautiful edifice couldn't be put together.

A daunting task had to be undertaken in order to function again as a human being. Would it still be along the line of an **unfinished justice**, or would it follow a completely new path?

Heloise was like a little child who had lost its mother in the middle of a huge throng. Totally helpless and crying, wandering around, and without a friendly hand guiding and sustaining her, she felt impotent.

Maybe the new location, faraway from the continental United States, and the new accommodation, her father's property, surrounded by peace and comfort, could bring some sense of purpose and some feelings of mental balance back into her life.

Now, it was time to adjust to living in comfort and luxury, unfortunately curtailed by a wheelchair and a constant need for assistance. The positive contrasted sharply with the negative. Never before had good and bad, light and dark been so striking. Never before had a desire to strive and a mental desperation tussled each other for supremacy.

Her floor-level apartment, easy to access, was equipped with all the modern necessities and amenities. Catherine was utterly surprised to see such spacious closets, such voluminous bathrooms, and such large LCD HD TV sets. Huge king-size beds, splendid lights and mirrors, and marvelous carpets noticeably increased the value of that already overpriced piece of property.

Everything was in style and magnificent. Nevertheless, what Heloise appreciated most was the view with the marvelous beauties spread by Mother Nature's generous hands. She couldn't stop admiring the vast ocean, with the Molokai island in the background, the perfectly manicured lawn, populated by tall palm trees, the alternating wind and breeze according to the time of day, the melodious chirping of the birds, and the immense serenity of those sandy beaches.

If paradise could be reduced to an earthly reality, that enchanting corner of the world would be the most perfect approximation to it.

By itself, it could cure thousands of spiritual and psychological wounds, reestablishing any lost equilibrium between body and soul. The only thing required was a tacit consent, or a willing participation by the human counterpart.

Heloise had a long way to go before surrendering unconsciously to this magic partnership and enjoying its ensuing benefits.

The staff, solicitous and attentive, helped the handicapped daughter of the owner and her assistant settle down, carrying luggage, opening doors and making sure that everything was in its place and nothing was missing.

Heloise and Catherine slept in separate rooms, one adjacent to the other.

They had two direct phone lines. One connected to the father's private line, the other to the office of Charles Kent, the head physician coordinating all the medical services.

The first days' timetable covered an hour of physical therapy in the morning and one in the afternoon. A counseling session, without time limits, took place in the evening. The physician in charge, Kent, visited his patient daily.

Everything was running smoothly. The only interferences were the numerous phone calls coming from family and friends.

Obviously, her mother and father wanted to be kept abreast of every little happening or development, while friends were the conveyors of the city news and the socialites' gossips.

Catherine's presence was the right balm for Heloise's wounds and pains, both physical and spiritual. They got along so well that they gave the impression of having lived together all their lives.

The other person that spent hours with Heloise was Ercole Bitossi, the multifaceted young doctor. A brilliant mind and passionate heart, he loved Heloise like a sister, after discovering that she felt no passion for him. They confided in each other. They shared an ardent thirst for knowledge and could communicate on a superior level.

Catherine and Ercole became the family Heloise never had, filling an immense void left by her blood parents.

After a week of this new life, where Heloise was pampered by humans and spoiled by nature, she was flown back to the mainland, in her father's private jet.

She was scheduled for a partial knee replacement, the first in a series of surgical interventions.

In order to literally put her back on her feet her father would spare no expense.

Under total anesthesia, the procedure was carried out with precision and complete success. When Heloise awoke, she was greeted by a broad smile from her specialist and by a kiss from her mother.

Everybody was happy. Nothing was more cherished by Heloise than her physical independence, and that was certainly the first step. To be back on her feet was a dream that would be followed by many other beautiful aspirations.

She spent a full day in the capital city, being visited by friends from the law office. During the few hours at her disposal, she paid a quick visit to Karina. The orphan girl, still uninformed of her father's death, was in good spirits, but her slow physical deterioration was visible and palpable.

Karina rejoiced at the surprise presence of that gentle fairy, whose smile could bewitch a ferocious beast.

She exuded hope of a quick recovery despite an increased stiffness in her left leg. Their conversation, cheerful and alive, was very brief.

An affectionate hug signaled their separation, leaving Heloise with an unexplainable chagrin.

Back in Maui, she spent a couple of days in a special program facilitating her legs' and knee's movement.

At the end of her second week in Kaanapali, she could walk without any help, from any mechanical or human source. What a feeling of relief to become independent again, since her car crash!

At the beginning, her walks were very short, because she was still healing from the broken rib. While the rib was mending slowly, she was taking pain relief medications. These were keeping her more comfortable, allowing her to take deeper and more effective breaths. Anti-inflammatory drugs, such as ibuprofen, were also very helpful in alleviating her pain.

Both Charles Kent, her primary caretaker, and his assistant, Ercole Bitossi, monitored Heloise's progress on a daily basis. A full Body Health Scan, performed on her by a licensed technician and reviewed by her primary physician, determined the complete healing of her rib and therefore the suspension of any further treatment or medication.

The Hawaiian divinities were looking down more benevolently on that foreign princess.

One important thing was still left, before proclaiming her complete recovery. Nasty scars marked her chin, nose and left cheek. Her beauty had been badly disfigured.

A partial facial reconstruction by a plastic surgeon was essential. Before beginning this last phase, scheduled for the following month, at the most renowned clinic in Beverly Hills, Los Angeles, she had abundant time for reflection and prioritization.

Sometimes in Catherine's company, sometimes accompanied by Ercole, she would stroll along the marvelous Kaanapali beach, sit down on the sand, and with her sight lost in the vastness of the ocean, she would meditate for hours on the tumbling down of her previous convictions, and the mental confusion about values and the meaning of life.

Would anybody be there for her? Would anybody guide her steps out of that dark night? If the physical and psychological sufferings had been excruciating, her new emptiness of ideals, aims and purposes was unbearable and insufferable.

Her previous vision of a world where bad people subverted the universal order, and with her profession, she would attempt every day to reestablish harmony, no longer made any sense.

The cultural belief, so widespread in our so-called religious society, that everything happens for a reason, that God either guides the destiny of our societies or allows people to make their own selfish decisions and try later on to generate some good out of an evil deed, no longer held true for Heloise.

The recent events in her life had clearly proven her ancestral belief wrong. There was no justification for the abominations she had witnessed lately.

How could anyone justify, or accept, the senseless death of her friend, Angie, Karina's degenerative illness, Brutus' suicide, her freak car accident?

What was the world coming to? What had she come back to? The harmonious and orderly world, in which she used to live, had crashed down obstreperously. She was back to an empty house, even worse to a frightening abyss. This was sucking away the last few drops of wisdom left in her soul.

Recalling her college years, she remembered participating in a lecture, where Leibniz's theory, "**We live in the best of all possible worlds**," was presented by a German professor and discussed among the participants.

In those days, when her naïveté was at its best, she wholeheartedly embraced Leibniz's theory, rejecting Voltaire's sarcastic criticism of the German philosopher's optimism.

In his famous book *Candide*, Voltaire tells the tale of a naïve young man, Candide (meaning "ingenuous"), who has been taught to believe in **Leibnizian optimism**, but becomes disillusioned after undergoing a series of extraordinary hardships during a luckless odyssey.

Overnight and as if by a miracle, she identified herself with the main character of that book. The many tragedies in her life opened her eyes and subverted her mind.

Overwhelmed by this sudden transformation, she consulted with her friend Ercole, well versed in Liebniz's theory, and more broadly in the widely held belief that "**everything happens for a reason**."

One beautiful evening, when the sun was setting in a majestic canvas of colors, they lay down on the sand and began philosophizing.

Ercole began his assessment of Heloise's personal situation by saying, "I see a menacing cloud obscuring the clarity of your soul. What is bothering you?"

"I lost control of my life," replied Heloise, "and I can't find my way out. Nothing makes sense any more. My orderly universe has become a chaotic entity, my vocation of pursuing justice, a quixotic adventure, my convictions and beliefs an insignificant pile of rubble.

Just as my body after the car accident was a pitiful, disfigured human hodgepodge, barely surviving in a vegetative state, the same way my consciousness and my mind are kept alive by a lethal dose of skepticism and a powerful couldn't-care-less attitude eating away the last fibers of my previous **optimism and faith**."

"Maybe," explained the young scientist, "you are falling into an existential crisis, which can result either in a beneficial ousting of your previous naïve outlook, or assume a defeatist attitude surrendering totally to irrationality and carelessness.

It is up to you to embrace this defining moment of your existence, and steer your ship into a safe harbor with a renovated and more adult approach to life."

With an imploring look, Heloise asked Ercole to guide her, through that stormy sea, to a safe haven.

Undeserving of such trust and with some hesitation in his voice, Ercole was about to embark on one of his most demanding intellectual challenges.

Holding Heloise's right hand, like somebody that wants to inspire total confidence in his thirsty listener, he opened his reasoning by saying, "In order to acquire a fresh understanding, we must first demolish a cultural and religious taboo, which impedes any critical mentality. This sacred cow, that must be slaughtered on the altar of reason, is the widely held belief that "**everything happens for a reason**" in its secular version, and that "**God is behind everything**" in its religious version.

In some major languages we find traditional expressions ("God willing," "God works in mysterious ways," "Si Dios quiere," "Non si muove foglia che Dio non voglia," "Kami no oboshimeshi", etc.) indicating in some degree or another God's participation or intervention in the history of mankind. From these or similar expressions emerges a clear conviction that God determines certain events, or actively allows certain others to occur.

Very often, people in the midst of calamities utter phrases like: "God, why me?" or "God, why didn't you spare my loved ones?" or "God, this is unfair!" or "I am saved, because God has a plan for me." The assumption behind this is quite clear. God is ultimately responsible for everything that happens in the universe. How many times have we heard the expression "This is an act of God"?

Moreover, it is not unusual to justify wars, forms of society, death penalty, types of education, number of pregnancies, disciplinary actions, etc. in the name of God, as if the Supreme Maker had put his personal seal of approval on all these human decisions.

Pushing a little further this theory of divine intervention, we are faced with expressions, like "God bless America," which is considered very pious and religious, but in reality it implies a distorted view of God's intervention. Indirectly, it suggests something never explicitly mentioned—that America was entrusted with a "Manifest Destiny" or "Divine Destiny" of expansion and supremacy. In this scheme, God would take sides, favoring one nation over others, as in the Old Testament.

After establishing the existence of this pervasive mentality of divine intervention in world affairs (so popular in Greek mythology, so overwhelming in the Old Testament and, obviously, undeniable in Jesus' convictions), we must ask boldly if there is any truth in it.

Doesn't it seem presumptuous to question a cherished tenet of our western civilization by posing the following interrogatives? How does God's will or plan relate to humans' wills or plans?

Are they complementary, contradictory, or do they run parallel to one another?

If they were **complementary**, we would verify a perfect identity of views, purposes and actions between man's free will and God's universal plan.

Evidently, this is neither historical nor realistic or imaginable, not even in Jesus' life. As a man, he felt a strong resistance, when confronted with his Father's plan of being sacrificed on the cross. In addition, all the historical atrocities would be attributable equally to man and to God. And this is totally repugnant.

In the second hypothesis of **being parallel** to one another, each would have his own project and his own will, with no interference of any kind. No one could claim superiority or dominance over the other.

This would square perfectly with **man's free will,** reclaiming his total independence from any external interference, but it would also contradict all those human expressions and biblical passages that imply God's direct participation in human history.

Thirdly, are they **contradictory** or mutually exclusive? Man's free will cannot coexist with God's plan or conform to any of his determinations; otherwise, it would contradict its own essence of being "free."

This third possibility would explain eloquently all human horrors, from genocide to infidelity, putting the blame on man and not on God. Again, the pervasive conviction that "God is behind everything" would be shattered.

The only hypothesis, where the widespread conviction of God's intervention in human history would find a probability of subsistence, would be the first one. However, being anti-historical and intellectually repulsive it must be discarded.

Left with the other two hypotheses, where there is no room for God's intervention, there is only one logical conclusion: God's will and plan, if any, don't interfere with man's **free will.** Therefore, man is the only one responsible for what takes place in the world. The cherished tenet of God's action in human affairs, although comforting at times, is groundless and leads to misinterpretation, illusion and confusion."

Ercole concluded his philosophical speculation with a hopeful note. "If there is a glimpse of God's plan or divine interaction in our history, we are totally unable to quantify or qualify it. We must humbly profess our shortsightedness and renounce our simplistic, almost voodoo mentality of God capriciously intervening in our affairs.

Whoever claims to know **God's will** [besides the generality of the Golden Rule "Treat others as you would like to be treated", and Jesus' Central Message of Love] at any nation's, society's, organization's or individual's crossroads is a liar and an impostor."

Heloise, spellbound by the young eclectic scientist's stringent logic, remained at a loss for words. Unqualified for any type of criticism of that theory, and absorbed in her thoughts, she kept gazing into the horizon, where the sun had long gone, leaving the surroundings in total darkness.

Despite that material obscurity, rays of hope and comprehension loomed large in her heart. Her deconstructive phase had begun. It wouldn't be easy to pass from an optimistic and credulous stage, to a critical and more sophisticated frame of mind.

Returning to a more domestic conversation, our two thinkers left the solitary beach, and walked back to their luxury accommodations, with the clear pledge of resuming their conversation on the central question of Leibniz's theory, whenever the opportunity presented itself.

This had just been an introduction to the central issue of "**We live in the best of all possible worlds**."

Was there any truth in that vision of a harmonious world, governed by eternal laws, where everything, even the most heinous, concurs to a positive result?

That was the crucial question tormenting our convalescent young lady.

Her physical progress was extremely encouraging, and Heloise anxiously awaited her partial facial reconstruction.

Leibniz's beautiful world had to wait before being fully explored. With her attractive features restored, it would probably prove easier to confront the hidden conundrums of our world.

In the meantime, Heloise made a serious effort to familiarize herself with what was going on around her. One thing that caught her attention was a very small group of doctors that included her own primary physician, conducting a type of life that could be described as cloistral at best.

Were they on a research assignment, on a relaxing prolonged vacation, or on a secret mission?

From references she collected, all of them were luminaries in their own field. Except for a few days of absence from time to time, their continual presence in that magnificent hotel could raise anybody's suspicions.

However, what intrigued Heloise more was their daily schedule. Upon a relentless observation, and artful interrogation of the housekeeper, in charge of cleaning their rooms, she got some rare pieces of information.

Apparently, from ten in the morning to one in the afternoon, and from two to six in the evening, nobody was ever present in those rooms, but nobody was ever seen exiting during those hours either.

What happened during those two periods? Did they leave from a secret door? Did they have a special power of walking undetected through thick walls and long corridors?

The mystery thickened when Heloise questioned her good friend Ercole Bitossi, Charles Kent's assistant. In his conviction, Charles and the other two scientists were presently working hard on some special project. Ercole could not pinpoint the exact nature of that research, because the contribution requested from him was marginal.

He had never been invited to their rooms. For his assignment, he received detailed e-mails on some restricted topics. Of one thing he was quite certain. No one could ever conduct those kinds of investigations without a state-of-the-art laboratory. However, to his knowledge, no sophisticated lab was present in those facilities.

Heloise had sufficient elements to launch an undercover investigation. She could not believe that stroke of luck. Finally, she had found something to occupy her mind and entertain her action, besides her health problems.

Was her father, Mark Centurion, the super-millionaire philanthropist, involved in some secret project, known only to him and his closest collaborator, Charles Kent?

If so, she could have stumbled across a pot of gold, moreover a gold mine of incalculable value. When she genuinely believed that all was lost, from the meaning of life to her purpose in it, spending her precious time in debatable discussions, she unexpectedly turned the tables, retaking into her hands the reins of her life.

This surprise turn of events cold be a false alarm, just a product of her vivid imagination. Probably, the reality, later on, would leave her disappointed and frustrated once again.

However, whatever lay in store for her in the future, it wouldn't hurt, at this stage, to once more follow her hunch.

She was barely able to move around, and already she had committed herself, in total secrecy, to undertaking a dangerous mission. This time, she was not playing with a Vatican financier or an economic wizard of a powerful religious movement, but with her own father's company and ambitions.

The stakes were high and the risks incalculable. Oblivious of her physical condition and her professional weaknesses for such a job, she threw herself body and soul into the cause.

Calmly, and rationally, she sat down at her desk, and jotted down some strategic moves, with alternative plans, in case of difficulty or failure.

She worked on the assumption that the prolonged presence of a small team of scientists was not there just for ostentation. Certainly, her father could afford such a waste of talents, but that was not his style. For a man used to treasuring breadcrumbs, that would suggest insanity.

The more likely explanation would be some innovative way of conducting research, away from indiscreet eyes, and safe from scientific espionage.

An endeavor of such magnitude would require a phenomenal lab, equipped with the most advanced instruments.

In conclusion, step number one would be to discover the exact location of such a lab, crack their secret code and get access to the information stored in the main computer.

For Heloise, Mark Centurion's daughter and a very special guest in that luxury hotel, nothing was off limits. She could peek around, without raising suspicions.

Nobody, not even Catherine or Ercole, would be informed of her undercover operation. With the help of the housekeeper, and on some plausible pretext, she would gain access to Charles Kent's living quarters.

She would patiently await his first absence from the island, and then she would implement her plan.

Under the cover of darkness, she would creep into that sanctuary and try to uncover some clues, leading to his mysterious activity.

During the waiting game that did not seem to come to an end, some significant events diverted Heloise's attention away from her secret mission.

One of them was her partial facial reconstruction. The procedure, eagerly awaited before, was embraced now without enthusiasm.

Back on the mainland and more precisely in Los Angeles, Heloise underwent a two-day operation. Her chin and nose assumed a more graceful form, considerably improving her overall appearance.

The plastic surgeon, after removing the bandages, handed her a mirror. She looked into it. Her face was not filled with any curiosity. A routine look into it was more than enough. No exuberant jubilation, no wows of surprise or admiration. Just a simple "thanks."

The skilled doctor was taken aback by that reaction. "You are not happy with the final result?"

"Oh, no. I like my new look. You did a great job. Thanks again."

Heloise's mother too was surprised by that unusual reaction, but she didn't say a word. Her daughter looked terrific, and she was ecstatic.

The compliments in Maui were lavish. Catherine was so moved by her sister's beauty, that she couldn't refrain from shedding a few tears of joy. She hugged her tightly, squeezing Heloise's cheek against hers, as a mother does with her child.

Here again, the new and improved beauty, resembling a movie star of the future, kept cool and impassionate, to everyone's surprise.

She had more serious things on her mind, and her attractiveness could be more of a hindrance than a help. Another reason of a different nature was at the root of her atypical attitude.

Her recovery days in Kaanapali were numbered. Having lost that marvelous opportunity, handed her on a silver platter by her father, she would never have a viable occasion of making startling discoveries.

The race was on, and Heloise was well aware that she was racing against time and all the odds.

Chapter XIII

Brutus' suicide, as unfortunate and deplorable as it was, didn't stop the ongoing investigations; on the contrary, it propelled the law enforcement agencies into a more active and dynamic pursuit of the truth.

Mark Centurion's assassination attempt, artfully disguised as a ransom-for-money kidnapping, proved very difficult to crack, while Brutus was still alive.

After his sudden suicide, many people, somehow connected to his activities, started breathing easily again. Among them, Atticus Bitter, his faithful assistant and unscrupulous henchman.

Free from the overpowering shadow of his boss, and pressured for more information by the relentless FBI interrogations, he loosened his tongue and spilled the beans. The whole yarn unraveled, disclosing Brutus' central role.

He had instructed Atticus Bitter to get in touch with a vicious Los Angeles gang, through his niece Ephemeris, formerly Rambo's girlfriend.

A considerable amount of cash was offered to Rambo and "*El Cholo*," the gang leader, with a detailed plan of brutally eliminating Mark Centurion, during his visit to Los Angeles.

Half of the cash transaction took place before the operation, thanks to the untraceable services of an offshore bank in the Cayman Islands. The other half would be deposited after the successful assassination.

The plan failed miserably. Ironically, who lost his life in that crude and amateurish adventure wasn't the intended target Centurion, but his mastermind "*El Cholo*."

Atticus Bitter backed up his story with some undisputable documents. Everything was there, in black and white: the amount of money, receipts, date of transactions.

This plain confession, long overdue, did not come as a surprise to the veteran investigators. It gave them an eloquent clue of interpretation into Brutus' character and his twisted operational mind.

His criminal profile was coming into focus, opening the door to other ongoing investigations.

The second investigation that had been going on for quite some time, without any tangible results, was Icarus Proctor's fatal car accident.

An enraged motorist had fatally shot the garage owner Carlos Carreras, suspected in the tampering of Proctor's brakes, after a heated argument, according to some eyewitnesses.

His mechanic, Pedro Almendarez, who performed a costly replacement and a general maintenance service, would swear on his mother's grave that he was totally unrelated to any dubious activity that might have taken place, related to the car.

If he was acting under fear, after his boss' unexpected death, he could have changed his version of the events and come out clean from that suspicious episode.

However, he kept, throughout the interrogations, an uncompromising attitude of total extraneity to the alleged accusations of involvement.

His version of the events remained the same. His boss' disappearance did not affect in the least his recount, sticking always, from beginning to end, to his original narration.

The police officers found themselves up against a brick wall. Now that the two main suspects, Brutus and Carreras, had been swept away by an untimely death, that line of investigation was dead as well.

Nobody could ever explain those mysterious phone calls between the two, at the exact time of the repair job.

Both had gone to their eternal rest, leaving behind a trail of suspicion, but not a single shred of evidence.

The alleged monetary transactions, could not be verified. If any perfect crime was ever committed, that appeared to be it.

The local law enforcement, despite all their efforts, and against their will, suspended the investigation and placed all their materials in a special box, labeled "unsolved," contiguous to many other boxes with the same label, but a different name and date.

If human justice was completely impotent concerning such cases, would any other justice, either human or divine, ever come to the rescue and make the wrong right?

A third undergoing investigation had to do with the unexplainable death of a cadet, Titus Potamous.

This inquiry, conducted by naval military officers, after many twists and turns, was landing in a total wasteland.

The medical examiner, with his lack of significant findings in his *post mortem* report, appeared to preclude any avenue to the Naval Academy investigators.

Discouraging appearances notwithstanding, the officers left no stone unturned. With their keen sleuth sense and smelling foul play, they began digging in every direction, both in time and space.

Titus Potamous, the dead cadet, extremely bright and dynamic, had a very difficult childhood. His family had some unspecified financial ties with Mark Centurion. Apparently, Mark was the one footing the bill for Titus' psychiatric treatment. He was also the one that suggested sending the troubled boy to the Naval Academy.

Brutus was instrumental in all this tortuous itinerary of getting the boy settled down. During his training period, he kept in touch with the promising cadet, who, finally, seemed to have found a way to channel his potential in a positive manner.

What startled the investigators was a one-line annotation by one of his instructors. Under the strict policy of "Don't ask, don't tell," the cautious naval trainer wrote, "Titus appears to show homosexual tendencies."

That observation, curious and suspicious at the same time, would never reemerge in the documents pertaining to the cadet formation.

The investigator believed to have found a clue of the highest importance that could potentially open the door into Titus' cause of death. However, with no hard evidence to back up their theory, everything went up in smoke.

Once again, Brutus seemed implicated in a human tragedy, but his connection was so tenuous, and so untenable, that no one would dare indict him on charges of murder, or on conspiracy to commit murder.

The case, never investigated and where the suspicion was running wild, was Angie's death.

Heloise firmly believed that the suicide theory was a total fabrication, and nobody could convince her otherwise.

The irony was that the husband was the main suspect, and who more than him would be interested in covering some potential tracks?

The medical examiner's report and Brutus' stonewalling attitude achieved the impossible. No investigating agency would dare to contradict those two qualified sources, and open a bogus investigation on an undisputable act of insanity.

However, that was exactly the point of contention for Heloise—her friend Angie was neither desperate nor insane. She loved life, she was full of energy, and she would not leave her daughter, Karina, an orphan for the entire world.

Divorce would have been the answer to her marriage problems. Maybe the motive for a criminal action could emerge from a serious examination of her marital life, and Angie's close friendship with Heloise.

Nevertheless, a most likely implicated husband conveniently swept any doubt or suspicion under the carpet.

Amazingly enough, in all these cases, except for Mark Centurion's failed assassination, there was a common element, never taken into account by the investigators, but attentively scrutinized and pursued by Heloise.

The invisible dots connecting those mysterious deaths had an unusual name, "*Moral Phalanx*," the alleged credit card that made Heloise tilt toward the murder theory.

Nobody could ever explain why the professionals—the FBI and local police—overlooked that unifying element, while a self-appointed detective/lawyer focused almost exclusively on that plastic.

For obvious reasons of physical impracticality, Heloise had suspended her frantic chase in pursuit of the elusive credit card's origin. Instead, she was about to embark on a new adventure, with no apparent connection with her previous mission.

In the eyes of the experts, this probably looked like something amateurish or wimpish, for Heloise instead, it meant to be true to herself and to her conscience.

Time for speculation was over; it was time to follow her gut feeling.

Unfortunately, she had to play a nerve-racking and nail-biting game, waiting for Charles Kent's absence from the island, or at least from the hotel.

She didn't have any big expectation of earth-shattering discoveries, or incriminating clues. She just had a basic desire of clearing up a very unusual and bizarre situation.

That, after all, was her father's finest accomplishment. Was there anything illegal or immoral attached to it?

Her new top-secret project engulfed her personality. An unusual air of uncertainty and trepidation exuded from her facial expression.

Her aesthetic procedure, so successful, failed to bring back her habitual charm and confidence. Both Catherine and Ercole noticed that state of affairs, which could no longer be ignored.

They mounted a concerted assault, pounding her with a series of questions, some very personal.

Unconvincingly, Heloise dismissed their concerns, shrugging her shoulders at times, and at others replying, "It doesn't matter!"

Totally baffled by her dismissive behavior, and afraid of some rush and unadvised gesture, a product of a creeping depression, according to their layman diagnosis, they took matters into their own hands.

Their main objective was to distract her, keeping her mind off whatever was troubling her. Catherine would take her to fanciful places, where she could dine at her leisure and admire the rare species of flora and fauna, while Ercole would seriously engage her mind in philosophical conversations, as he had promised on past occasions.

Catherine wasn't lacking places at which to occupy Heloise's eyes, and Ercole didn't lack arguments to amuse her intellect.

Their combined effort seemed to produce some positive result that made them proud and hopeful.

However, what struck a sensitive cord with Heloise, relieving her of undue pressure, was Ercole's presentation of Leibniz's theory preceded by brief annotations on "**love and faith**."

Heloise possessed an insatiable curiosity on those two subjects, for the simple reason that she never had any first-hand experience in either one.

Frigid as she was, total and complete love was an empty word for her. Likewise with faith. Without a formal affiliation to any organized religion, she had a hard time understanding certain religious manifestations, so out of the ordinary and so irrational.

In the presence of a soothing cascade, surrounded by luxurious vegetation, and entertained by the sounds of the wild, Ercole did not have any difficulty putting forward some reflections on the abovementioned topics.

Skipping any preamble, Ercole initiated his reflections. "Love and faith have much in common. Their nature and dynamics are so similar that they might be considered twins.

Neither one is based on reason; both, actually, are irrational and blind. Love follows basic instincts, like attraction, while faith gets its strength from somebody else's word, whether it be God or man.

Both can propel men into sublime actions, like sacrificing their own life on behalf of others, or driving them insane, committing despicable acts.

Without love, a man withers away; a man without faith becomes paralyzed.

These two powerful drives, essential to any human existence, must be kept in check by a sensible dose of rationality. Left on their own, they will cause incalculable damage.

Every day we witness the devastating results of an excess love or a misguided faith.

Without reason, love becomes hatred, and faith, fanaticism. On the other hand, reason without love and faith will convert life into a desolate reality, unpalatable and unbearable."

The last statement left Heloise shaken up. A self-professed frigid woman, without an official religion, was she reduced to some unpleasant creature, incapable of loving and believing passionately?

Ercole guessed her sense of loss and inadequacy and came to the rescue with a further elucidation.

"You don't need to get married and have a family in order to experience true love; neither need you belong to an organized religion in order to possess faith.

Your love for **mankind and society** is admirable; similarly, your faith in **justice** doesn't leave anything to be desired.

Contrary to any perception of inadequacy, you are perfectly grounded and masterfully adjusted. Cheer up! Maybe your situation is far better than that of any common mortal, because the object of your love and faith is far superior to what you think is normal."

Reassured by these words, Heloise smiled thinking how naïve she used to be.

Ercole's words of wisdom, whether philosophically sound or not, were opening new horizons, and instilling confidence.

However, what really brought intellectual newness into her shattered life was the lengthy presentation of Leibniz's theory.

She would never forget that gorgeous afternoon, sitting on a boat, in Ercole's company, not far from the beach, being rocked gently by the ocean waves. That incessant movement of the salty water, by which she was completely surrounded, was a perfect picture of her inquisitive mind, in search of a satisfactory explanation of the universe and the world.

Leibniz's theory of **universal harmony** no longer squared with her life experience, or her broken dreams of a just and fair society.

Too many irrational and unacceptable things had happened; too much mud had piled up on her crystal clear image of people and nations.

The time had arrived for a massive conceptual cleanup, an ideological metamorphosis, and a reinvention of her persona.

Ercole had been waiting for the right moment, and this special **kairos** was there, impatient to be explored and taken advantage of.

Refreshing Heloise's memory, he briefly summarized the German philosopher's theory, which is referred to as "**We live in the best of all possible worlds**," so criticized and even ridiculed by thinkers.

"The theory of **pre-established harmony**," Ercole began by saying, "stems from a fundamental belief: God, who is perfect, created the universe, and this universe **functions perfectly**. Those who assume that the Creator constantly intervenes in his work, regard God as an unskillful watchmaker, who cannot make a perfect machine, but must continually repair what he has made. Not only does God not intervene at every moment, but he never intervenes.

Leibniz forcefully rejects the theories of people who support God's constant interference in his creation. However, this does not mean that the world is left abandoned to its whims. No, God created a perfect machine that can work without his intervention.

If some imperfections occur along the way, they will be mysteriously corrected, reestablishing order and harmony. The ending will always be a happy ending. "**Everything happens for a reason**."

Leibniz seems to suggest that despite all the atrocities and iniquities soiling our societies, somehow, in the long run, everything will work out for the best.

The German philosopher is not an **interventionist**, seeing God's finger in every twist and turn of our history, but he is a **radical optimist**, based on the belief that God is perfect and His creation bears this inherent quality.

His theory is perfectly logical and coherent. A Perfect Maker cannot produce anything but perfect creations. Therefore, our world is the best of all possible worlds.

Intellectually and based on his Christian faith, he reaches this astonishing conclusion: this world is the best of any possible world, because something inferior would be an insult to His essence, and something superior a metaphysical impossibility. God always operates at full capacity, which is total perfection.

Leibniz, faced with the scandalous and revolting atrocities of our history, **makes a leap of faith**. He cannot ignore them, because they are blatantly there for everybody to see, but he tries to justify them, proclaiming that they happen for a reason that we do not know, but God knows. At the end, **God can derive good from evil**.

In our modern day, Christians come up with new theories to justify the active presence of God in our universe. The latest one is called "Intelligent design."

Intelligent design is the assertion that "certain features of the universe and of living things are best explained by an intelligent cause, not an undirected process such as natural selection."

This powerful conviction of a God Creator and Provident Administrator, has through the centuries inspired an antithetical and mutually exclusive attitude in Christians.

Some, considering the world dangerous and corrupt, assumed an escapist posture. Abandoning society, these Christians have founded convents and monasteries, in which to live a perfect Christian life, far from any mundane and sinful ways.

They tried to build the perfect City of God, where their faith would be expressed without any restraint.

This posture not only contradicts Leibniz's theory but is founded in a great illusion. To assume that four walls can keep out corrupt human tendencies is a travesty of the facts. Truthfully, we have greed, corruption and even murder in the sacred enclosure of convents.

How can you honestly dream of escaping from a world that is inside your own heart?

This notwithstanding, such an option is still considered valid and viable.

The opposite attitude, generated by the belief of God's active presence in our midst, is to transform the existing society into a perfect Christian society. God's action, in fact, is not enough. The Church's laws will become society's laws; Christian authorities will be society's authorities. This model of a Christian society, implemented during the Middle Ages with the Christian Roman Empire, and resurrected in some form or another in the following centuries, has historically failed.

This does not mean that Christians throughout the five continents have given up on the idea. On the contrary, their Christian commitment pushes them to work incessantly in favor of Christian projects (Christian presidents, Christian social programs, Christian laws, etc.) in order to conform society to the parameters of what is considered Christian.

This attitude not only belittles Leibniz's theory that **"everything happens for a reason,"** but also works on the assumption that they know God's plan for humanity, and their programs coincide perfectly with that plan.

Both historical currents with their actions undermine their own belief. Either God is actively present in our human history and does not need our cooperation, or He is absent, and our commitment to establish a new order is indispensable.

A third position of man collaborating with God in building a new society implies something difficult if not impossible to accept. In order for man to collaborate effectively with God, he needs to know in every circumstance God's specific will. Who, among mortals, can claim this gift? As was said before, whoever asserts this privilege is a liar and a cheat.

Furthermore, it requires man to sacrifice his own interests, if they contrast with God's interests. This too appears very improbable.

Nothing can be further from the truth than Leibniz's theory. Albeit reassuring, it does not give a satisfactory explanation of all the cruelties and injustices in our society.

We can't hide the fact that nobody, as far as we know, has given a satisfactory explanation of the existence of evil and suffering in our midst.

Original sin, the central tenet in Christian theology, offers an all-comprehensive explanation to Christians.

For them, original sin subverted the natural order established by God in our universe, introducing evil and disorder. This dogma, based on faith, can't be discussed. Either it is accepted or rejected."

Ercole was painfully aware of his Christian upbringing. He could not openly disregard his religious beliefs. He had to come up with something acceptable to believers and non-believers alike.

Gazing intensely into Heloise's eyes, he detected anxiety and insecurity in that noble soul. He did not want to disappoint her, giving some religious dogma or some common platitude. He had to feed her reason, and that was what he intended to do.

Just as parents guide their children through the difficult stages of life, so Ercole made a supreme effort to shed some light on the most intricate human mystery.

"I do not possess," he continued, "any original theory on the intrinsic nature of our universe. Nor can I offer you a satisfactory explanation on the troubling and perplexing existence of **evil and suffering**.

Instead, I will try to proffer an **empirical analysis** of the reality in which we live. It is ascertained that **faith presupposes reason**. Therefore, I will just lay the groundwork. If later on you wish to proceed beyond the realm of reason, you will definitely need a different guide, more competent and enlightened in theological issues.

Here are my poor reflections on the **universe** in which we live. Scientists are debating the origin and nature of the cosmos, perfecting their theories along the way.

What we know for sure is that our universe had an origin and very likely it will have an end. It is composed of matter, therefore is quantifiable, and it is immersed in time and space. These elements: quantifiable matter, space and time constitute its essence. Anything that exists in it, man included, has the same characteristics.

Without being exhaustive, these are some of the main characteristics: imperfection and limitation; order and violence; birth and death; composition and decomposition; growth and decline, etc.

From that essence with those characteristics stems, as a necessary consequence, all the best and all the worst human nature and our universe have to offer.

Love and hatred, joy and pain, health and disease, comfort and suffering, justice and injustice, use and abuse, order and chaos, creation and destruction, war and peace, hope and desperation, trust and mistrust, truth and error, sincerity and lies, and so on.

The most peculiar thing in this litany of antonyms is that one cannot subsist without the other. Moreover, one requires the other as an intricate fiber of its essence, which is imperfection and limitation.

If you are imperfect and limited, you cannot have absolute love, otherwise you would be perfect.

Therefore, given our limited nature, it seems impossible to dream something different, better or worse.

We are what we are, and nobody will ever change the intrinsic laws and tendencies of our universe and those of our human nature.

The beauty in all of this is that there is room for sublime actions and heinous crimes, for heroic virtues and despicable vices, for redemption and condemnation.

Reflecting a little deeper on this mixed bag of blessing and curses, we discover a baffling reality. Only the existence of death gives total meaning and consistency to life. Only one who has stared death in the eyes can appreciate life. Only one who has been cheated can appreciate faithfulness, etc. The positive and the beautiful takes consistency and true meaning from the negative and the ugly.

To experience something negative in our life shouldn't be a handicap, but an asset to be treasured. There are no bad situations from which we cannot profit.

It is not our intention to advocate disasters and misfortunes. We just try to underline the astonishing mechanics of our nature, and make the best of it, without blinding ourselves with pseudo-religious explanations or voodoo solutions, or cursing our calamities, making God responsible.

Either we fight for survival (an imperative in every living creature), and struggle to better and improve all that surrounds us, or we succumb to the constant assaults carried out by negative elements (whether natural or human), lying in wait.

There are no absolute saints or absolute sinners, **because relativity is an integral part of our human essence**. There are human beings with more virtues than vices, and there are human beings with more iniquity than righteousness. In everybody there is a rescuable side, which must be utilized if there is any hope for true dialogue.

There is no happiness ever after, or immunity from pain and weakness ever after. There is a perpetual battle for superation or degradation, a constant turmoil between good and evil, agitating the whole creation.

Nobody is immune to this cosmic conflict and everybody, willy-nilly, gives his contribution. The pursuit of happiness is not an end in itself, instead it should be the result of everybody's commitment to this phenomenal struggle for **justice, peace and love**.

Our universe is harmonious and beautiful, yet at the same time scary and cruel. This is its essence.

Without mentioning God, or worse without implicating Him in the ugliness of our existence, our empirical vision of the world is fairly reasonable and fundamentally Christian, advocating a sincere commitment to save the planet by establishing more humane conditions for every living creature.

"Not everybody who says to me, '*Lord, Lord*' will enter the kingdom of heaven, but only the one who does the will of my Father in heaven." (Matthew 7:21)

Only one who fights fiercely and works tirelessly for justice is a true human and a true believer.

Whoever goes around mouthing the name of their God, and proclaiming **holy wars** in his name, in the judgment day will hear those tremendous words, "I never knew you. Depart from me, you evildoers." (Matthew 7:23)

Ercole, in an unprecedented move, ended his reasoning by quoting some biblical passages from the New Testament.

Unconsciously, while asserting his Christian roots, he was making an appreciable effort to appeal to a wider range of readers.

Heloise, who all along had listened attentively without interrupting, remained breathless. She had a worried look on her face, of somebody that had lost something precious.

Her harmonious universe, her orderly society, had crumbled into the dust like a huge building demolished by a complex dynamite coordinated implosion.

In its place there was only rubble. A scary sense of emptiness and disorientation took hold of her.

If her world vision had been mercilessly crushed, one thing stood upright, like a monument to the fallen. That was her **unshakable commitment to justice**, her intrepid and fearless pursuit of the truth, regardless of who, what or where.

She felt stripped of her ideological garment, but armed with a powerful weapon. For the time being that would be more than enough to spur and motivate our warrior.

The battle was raging all around her. It was time to join the fight and make a difference.

Chapter XIV

"Impatience" is not the appropriate word to describe Heloise's psychological attitude at this stage of the game. "Panic" would better explain her frantic waiting.

Her recovery on the beautiful island of Maui was almost over, and the time was running out faster than the last additional minutes of a soccer game.

Charles Kent, the experimental drug expert, with his unusual and peculiar presence, had raised serious doubts on the legality of his activities.

Being her father's most trusted researcher, she felt entitled to dig into his operations.

She was waiting for an opportunity to get quick access to his room and conduct a thorough search. Any considerable absence from the hotel would be more than welcome. But, Kent, like a Swiss watch, was inexorably marking his entries and exits from his room.

If destiny and luck were not on Heloise's side, fortune would be bent and forced to work in her favor.

She asked Ercole, Kent's assistant, to organize an event, outside the hotel, that would require his boss' participation.

The genial assistant, endowed by nature with imagination and inventiveness, did not waste any time in coming up with a brilliant idea.

On the other side of the island, in Hana, a group of retirees, owners of timeshare real estate, were meeting to discuss some health issues. They needed a keynote speaker. Who better than Dr. Kent to present the last findings on the subject?

The retirees were enthusiastic at the idea of having among them such a celebrity, and Kent was glad to have an eager audience, instead of the usual four mute walls.

The window of opportunity for Heloise would be on a Sunday evening, from three to eight p.m. Finally, her secret vocation of detective would be reactivated. She did not have a clue what was in store for her.

That famous Sunday afternoon was there to be taken advantage of. Ercole, kept in the dark about Heloise's real intentions, would inform her of Kent's every movement, while Catherine, equally ignoring the existence of a special mission, would follow her normal schedule.

It was barely midday, when Heloise received a phone call from her father, asking about her recovery process. With a hesitant voice, she reassured him that everything was proceeding as expected, although slowly.

Hoping that no further interruption would distract her from her secret endeavor, she contacted the weekend housekeeper.

After obtaining the key to Kent's room, under false pretenses, she pocketed her mini camera, a pen and a notebook.

Kent had left the hotel around noon, and soon after that, Heloise was off on her unauthorized undercover operation. Taking all possible precautions to protect herself from indiscreet eyes, she entered the forbidden room.

At first glance, nothing out of the ordinary caught her sight. Everything neatly occupied its space, and every space was orderly and functional.

Curiously enough, Kent did not have any computer on his desk, nor piles of documents, nor any other object that would reveal his profession as a researcher.

Meticulously, she inspected every single drawer of every piece of furniture, but came up empty-handed. Despite wearing white surgical gloves, she was afraid of leaving traces of her presence, by changing the position of objects or just by touching them.

Confronted with this insignificant reality her adrenaline rush had totally subsided, leaving feelings of frustration and disappointment.

As in the past, she appeared cursed by blind fate. Unlike in the courtroom, where she reaped reward after reward, here, in her improvised function of detective, she faced failure after failure.

The study and master bedroom were connected by a corridor, having on one side a large bathroom with sanitary facilities, and on the other, an enormous walk-in closet.

As soon as she slid open the huge door, an unusual scene popped up as if from a children's book. Jackets, pants, sweaters, shirts and neckties hung in an impeccable order, following a strict color pattern, from dark to bright.

The same way, socks and shoes were kept on shelves placed conveniently below the clothing line. No order freak in the world could have expected such neatness from a human being and much less from a scientist.

That would raise serious questions on the psychological makeup of that particular owner. He certainly possessed unmistakable traces of a compulsive and obsessive personality.

Heloise wasn't there to psychoanalyze the man. Her precise objective was to uncover his real line of work.

Would she check thoroughly any piece of clothing, in a desperate attempt to find some revealing clue, or would she abandon that wild goose chase?

Heloise still had plenty of time on her hands, since only half an hour had passed.

She stood motionless a few seconds. She closed her eyes, reflecting on what to do next. Absolutely, nothing came to light up her mind. Frustrated and annoyed by her poor investigating skills, she opened her eyes and kept staring at that aberrant display of clothing.

All of a sudden, a ray of hope flickered in her imagination, when she observed a different length of space between two hand-knitted white sweaters.

Was that an unforgivable oversight, or a real opening into the unknown? With a trembling hand Heloise made the separation wider, and looked intensively at the wall behind.

At first sight, nothing abnormal or original stood out. However, upon closer observation, she noticed a slightly different floral design in the wallpaper.

At this point, her anxiety level matched the speed of light. Was she really close to discovering a mysterious world never seen or imagined before? Conversely, a shabby wallpaper job by a disgruntled interior designer?

By applying considerable pressure with the palm of her gloved hand here and there, she expected something to move magically, as in a fairy tale.

To her bitter disappointment, nothing happened. On the contrary, a loud noise, coming possibly from the corridor, made her heart jump and her blood pressure shoot up.

Immobilized by fear and terror, Heloise held her breath. She tried to hide behind the hanging clothes, in case somebody dropped in unannounced and unexpected.

To be discovered as an intruder would be the ultimate insult to her detective ambition, and very likely the end of that misguided calling.

A few minutes passed, which seemed an eternity. Fortunately for her, it was a false alarm. She let out a sigh of relief and tried to compose herself. It wasn't easy.

Still shaken up, she resumed her gentle patting on the dry wall. No sign of any hollow spot, or cavity of any kind.

When all attempts appeared futile, Heloise, by accident, hit the lower part of the wall with her right shoe.

Surprise! Surprise! Something began moving, noiselessly and effortlessly. The entire section of the wall slid to one side, introducing her to a secret chamber, furnished with an elevator.

Her intuition was beginning to pay off. Inside the elevator, Heloise took the only way allowed—down. Now, she was traveling into the bowels of the unknown.

At the end of her descent, a surprising reality opened up in front of her eyes. It was a huge laboratory, equipped with state-of-the-art equipment.

She had never before seen such a dazzling array of scientific tools of different sizes, shapes and colors. What impressed her most was how immaculate the place looked. Was it a real scientific lab or just a display of the latest gadgets in the field of research?

Obviously, she wasn't there to admire the profusion and overabundance of objects, or the freakish and compulsive cleanliness of that surreal facility.

Her mission was to unveil the secretive activity of the doctor responsible for her rehabilitation, and her father's concealed business.

She was about to stumble upon a piece of evidence that would turn her world upside-down. Up to this point, she had experienced nothing, compared with what was lurking for her just around the corner.

Extremely careful not to leave clues of her presence, she turned on the main computer. Inputting numerous keywords, none of which served as a password, she was denied access to the programs and information.

Her patience was put to the test. Despite being surprisingly calm, after an hour of frantic attempts, Heloise had to abandon the idea.

Undiscouraged by the useless tries, she began rummaging through the drawers and shelves in search of any shred of paper with anything written on it.

In the meantime, the clock was ticking, and the search was running out of steam.

Contiguous to Kent's mahogany desk, she observed a stand with a handy storage compartment. Unfortunately, it was locked. She had no choice but to force it. Using a metal letter opener, like a professional burglar, she disabled the lock and pulled it open.

A brown folder, labeled "Top Secret Project," instantly grabbed her attention. She opened it. The first page carried an astonishing title—"*Moral Phalanx.*" Was she dreaming, or was a powerful flashback flooding her imagination, obliterating the present and recreating a disappointing past?

She touched it repeatedly to make sure it was real, and her fantasy wasn't playing tricks on her. She was neither deceived nor deluded; it was real, written in black and white, and with capital letters.

Yes, believe it or not, it was "*Moral Phalanx*," the mysterious credit card that had intrigued her since Angie's death, and prompted her to undertake the investigative mission that almost ended her life.

Instantly, the meeting with her father came to mind. She remembered Mark professing total ignorance about that special card. Also, she couldn't forget his body language, unmistakably denying what his mouth was saying.

Not only did he know it; he was its primary instigator. What a monumental lie! What a colossal deception!

Poor Heloise! The shock and surprise were just startling. She had only touched the tip of a cavernous polypoid monster, whose tentacles reached the whole wide world, suffocating genuine human lives.

As soon as she began glancing at the pages and reading the contents of that project, her jaw fell, remaining almost paralyzed.

Moral Phalanx dealt with the manipulation of a basic human tendency—**sex drive**. Its clear aim was to diminish or totally suppress its powerful forces by targeting, through new pharmacological products, the sources (testes, ovaries, glands, etc.) of testosterone and other steroids.

The demented objective was to create a new breed of humans (the new Moral Phalanx), able to withstand widespread sexual corruption and form a new army that would take over the destiny of the world.

Mark Centurion, an army man, was thinking in military terms, and planning with an army ideology. Brutus, insensitive and detached, had been his material executioner, while Charles Kent, the brilliant medical wizard, was in charge of creating, experimenting and perfecting the new wonder drug.

The experiments had been going on for many years and the list of human guinea pigs was extensive. If Heloise had been deeply troubled in discovering the secret project, there were no words to describe her tumultuous feelings of fear and dismay when she saw her name in that infamous list.

What a cruel blow for the young lawyer! Instantly, time and space disappeared from her perception and an air of unreality hung over her undercover mission.

Not only had her father been a supreme manipulator, with messianic dreams of redemption for a mankind gone astray, but a real bastard and criminal, who would stop at nothing, not even his own flesh and blood.

One paragraph of that secret project turned her pale with bewilderment and terror: "Any experiment that does not succeed, will be promptly terminated. Natural selection is carried out by nature regardless of ranking or species."

Now, Heloise had a clear clue on those premature deaths, from Angie Barker to Titus Potamous. Somehow, they were experiments gone sour. The creator of that aberrant and diabolic project, according to his own philosophy, had no other choice but to cut down the dead branches if he wanted his tree to survive and prosper.

The problem was to find out why those people were considered failures, and how their life was cut short, without leaving a trace.

She kept reading the explosive document, but she found no answer to her burning questions. However, one thing stood out incontrovertibly—**the alleged credit card "*Moral Phalanx*" was not a credit card, but a simple identification card**. Mons. Marcikkus had hit the nail on the head. He was unwittingly right.

This significant discovery that had prompted Heloise's initial crusade as an undercover agent and meant the world for her in those early days, at this point in time had lost all urgency and meaning.

The gruesome reality behind that piece of plastic made everything pale into insignificance when compared with her original doubts and suspicions.

No sooner had she recovered from her bitter dismay than she extracted her tiny camera and began taking pictures of the highly incriminating material.

Then and there she hadn't the faintest idea of what to do with that evidence, but she was sure it would be of some use in the future.

While photocopying, a sudden inspiration crossed her mind. Without delay and following her instinct, she went back to the computer, using "*Moral Phalanx*" as the password. Miracle of miracles—it worked!

Heloise was about to lay her hands on Charlie Kent's secret research. Nobody could imagine the excitement of that young lady. *Too much luck for one day*, she thought.

Probably, the computer could reveal the answers to all her problems. Scrolling through the list of files, she noticed something unusual; the words appeared to be not scientific terms, but an unintelligible rebus.

She clicked on one of them, and the ephemeral hope raised by the successful password was dashed away in the blink of an eye.

All the research documents were encrypted to prevent unauthorized people gaining access to or stealing the extremely sensitive material.

Had she been able to open the door into that forbidden kingdom, what dark secrets and frightening realities would she have unveiled? Nobody would ever know.

Mortified and still numbed by her ghastly discovery, Heloise made her way back toward the elevator. The exit strategy didn't need any special tactic, just extreme caution and some more confidence.

The mission had been successful, and her dream of getting to the bottom of her dear friend Angie's death realized.

Back in her luxury quarters, without raising suspicions of any kind, Heloise sat down to reflect on the daring operation, just carried out.

A mixed bag of feelings and emotions troubled her soul. On one hand, a sense of accomplishment for accidentally discovering the origin of the "*Moral Phalanx,*" the crux of her undercover activities.

On the other hand, disappointment, rage and fury against her father, for violating and destroying the most sacred part of her individuality: her femininity. She would never know what it is to be a nurturing mother, an affectionate wife and a complete woman.

She wasn't the only one affected by that deranged project. How many other human beings, males and females, had been deprived and stripped of their full humanity? How many had paid the ultimate price for that insane experiment? She was still lucky to be alive.

Her passion for justice, one of her overriding feelings, left her deeply agitated and in a convulsive panic.

Heloise was simply terrified just thinking about the consequences of legal action against her father. That could alienate and destroy her entire family, starting from her father.

Could he survive the total humiliation of being dragged through the mud of a lengthy trial and a very likely conviction?

Her mother, so fragile and sensitive, who was finally enjoying a few years of relative peace, would she succumb to such an ordeal?

What about Catherine who secretly worshiped her father? Would she turn against the only sibling she had? It was a real nightmare scenario.

Would she wait and let the events play themselves out, convinced that "what goes around, comes around"? Wouldn't that be considered cowardice and weakness? Whichever way she turned, total catastrophe loomed large on her family's horizon.

Gripped by this dilemma, Heloise found herself incapable of any reasonable decision, and immobilized by fear.

While Heloise was still brooding over the terrible consequences of her findings, Charles Kent was administering a lavish dose of his gerontic philosophy to the timeshare owners on the opposite side of the island.

The audience wasn't huge, but it had been carefully selected. Every single one of those participants was extremely eager to listen to what Charles Kent had to say. At his arrival the seniors broke into rapturous applause.

Charles began with a clear voice and a commanding attitude. "I'm not going to make a sugar-coated speech. I will present some reflections, based on the crude reality of our daily living.

In this day and age when everything is changing rapidly, when myths are dispelled, and heroes of any kind are falling (from religious leaders, sports champions and entertainment superstars), we need to take an honest look at what is called the third age.

Putting it mildly, aging is neither easy nor pleasant. The euphemistically called **golden age**, should be more accurately designated as the final stage and the **age of diminishing capacity**.

Final, because it is the very last season. There is no other period to look forward to.

The age of diminishing capacity, because every energy, whether physical, mental or spiritual, will slowly and irreversibly disappear, until nothing is left.

Independence and freedom of movement, so dearly treasured and fiercely defended, will be substituted by progressive dependence and degrading impotence. Even our most basic bodily functions will be in need of assistance.

Man will reach the point of begging for a mercy killing either by nature or by technology, if any consciousness is still left in him.

Science is trying its best to postpone as long as possible this dreadful stage, slowing the aging process and virtually maintaining one's self-sufficiency.

The daring techniques (organ transplant, partial reconstruction, stem cell regeneration and reproduction) used so far, are nothing, compared with what science will lead to in the near future.

However, science alone cannot reach this ultimate goal; it needs man's conscious effort.

It is here that your input is indispensable and absolutely invaluable. You must take your destiny into your own hands.

Despite the enormous difficulties of reversing any habit at your age, you must practice a lifestyle in accordance with new guidelines.

Eat right, breathe right and exercise right are the three fundamentals, essential to slowing the aging process.

By **eating right** we dearly encourage people to produce and cook their own food. As far as is possible, everyone should grow their own vegetables and fruits and raise animals, embracing an agrarian way of life, extremely beneficial to both body and soul.

In your position, with a considerable amount of money and time, this project is not only reasonable, but also feasible and achievable.

Breathe right. Far away from the polluted industrial centers, choose a piece of land where the contamination of air and soil hasn't yet reached a dangerous level.

On top of that, with a new technique of measuring your **inhaling and exhaling**, not only can you improve the lifespan of your lungs, you can also reduce your blood pressure. As a result, the benefits for your heart and brain will be incalculable.

Finally, **daily mental and physical exercise** will keep the machine of your body fine-tuned and in perfect condition.

If the slowing of the aging process has to occur in your lifetime, you must gain full control of your eating, breathing and exercising habits.

For many of you, this project might seem out of reach, full of obstacles and unfeasible. But, whatever you can do in that sense, even on a reduced scale, it will be exceedingly rewarding.

My best wishes for a world of health and prosperity."

This presentation originated a very vivacious round of questions and answers, that occupied the speaker for quite a long time.

A sumptuous dinner followed the very lively discussion, where bottles of generous Bordeaux were being emptied no sooner than they arrived from the cellar.

Relaxed, a rare psychological condition, Charles Kent made his way back to Kaanapali.

In an exuberant mood, he went to bed, dreaming of international meetings, where his scientific findings and pretentious theories would be hailed with enthusiasm by his admirers.

Unfortunately, under the influence of wine, he forgot a particular piece of routine that he performed faithfully every night before hitting the pillow.

Customarily, Charles would check the security tape to see whether anybody, during his absence, had broken into his lab and violated his scientific sanctuary. However, that unfortunate evening he totally forgot.

Monday morning, he awoke with an annoying hangover. His mood had gone from exuberant to somber. With his mind clear of alcoholic fumes, he instantaneously remembered the previous night's memory lapse.

Immediately, he went down to the lab and, switching on the invisible electronic eyes, ran the last segment recorded.

It is impossible to describe his astonishment when he saw the intruder laying her hands on the secret document "*Moral Phalanx.*"

All hell broke loose in that insignificant corner of the universe. The poor researcher felt as if his irate boss had caught him neglecting his most sacred duty of protecting and defending with his life the top secret project.

Unprepared for that eventuality, his first reaction was to end his existence using a suicide pill, which he himself had created.

This extraordinary pill had a great advantage over any other rival of that kind. In a matter of an hour, it would be undetectable, leaving no trace in the blood or any other organ of the body. It would be the perfect weapon to eliminate any person who dared to oppose his boss' course of action. It had already been used with considerable success. Some unexplained deaths, where the autopsy was inconclusive, were the results of that powerful pill.

Charles, distraught, upon reflection changed his mind. He abandoned the idea of suicide; instead frantically dialing Mark Centurion's private number.

It was almost midday in Washington, D.C. and Mark was preparing for a quiet lunch with his wife. After a few rings, he picked up the phone and answered calmly.

"Hello, Mark here."

"Mr. Centurion, Charles Kent here. I'm afraid I have terrible news. Yesterday afternoon, while I was entertaining a group of seniors in the resort city of Hana, Heloise, I don't know how, gained access to the underground lab. What is worse, she found the project "*Moral Phalanx*," and took pictures of it.

I knew your serious concerns about Heloise snooping around in search of the origin of the alleged credit card. Unfortunately, your fears have materialized. I am responsible for that breach of security, and I am ready for your punishment."

Charles waited a few frightening seconds for an answer, finally, from the other end; a cavernous voice, never heard before, said, "I hoped we would never need to resort to this. But, we don't have any other choice. Knowing the puritan sense of justice of my daughter and her messianic push to right any wrong, we must think about our survival and the continuation of our project.

The only way to achieve this is her complete elimination. **Everybody knows that mankind's interests take precedence over personal ones**, and fatherly attachments and feelings must be superseded by company duties. In view of all this, and much to my chagrin, this death sentence must be carried out without any delay.

You will be the official executioner, since Brutus Barker is no longer among us. You will use the right dosage of your untraceable pill. It must look like a natural death. Not a shred of evidence must be left behind. Immediately after that, the camera with the pictures has to be found and destroyed.

You caused this mess, and you must clean it up. This is a strict order. Goodbye."

Mark, as a military man, faced with the most disastrous eventuality of his existence, did not hesitate a second, and in a calculated manner and with a bloody determination, pronounced his daughter's death sentence.

Who would have ever thought that a famous captain of industry, a great philanthropist, would possess such a criminal mind and reach the point of murdering his only daughter, appealing to a moral principle ("**mankind's interests take precedence over personal ones**") of dubious validity?

Fame, power and riches blind people, making them insensitive and unresponsive to basic human instincts.

Charles Kent, shaking like a leaf due to the awesome responsibility, hung up the phone, and rushed to his lab to concoct the deadly drug.

With his judgment clouded, emotions running high, and mounting pressure, he wasn't in the ideal position to perform the delicate operation. Any small variation in calculating age, weight and height of his intended victim could have disastrous consequences. The dosage in order to be effective, in other words lethal, causing complete and permanent cardiac arrest, had to be very precise.

Moreover, Kent's window of opportunity was extremely reduced. By breakfast time Heloise should have ingested the deadly medicine.

Every morning with her tea, the convalescent young lawyer took a few tablets. It wouldn't be difficult to slip in her beverage an extra one at the time of serving her orange juice.

In this way, Heloise wouldn't have time to confide in anybody, exposing the damaging secret of her discovery.

Kent was well aware that time was of the essence. Moreover, his life and reputation were at stake.

As a scientist and researcher in the medical field, he never had anything to do with the operational inconveniences of carrying out an execution of a real live human being.

This was against his principles and his Hippocratic vows. However, scary as it was, he had no choice if he wanted to survive.

Despite having on his conscience an enormous weight, he went full steam ahead. Like the Nazi physician, Josef Mengele, he would shortly become the Angel of Death, putting the Angel of Justice to sleep for good.

Ironically, his murderous mission was intended to benefit mankind **"because mankind's interests take precedence over personal ones."**

For breakfast time, the deadly medicine was ready. Heloise was sitting on the veranda of her apartment, reading the morning paper and waiting for Catherine to bring the usual toast with the usual drinks.

On her way to serve her sister, Catherine bumped, accidentally, into Dr. Charles Kent. With a big smile on his face, he asked if she hadn't forgotten anything.

"I don't think so," she answered.

"Let me hold the tray," he added, "while you open the door." Obediently, she handed him the tray, and proceeded to open the door.

In that very instant, the lethal dosage was dropped into the glass of juice, without Catherine noticing anything. She thanked Professor Kent for his genteel manners and entered the room.

Heloise, overwhelmed by the previous day's discovery, wasn't in a conversational mood. Looking at her sister with affection, she thanked her and resumed her reading, while nibbling on the toast and drinking her juice.

Catherine, reluctant to intrude in her sister's world of feelings, took her leave saying, "I'll check on you later, to see if you need anything."

Immediately, she left her sister absorbed in her morning reading and personal worries. This wasn't the Heloise she knew. Something was happening.

She would never have imagined the drama unfolding inside and outside the poor girl. Heloise put a stop to her reading and finished what was left of her breakfast.

Feeling a little tired, and with some nausea and difficulty in breathing, she lay down on her bed and closed her eyes. What happened next she will never know.

Only two people could predict the chain of events that would follow. Thousands of miles away, Mark Centurion, visibly nervous, couldn't sit down for any length of time. Charles Kent was waiting, impatiently, for a commotion to break out.

Three full hours had passed and no sign of anything abnormal in the Kaanapali hotel.

Around eleven, Catherine went back to her sister's room. Usually at that time they took a stroll along the beach. She knocked on the door, but no answer came from inside. She knocked for the second time, with the same result.

Curious and suspicious, she turned the doorknob, which was unlocked, and entered the room.

Heloise lay in bed, immobile and pale. Catherine tried to wake her up, gently. All attempts were fruitless. In despair, she checked her pulse and respiration. There was no sign of any life in that motionless body.

Immediately, she extracted her cellular and dialed Ercole's number. The assistant physician rushed to Heloise's bedside, and with indescribable consternation he could do nothing else but confirm Catherine's findings.

The young, beautiful patient, for whom he felt so much attachment and admiration, had passed away a few hours earlier. On the spot, he notified his boss, who did not show any surprise. He, in turn, immediately called Mark Centurion. A huge sigh of relief came from both of them.

They had averted the biggest disaster of their professional careers. Now they could sleep peacefully. The voice of justice had been silenced.

Not only had a heinous crime been committed on that enchanted island of the Pacific, but **injustice was**

beginning her triumphant march on the land of justice.

Chapter XV

Heloise's mysterious death caused quite a stir among the hotel's adventitious population.

Indubitably, she was well liked by people who had the privilege of dealing with her. That news was like a stab in the back, leaving them petrified.

However, no pain or suffering could be compared with Magdalene's and Catherine's grief and torment.

The mother had just come out of a paralyzing depression, fruit of the trying times she had gone through lately, and Catherine was beginning to enjoy her sister's return to normality, when such a merciless blow came upon them like a devastating tornado, forever altering their lives.

The angel that had graced them with her presence, had been taken away by some vindictive hand, jealous, maybe, of so much virtue and integrity.

The only one who showed neither overwhelming emotion nor visible perplexity, was Charles Kent. Treating that unfortunate episode as a normal occurrence among mortals, he called in the local medical examiner.

As Heloise's personal physician, he could have conducted the examination of the corpse himself. However, to avoid any arousing suspicion, he preferred to bring in the local medical authority.

While mourners displayed their deepest sentiments, Kent didn't waste any time eliminating incriminating evidence, particularly the camera, where the lab intruder had stored pictures of the secret project.

Everything seemed wrapped up marvelously, and in record time, especially when the autopsy ruled out any foul play, proclaiming the cause of the sudden death, an atypical heart attack.

Kent, the ruthless executioner, needless to say, was bursting with satisfaction. Not only had the deadly dosage produced the expected outcome; it hadn't left any suspicious trace in the blood.

In total agreement with his boss, he immediately made arrangements with the funeral home, where the body would be embalmed. It would stay overnight on the island, to be flown home the following day.

No ceremony with an open casket in Washington, D.C. Just a private burial in a family columbarium. However, Catherine and other close relatives and friends could have the possibility, an hour before going to the cemetery, of paying their respects and saying their final goodbyes.

All was meticulously planned by Mark, who seemed more in a hurry to get rid of his daughter than to mourn her properly.

Nobody, not even the most observant, took notice of that out-of-character precipitation. Only his wife experienced something sharp like a spear piercing her heart. However, knowing her husband, she was extremely cautious not to utter a complaint.

In the meantime, back on the island, the outpouring of condolences and the manifestation of affection for that beautiful flower, cut short by a cruel destiny, went on for hours.

If Ercole was stoned, Catherine remained in a state of shock, never experienced before, not even when her mother passed away.

Anyhow, snapping out of that kind of fourth dimension, where everything was surreal, she busied herself with the preparation of her sister's remains.

She gently washed her body, dressing it with the best attire she could find in her closet. With a motherly fondness, she combed her sister's delicate hair, propped up her head with an extra pillow and applied some makeup to those pale cheeks.

That inanimate corpse, so simply fixed, gave the favorable impression of an angel, sleeping in an ocean of serenity and peace, ready to come back to life at any moment.

Moreover, that corpse was the loveliest corpse ever. Finally, its femininity, so brutally manipulated and defaced by a deranged experiment, seemed to spring out of those lifeless limbs and irradiate the room with an irresistible charm.

In such a surreal presence only one question arose spontaneously. Had Heloise left this earth forever? Only people out of their mind would assume the contrary. Was her mission of justice lost in the chaotic vicissitudes of human history? All credible signs pointed in that direction.

What would she genuinely think, if she were able to assist her own demise? Would she still have faith in humanity, or would she give up her indefatigable quest for justice?

Could she have predicted her brutal elimination, after discovering the secret project and having serious doubts on those mysterious deaths, upon which she was determined to shed some light?

Whatever the answer to these questions might be, the fact that she was swept away like a twig by a merciless cyclone leaves the unpleasant situation incomprehensible.

The forces of darkness and evil had prevailed and nothing could change that. She was gone without big headlines in the media and without a clear legacy.

Her presence on this earth, despite touching countless people, had been like a delicate dawn that quickly gives way to a glorious sunrise. Just a fleeting moment of splendid pinkish colors submerged by a flood of white lights of an emerging triumphant sun.

What a terrible sense of injustice hovered in the air, and what sharp pain was eating away the sanity of every simple mind!

All of a sudden, for common people like Catherine, Magdalene and many others, justice had become an elusive chimera, a figment of our human imagination, praised and proclaimed from rooftops, but rarely carried out in the courtrooms.

Probably, Heloise, if still alive, would have suffered the same frustration and disillusion, giving up her lawyer toga, and pursuing some other career, less hypocritical and more genuine and honest.

Would the perpetrators of this heinous crime go unpunished? Or would some natural stabilizer fill the vacuum created, obeying a mysterious law of compensation?

Unfortunately, for now the only thing visible and palpable was the unexplained departure of a marvelous human being, and the triumph of an alleged violence, asking heavens for vengeance.

While Catherine was trying to compose herself, a persistent doubt kept coming back. She remembered Heloise's detached and worrisome attitude during her last breakfast, so alien to her pleasant demeanor.

Did she have a foreboding feeling that something was terribly wrong? Was she filled with a sense of impending doom?

If Heloise was dreading something or someone, why not open up and confide in her? Was her secret so big and so dangerous that she couldn't afford to involve anybody else?

Definitely, in her sister's death, there was something wrong that wouldn't go away easily, despite the autopsy's results.

Was it connected with her previous investigation about the origin of an unknown credit card and the death of her best friend?

They had talked about that on several occasions, but, after the car accident, to her knowledge, she had suspended all undercover activities.

Catherine, unable to come up with a satisfactory answer to her burning questions, approached her friend Ercole, pouring out her troubles to him.

He too was deeply disturbed by Heloise's unexpected death. Besides, there was something odd about his boss, and unfortunately he couldn't put his finger on it.

Unlike Catherine, Ercole had been trained to expect the unexpected. If he had to undertake a thorough investigation, he wouldn't rule out anybody, not even Charles Kent. On the contrary, being Heloise's personal physician would be all the more reason to perpetrate the perfect crime.

However, what could possibly be the motive? Ercole had to confess total ignorance on this. With regard to the weapon, the possibilities were numerous. Ercole knew that his boss was working on the production of powerful drugs that could induce suspended animation in animals and humans. He himself had produced a paper on that delicate field.

He would be horrified to know that his research could have contributed to somebody's death. He had exercised considerable restraint in the past in talking about his scientific work. Now, with Catherine, he didn't show any scruple or hesitation. He was eager to open his mind and expose his fears.

Catherine, unlike her sister, didn't possess a knack for undercover activities. Moreover, on foreign soil, she couldn't even dare to think about it. She didn't have her sister's ardent desire for justice. Their emotional and intellectual worlds were light years apart from each other.

But, an endearing affection united those two noble souls. With Heloise's disappearance, Ercole became for Catherine the new shoulder to cry on. Until then, he had been a teacher and a guide. From that day forward, he would be her only true friend and confidant.

She listened to his wild speculations with bewilderment, because the eventuality of Kent being a bloody murderer was very difficult to swallow.

Anyhow, she was impressed by that little world of intrigue, and was more than willing to give him her approval. Whatever he could do for her loving sister, she would welcome it.

However, he shouldn't expect any collaboration from her, just moral support. In fact, anything in the realm of investigation was alien to her nature.

Ercole, on the other hand, anointed himself the new prophet of justice. Just as Elisha had received the prophetic cloak from Elijah, so would Ercole be invested with Heloise's mission.

Would he succeed where Heloise had failed? He surely needed superpowers or a miracle. Nothing short of that would help him.

He genuinely thought of himself as a mole planted in his boss' quarters. He would take up the active role of scrutinizing Charles Kent's secret activities. Incessantly, he would ask questions, examine documents, observe movements, and capture the hidden meaning of every word. Silently but efficiently, he would leave no stone unturned, until he got to the bottom of that quagmire.

It was impossible to predict the end of that slippery road. Nevertheless, he deemed worthwhile any risk taken on behalf of his dear friend Heloise.

That calamitous day, impossible to forget, was the eve of a big national holiday. Everybody out there was hitting the road, early. The frenzy to reach familiar destinations bore little relation to what was going on inside the luxury apartment, where Heloise was receiving the last respects.

A steady stream of visitors, that lasted hours, was a welcome surprise. Nobody could have ever imagined such a spontaneous and remarkable outpouring of affection.

When the procession of mourners trickled down to the last few people, Charles Kent made arrangements for the transportation of the corpse to the funeral home.

It was almost five in the evening when the hearse left the hotel with the coffin. They couldn't have chosen a worse moment, as a result of the intense traffic that had reached its peak.

There was no police escort, because it wasn't a funeral. It appeared that an unconscious reluctance was keeping the hearse from reaching its destination.

Finally, after ninety minutes of fighting that rush-hour madness, the coffin was deposited in the funeral chamber.

This had been ready for quite a long time, with numerous burning candles and multiple wreaths of flowers. The smell of wax mixed with the perfume exhaling from roses and lilies was overwhelming.

Among the many wreaths, one stood out not only for the mastery in the layout of the precious and rare flowers, but mainly for the ironic and truculent content of the dedication: "To my loving daughter. Mark C." Nobody could have ever fathomed the miserable treachery behind those words. It was the ultimate insult to a normal father-daughter relationship.

Unfortunately, the embalmment couldn't be performed that evening. The mortician, in effect, had already left for the long holiday. It would be carried out first thing in the morning, before flying the corpse to Washington, D.C.

Since there were no relatives on the island (nobody knew of Catherine's blood relation), all the pertinent decisions were taken by Charles Kent and the funeral director.

At the risk of appearing intrusive and, at the same time, a simpleton, Catherine asked the director to leave the casket open. She explained to the astounded listener that Heloise was terrorized by enclosed spaces.

Afraid of being rude and insensitive, even if the request was childish and without merit, and was going against the house regulations, the director agreed to the demand.

Catherine showed gratitude to the man in charge. After kissing her sister, her face stained with tears, she left that sad place in Ercole's company.

On the other hand, Charles Kent, exuding confidence, and almost triumphant, with a smirk on his face, made his way back to the hotel.

Night was fast approaching. Families all over the great nation were getting together to celebrate. Catherine had neither family nor celebrations. Actually, she was in no mood for popping champagne corks or any other festive manifestations.

She was not a lady that would cry at the drop of a hat, but that day had been an unbelievable rollercoaster of tears and sobs.

While lying on her bed exhausted, yet unable to fall asleep, the image of her sister, so serene, kept coming back, comforting and reassuring her.

In the meantime, Heloise, in the funeral home, was sleeping the sleep of the righteous. Nevertheless, the night watch, in charge of keeping a vigilant eye, wasn't sleeping nor was he righteous.

When everything quieted down, he inspected for the last time the premises. The open casket, with the beautiful lady inside, attracted his attention.

What enticed him most wasn't the lady's beauty, but her marvelous ring, with a precious gemstone. The temptation to substitute it with a similar fake one was something he couldn't resist.

Without wasting any time, he went back to his station, grabbed the counterfeit ring and returned to the coffin to carry out his criminal intent.

To his greatest amazement, a substitution that he believed simple and easy, turned out to be awkward and frightening.

The swollen finger, in fact, rendered the removal nearly impossible. Then, the determined casket thief, instead of abandoning the abominable desecration of the corpse, began squeezing, as hard as he could, the inanimate finger.

During the uphill struggle that lasted interminable minutes, the sacrilegious night guard, totally absorbed in his unscrupulous act, did not realize that the corpse was no longer a corpse.

The lifeless body, condemned to the underworld by a deadly dosage of a powerful drug, had refused its final descent among the dead.

Under the intense pressure of the squeezing, the suspended animation came to an end, and Heloise opened her eyes and began to breathe. That reanimation, witnessed by no one, not even the robber, was nothing short of a miracle.

The acrid smoke of the candles mixed with an undefined perfume of flowers, the soft flickering of the lights, and the intense pain in her finger created a supreme state of confusion in the just-resurrected young lady.

If she couldn't determine yet where she was and why, she didn't fail to assess that somebody was attacking her. No sooner had the face of the assailant become clear in her vision, then she slapped him vigorously with her left hand.

The poor lad, terrorized by the unexpected blow, jumped back, expecting to face a co-worker or an intruder. What he saw instead was the dead lady sitting up and screaming at him.

Scared and ashamed, he did not run away. On the contrary, quite taken with that prodigious event and Heloise's disoriented attitude, he reassured her that he wasn't a threat.

Holding the hand that slapped him, he explained to Heloise what had happened to her and where she was. She could hardly believe her luck. Trying to remember the last moments when she was still alive, and how bad she felt, it wasn't difficult for her to reach the dreadful conclusion that somebody made an unsuccessful attempt on her life.

Reacquainted with space and time, she quickly reassessed the situation, and in a composed manner, asked for a glass of water.

After that, with the help of the assistant, she stepped out of the coffin. Holding his arm firmly, she looked intensely at him and said, "Don't be afraid. I'm not going to accuse you of anything or bring you up on any charge. On the contrary, I thank you profusely for bringing me back to life. Since I am in grave danger, I need you to ignore completely what happened in here tonight.

You will tell the police and anybody else that you don't know what occurred to the corpse. As a token of my gratitude I'll give you this ring that you attempted to steal and later on a substantial reward. Do you promise me absolute silence?"

The night watch, still embarrassed and fearful, gave her his word of honor, for what it was worth. Moreover, the man, captivated by her gracious and magnanimous gesture, was more than willing to protect her with his life.

At last, he felt valued and an important part in an intriguing conspiracy that could have significant repercussions in the future.

The stage was set for exciting developments. Heloise left the funeral home for an unknown destination, while her co-conspirator resumed his boring surveillance duty.

It is nearly impossible to describe what was going on in the mind and heart of the young lawyer who, for the second time, had miraculously returned from the dead. Her first impulse was to communicate with Catherine and Ercole. However, she had to give up the idea immediately because she didn't have her cellular phone or any other means of getting in touch. Mom was also first on her priority list, but there too she had to refrain from any rush decision.

The important thing for her was to lay low for some length of time and wait for some startling event to take place.

The night assistant, responsible for the prodigious happening, could barely wait for his shift to end. Finally, after some tedious hours, his seven o'clock replacement came in.

Without any explanation and with the usual comment that "everything had been quiet," he turned in the keys and vanished.

Being a national holiday, the new man in charge didn't expect any dramatic movement, let alone complications. Nevertheless, he was deadly wrong.

At nine o'clock, as had been planned the previous day, Professor Charles Kent came with a limousine service to reclaim the corpse that was supposed to be flown to Washington, D.C.

Imagine his shock and anger when he discovered the empty coffin. Immediately, all hell broke loose.

The funeral director, the night assistant, and the police were called in. Interrogation after interrogation failed to produce any plausible explanation or clue of what had happened.

The mystery was deepening and Kent's fury was raging. How could he justify to his boss that gross negligence and that unforgivable loss?

There were only two possibilities. Either the corpse walked away using its own power (and that would mean one thing and one thing only: the administered dosage was wrong and Heloise was still alive), or some dark force stole the body with the intention of creating serious damage.

In either case the future was very bleak for both Kent and Mark Centurion. Their victory song had been premature; a colossal catastrophe loomed large on the horizon.

Meanwhile, the police would carry out their investigation, and it would take some time before reaching any definitive conclusion.

Time was exactly what Kent needed. If Heloise was alive, worst possible scenario, there was no salvation for him or Mark Centurion. She knew too much. The only way out was to destroy any compromising evidence, and meticulously cover any incriminating tracks.

To say that job was staggering is a mild euphemism. Under cover of pressing matters, and despite the sacred holiday rest, he hired skilled professionals to seal off the lab and its entrance.

At the same time, with the help of two other associates (certainly not Ercole), he transferred the astounding amount of data to a secret lab in Switzerland. All the lab materials, including the costly instruments and computers, were transported to a remote location, where they were disposed of.

In record time, that scientific sanctuary, where the modern-day Mengele had performed the most daring human experiments, had become an empty space, with no entrance, no ventilation and no connection to a power source.

While all this was going on in the utmost secrecy, the news of the corpse's disappearance spread like wildfire, resurrecting ancient local legends of dead people walking and scaring the shit out of the living.

When Ercole got the dreadful news, he didn't waste any time sharing it with Catherine. This was like rubbing salt in an open wound. Her pain, somehow subdued during the night, revived all of a sudden, and became excruciating. Fresh new tears were brought to her eyes, and a new stage of depression darkened her outlook.

Bracing herself for the worst, and still brooding over that undeserved cruel joke, her cellular phone came alive with a joyful ring. Looking at the small monitor, she didn't recognize the number. Was it a wrong number, or a prank? The only way to find out was to answer. What was there to lose, by answering it?

With a shaky voice, she said. "Who is it?" What followed almost caused a heart attack in the poor, dejected Catherine. A familiar voice, so cherished, reached her ears.

"It is I, Heloise, in the flesh. I need you to listen carefully to what I'm going to say."

With the usual soothing persuasion and a unique captivating affection, she warned her sister not to say anything to anybody, except Ercole. In the greatest secrecy, they should reach her, as soon as possible, at the given location. Once there, she would explain everything.

New tears were shed from those swollen eyes, and this time they were tears of an ebullient joy and exhilaration.

Catherine didn't have time to adjust her gears; she was on automatic pilot, impatient to get to her sister. Ercole, rendered speechless by the best surprise of his entire life, didn't waste a second in getting into his car with Catherine, and dashing off to meet the lovely Heloise, believed dead and gone by all.

Speeding was the last of his concerns. All he thought of was hugging and kissing her, as if it were the last time he would ever hug and kiss a human being.

The streets were quiet, compared to the previous evening, when the islanders seemed to have gone mad.

The reunion of the three was the sweetest thing in the whole wide world. There was no need for words; the embraces and kisses were eloquent enough. No high definition picture could have ever captured the intensity and depth of that unforgettable moment.

Time stood immobile, the earth stopped spinning, and the blue sky matched the color of the unsettled ocean waters.

None of them ever knew how many minutes elapsed in that mystic effusion of love, in that self-abandonment to inexpressible emotions.

As soon as the jubilant celebration had run its course, and the joyful trepidation of their hearts had simmered down, Heloise narrated her story and the terrible suspicions behind it.

The unbiased accusation against Charles Kent, her personal physician, and Mark Centurion, her father, coming from her mouth, appeared so unpalatable and distasteful to Catherine, that she entered into a new cycle of fear and depression.

Such a gruesome atrocity was inconceivable for a simple-minded teacher from Italy. On the other hand, for Ercole, it seemed more likely than not, being in consonance with his original intuition.

Heloise explained to her two astounded friends that they shouldn't waste any time. They should go straight to the police station and press charges against Charles Kent.

Any major delay would favor the diabolic professor, who could eliminate any incriminating evidence. In that fluid situation, time was of the essence.

Without paying much attention to objections, Heloise asked Ercole to take her immediately to the police station.

What a surprise for the investigative division to see the alleged dead woman alive and kicking under their noses!

Obviously, against the smashing evidence of that presence, they could not object to anything, except entertaining themselves, later on, with some extemporaneous jokes.

They prepared an accurate report, taking down all the allegations presented by Heloise against Kent and Centurion. They promised to begin in earnest a full investigation the following morning.

Immediately after that, they rushed back to the hotel. Heloise's first and biggest concern was to retrieve the camera with the pictures of the secret project.

What a feeling of frustration and bitter disappointment when the camera was nowhere to be found!

On the spot, she realized that she was one step behind her enemy. Kent had taken every precaution in the book to protect his back. With a scientific method and surgical precision he had carried out the most thorough job in the history of criminal investigation.

The crime scene was literally wiped off the map. Not a shred of a document, nor any minute evidence of a lab could ever be found, let alone any criminal intent of murder.

The news of the resurrected Heloise not only caused great commotion among the hotel population, but also excited the islanders' insatiable curiosity as soon as it was aired.

Kent's worst fear had come true. He had made a tremendous mistake in the preparation of the dosage. Now, he had to face dire consequences.

He had just come off the phone with Mark Centurion in Washington, D.C., communicating the disappearance of the body, when Heloise's return was announced on the radio. Frightened to once again face his irate boss, he went through some scary moments of indecision, never experienced before.

Did he have the stomach to reactivate the line and confess his incompetence? What would be Mark Centurion's reaction?

As the ultimate sign of his allegiance to the man, who had been a Maecenas for him, he took his courage in both hands and dialed his number.

On the other end, the voice sounded annoyed and extremely irritated. The few words Kent had prepared remained frozen in his mouth.

Stuttering like a scared child, he managed to convey the devastating news. No sound came from the other end of the line, just the confused noise of a man gasping for breath and then a deafening thump.

Kent would later learn that Mark Centurion had a stroke, leaving him half paralyzed and unable to speak.

The man who had overcome insurmountable difficulties and vanquished vicious foes, didn't have the courage to face the accusing finger of his only daughter. Not unheard of, but utterly barbaric, he had attempted to murder her on the altar of an alleged Greater Good, after callously disfiguring her femininity.

Ironically, a little pebble had brought about the giant's downfall. At the same time, involuntarily and by sheer coincidence, Heloise had rendered difficult, if not impossible, his criminal prosecution, due to his irreversible physical condition.

It was a dark day for Centurion and an even darker day for justice.

That national holiday was equally dark and bitter for Magdalene Centurion, Heloise's mother. She hadn't recovered yet from the double impact of her daughter's death and her corpse's disappearance, when the collapse of her husband sneaked upon her with devastating fury. She became hysterical, screaming for help. A domestic worker called the paramedics.

Centurion was transported immediately to the emergency room of a nearby hospital. The same evening he was put into the intensive care unit, with a respirator and an intravenous syringe.

The high and mighty man had been reduced to a vegetative state, still alive but showing no sign whatsoever of brain activity.

Magdalene, at his bedside, in a very short period, had been to hell and back. Now, she was so distraught that she couldn't take in anything of what was happening around her. She could not shed a tear, pronounce a word, or look straight into anybody's eyes.

Unexpectedly, her cellular phone rang. Without a blink and like a robot she answered it. Her heart missed a beat when the sound of a familiar voice reached her ears, and instantly her eyes became focused.

It was her daughter talking to her! At first she thought it was a bad joke and wanted to hang up. However, the voice was so insistent and full of love that she surrendered to such a beautiful dream.

Heloise, in fact, understood at once her mother's disbelief and incredulity, and pleading like a defenseless child, she reassured her that she was alive and well. She would be in Washington, D.C., as soon as she had straightened out some urgent business on the island.

She was looking forward to seeing her, and had many discomforting things to tell her. Surprisingly and contrary to her custom, she did not inquire about her father.

The poor mother, back in heaven by who knows what miracle, experienced new and conflicting feelings, so alien to her simple nature.

Her daughter, believed gone forever from the face of the earth, had made a miraculous and surprising comeback. She was hanging onto that feeble reality like a survivor from a shipwreck.

Finally, that memorable national holiday, so full of surprises for every single one of our protagonists, came to an end. If only they had known what the future had in store for them!

The following morning, a team of investigators were more than eager to conduct a professional examination of the premises, where Heloise believed an illegal lab was operating.

Nobody realized, except Kent and his workers, that the alleged lab had completely vanished overnight.

Heloise could hardly wait to show the detectives the secret passage. Under her guidance, they reached Kent's apartment. With the usual cockiness, they knocked at the door.

The professor, still wearing his pajamas, opened the door and affably, as if expecting their visit, received them.

Without indulging in explanations, they showed him the search warrant and began combing the place.

Nothing was left untouched, not even the personal hygiene objects, like toothpaste and toothbrushes.

The crucial moment arrived when they opened the huge closet and Heloise indicated the exact spot where the secret entrance was.

They pressed, they pushed, and they kicked every inch of the wall but nothing opened. Heloise remained so flabbergasted that she couldn't even open her mouth. She stood sealed like the impenetrable wall.

The agents tried and retried so many times that they got tired. Not even a hollow sound, or a small indication of some patching up. There was absolutely nothing. All was solid concrete.

Their initial arrogance had slowly simmered down to the point of transforming itself into an apologetic attitude when they decided to excuse themselves and leave.

Heloise's confidence has disappeared too, leaving in its place embarrassment and total humiliation. What a fiasco! She had never felt so degraded and disgraced before.

Her arch-enemy was not only always a step ahead of her, but he had covered his tracks masterfully.

She stood there looking like a complete idiot. There was not a shred of evidence to support her accusations.

Had she fabricated the whole story in a moment of anger and rage against her personal physician, who allowed her, and possibly caused her, to end up in an expensive coffin? The investigators entertained similar thought, but they turned a blind eye to such an eventuality.

Catherine and Ercole made every effort to lend Heloise moral support, but it was no use.

Just when she believed she had reached her final destination—discovering the perpetrators of multiple murders and their diabolic plan of altering human tendencies—she found herself empty-handed and ridiculed.

Her powerful battle cry for justice—"Let justice be done on earth as it is in heaven" —wasn't a cry any longer.

It had been lost, submerged in the mud of human passions. Her passionate crusade for justice had suffered the worst defeat.

Also, her personal dignity had received a deadly blow, from which it would be extremely difficult to recover.

What was left was total devastation and absolute desolation.

All her life she had the conviction of being in control of her destiny, deciding at every turn what to do and how to proceed. At this point in time, she was no longer sure. Like many other previous convictions, this too seemed to vanish in a puff of smoke. Lately, she wasn't dictating the course of her actions. Major events, unwanted and unexpected, were tossing her around, like a child tosses his inanimate toys into the air.

Certainties, convictions and beliefs were crashing against the abrupt cliffs of an unforgiving destiny. The scattered debris littered her mind and soul, creating a frightful insecurity.

Chapter XVI

Heloise thought the world revolved around her. However, at this point in time and much to her regret, she found herself revolving around people and events against her own volition.

Would she be able to stop that overwhelming trend, or would she be swept away by its irresistible forces? Her previous life had been a strange voyage in a dangerous land, punctuated with difficulty and pain, but still attractive and enjoyable.

Now, in the aftermath of her return from the valley of death, devastation and unbearable suffering would be her inseparable companions.

The brutal image of a father altering her femininity and ultimately murdering her, in order to cover up his failure, would be a constant reminder of a human depravity that knows no bounds.

The enchanting paradise island of Maui had become a frightful nightmare. Moreover, her whole world had changed into a modern Auschwitz, where a new holocaust was being carried out by unscrupulous men, under flimsy justifications of bettering mankind.

In a hasty decision, she called her mother in Washington, D.C., letting her know that she would be there shortly. With the same firmness, she notified Catherine and Ercole that she was packing up.

Two days after the memorable holiday, Heloise was back on the mainland with Catherine. Ercole would remain in Kaanapali, with a huge decision to make— whether to leave his boss and start his own research, or continue what he had begun.

For Heloise, the task to be undertaken was a daunting one. Would her sensitive mother withstand the unmerciful blows of discovering that her husband was an adulterer and a murderer?

He was lying in bed, unresponsive and ready to face God's wrath. Under those dramatic circumstances would she have the courage to present her half-sister and expose his father's diabolic activities?

The moment she saw her mother, welcoming her at the airport, she ran and hugged her with all the emotion and passion she could muster.

Her mom responded in kind. In that fervent embrace, the two women experienced a unique bond, far superior to any common attachment.

Magdalene looked into her daughter's eyes. An ocean of pain and sadness transpired from them, while tears streamed down her cheeks.

"Why are you so sad?" her mother asked. "You are not happy to see me? Or, perhaps, your father's condition is overpowering you?"

"Neither one," Heloise answered, with a halting tone of voice. "Unfortunately, I have something extremely dark and hurtful to reveal to you. However, this is not the right moment. Let us go home and enjoy each other's company a little longer. In due time, I will open up in all sincerity."

Magdalene realized that she hadn't spoken a word to Catherine, a silent witness of that mother and daughter's emotional reunion.

She apologized profusely, and holding her hand said, "Welcome among us!"

After that, the three women were whisked off in a limousine to the Centurion's residence.

On their way home, the conversation was unsubstantial, jumping from one topic to another with no connection.

All of a sudden, before arriving at their final destination, something awkward happened. Magdalene asked the limousine driver to stop at the hospital, where Mark Centurion was lying in an unconscious state.

Heloise showed some reluctance to step out of the car and visit her father. This came as a complete surprise to the poor mother, who never expected such an attitude from her girl.

Heloise, in the presence of her father, did not kiss him, or hold his hand. She did not show any feeling. She stood there, like a frozen statue, staring at that human being, incapable of recognizing anybody.

On the other hand, Catherine, without betraying her secret blood relation, could finally express her love for the man who had brought her into this world. She kissed him repeatedly, whispering sweet words in his ear.

Magdalene did not understand one iota of what was going on. The daughter was refusing to see her father, while the foreigner was pouring out her affection onto him.

Indubitably, it was a bizarre scene, without precedents in her personal history.

The old man, incapacitated by a stroke, did not show any sign of recognizing people. He maintained a lost stare into space with some blinking of the eyes. This was the only movement, with some faint breathing, that could be perceived.

Magdalene, following her maternal instincts, rearranged delicately some white hair covering the patient's front, and after a tender kiss, she left the room.

In complete silence, the three women reached their transportation and proceeded to their destination.

As soon as they were inside the house, Heloise broke her superimposed mutism and apologized to her mother.

"Mom, I'm sorry for my behavior. I'll explain the reason later."

"Maybe that will help me," said the uncomfortable mother, "make sense of these incomprehensible happenings."

"Before touching the main subject," continued Heloise, "I need to tell you something that will partially explain what occurred at the hospital.

Sometimes, the truth hurts and this time it might hurt real bad. Catherine, whom I love so dearly, is my half-sister. My dad, while serving his country in Italy, had a relationship with a woman, Caterina Longhi. From that relationship Catherine was born. She never knew her father, and her mother passed away a few years back. I possess the DNA test to prove my assertion."

Heloise was still explaining, when Magdalene interrupted her with certain vehemence. "I don't believe a word of what you're saying. Your father was a good man and a patriot!"

Immediately, she plummeted into a chair, hiding her face in her sweaty, shaky hands. The man she had loved with all her heart had betrayed her. That was extremely hard to swallow.

Even if her reaction was predictable, the impact had been unforeseen. After reflecting on that stunning revelation, she understood that her daughter wouldn't come up with such a lie, just to inflict pain on her, a woman already devastated by tremendous tragedies.

All became dark and unpleasant in that previously luminous and comfortable residence. Love and affection stopped emanating from those cold walls. Life had turned, in an instant, unbearable and asphyxiating.

An interminable pause followed, after which Heloise resumed a one-way conversation.

"Mom, I'm so sorry, but I had to tell you the truth about Catherine. It was the only way you could understand what's happening around you.

To burst your perfect bubble world was cruel, but necessary and urgent. Cheer up, Mom! You have a stepdaughter that loves you more than anything in this world."

Magdalene couldn't find any words to express the pain and shame she was experiencing. She looked at her daughter as if she were an intruder. An invisible barrier separated her from the rest, and no words of encouragement could overcome that obstacle.

Heloise put an end to her soliloquy. "Mom, if you need anything, just let me know. I'll always be at your side, no matter what. Now, I'll leave for my apartment with Catherine, but I'll keep in touch with you. I love you. Bye."

No previous goodbye had been heartbreaking like the present one. No solemn proclamation of love and affection could have changed the coldness of that strained relationship.

Back at her apartment, Heloise was forced to confront her determination to speak the truth. Was it so important to manifest an uncomfortable reality, running the risk of seriously jeopardizing a superior good?

Was it always accurate that "the truth sets you free?" Apparently not. Many times, the truth enslaves people to fear, disappointment and resentment. More often than not, it destroys perfect relationships, and sinks good family unions.

The price to be paid is, sometimes, far greater than the benefits derived from an act of sincerity.

In view of these reflections, Heloise rethought her plan of unveiling her father's true nature.

She wouldn't gain anything by exposing her father's diabolic enterprises; on the contrary, she would further alienate her mother. Moreover, instead of cleansing her soul with a spontaneous act of honesty, she would be irreparably mud-slinging her family.

She was still reflecting on this intriguing topic, when the phone rang. The hospital had just called her mother, announcing her father's passing.

Her mom, in turn, conveyed the news between tears. Heloise appeared to be struck by lightning. The deep hatred gave way to shock and confusion. The unmentionable enemy had suddenly become a momentary shadow, an insignificant worry.

His devastating campaign of modifying human nature, his sequence of murders, direct results of his failures, had vanished like a solitary cloud in the sky.

For Heloise the monstrous nightmare was over. Nevertheless, unresolved issues and conflicting feelings disquieted her tranquil nature and destroyed her peace of mind.

The overriding concern was that death had spared her father from human justice. In his case, justice had not been served. His heinous crimes would remain unpunished. His victims would never receive satisfaction and their families would never have proper closure.

At this point, nothing she could do would make any difference. She felt impotent and worthless. The servant of justice, so proud of her profession, sensed that she had touched bottom.

Her own father, with his megalomaniac dreams of improving human nature, had not only annihilated her femininity, but also shattered her vocation and her illusions of justice.

Tragedy after tragedy was piling up in Heloise's and Magdalene's lives. Neither one felt safe or secure.

The man who had driven a wedge between the two, with unforeseeable consequences, had ceased to exist. Regardless of his terrible legacy, now, mother and daughter had to fend for themselves.

Once more, the circumstances dictated what to do. Any plan Heloise formulated had to be scrapped. As a result, it was back to the drawing board.

She left everything. In total shock and bewilderment, she reached her mother. They looked at each other with compassion. A mutual acceptance and understanding seemed on the horizon. Truthfully, the reason for their discontent and disagreement no longer existed.

What a difference a few hours made! The man who had divided them in life would reunite them in death.

During the two customary days before the funeral, Heloise maintained a wait-and-see attitude. She was anxious to know whether her father's ruthless henchmen, the secret lab's medical crew, would attend the ceremony.

Her mother, Magdalene, was preoccupied too, but for a totally different reason. Catherine's presence was keeping her on edge, because she was a constant reminder of her husband's infidelity. Even if nobody knew, except for her daughter, she couldn't get rid of the shame brought on her family by the deceased.

A public funeral is always a reliable indicator of the dead person's popularity. This was no exception. Countless people, from the four corners of the earth, came to the exequies, and an even larger number attended the religious rites in the cemetery. Among them, dignitaries of every class and rank, from businessmen to politicians, from military representatives to religious authorities, from professionals to uncharacteristic street people, all bonded together by a common sentiment of respect and admiration.

The murderous medical team, with their chief Charles Kent, occupied the first row, next to the wife and daughter.

It was an incredible sight for a thriller movie. Charles rubbing shoulders with Heloise. Murderer and victim praying to the same God for the same impenitent departed. She felt such a repugnance that during the eulogy, conducted by Mons. Paul Marcikkus, she excused herself and left the religious ceremony.

Nobody knew the real reason. The current explanation was a sudden physical indisposition accompanied by overwhelming grieving feelings. That did not seem far-fetched, given Heloise's sensitive nature. Even her mother bought that plausible excuse without flinching.

The refreshments after the ceremony were subdued and composed.

The following day, when everything appeared to have returned to normal, a strange occurrence marred the alleged normality.

Ercole, the brilliant young researcher and affectionate friend, called Heloise from his hotel room and requested a private meeting. His voice had lost its bubbling vivacity and its phrasing had assumed an impersonal style. What was happening to that enchanting little brain, so stimulating in the most adverse circumstances?

Surprised and uncertain, she agreed to see him, but with some mental reservations. She would be on high alert. She would not accept any offer, no matter how enticing it might be and distrust anybody with a proposal of peace and reconciliation.

Once a rat, always a rat. This was applicable to his boss and to anyone forming part of his inner circle, including Ercole.

In an elegant suit, the man showed up punctually at her apartment. His handshake was cold and unconvincing, his demeanor professional and distant, and his look roaming in a different dimension.

No doubt in Heloise's mind, there was definitely something wrong with her friend.

Ercole didn't even open his mouth, and Heloise already smelled foul play in his conduct. With a tone of voice that sounded to her like role-playing in an acting class, he began a well-rehearsed speech.

"My boss, Charles Kent, deeply regrets all the misunderstandings that took place lately. He assures you that there is no ill will toward you. He offers you an olive branch, and invites you to a reconciliation dinner at a restaurant of your choosing. He intends to honor the memory of your father with a lavish celebration. You don't have to decide now. When you are ready, just give us a call. Here's the phone number. It's a pleasure to see you again. I hope you will delight us with your presence soon. Goodbye."

In saying, he was ready to leave. Nevertheless, Heloise, who refused to be ensnared by his subtle charm and false diplomacy, forced him to face reality.

"Dear Ercole, the change in you is totally beyond me. The man who was appalled, a few days back, by his boss' criminal actions, all of a sudden has jumped ship, and joined the enemy. Have you been brainwashed by some powerful drug, into believing that Charles is a modern-day Messiah, capable of transforming humankind? I will never sit at the same table with a bunch of criminals and fanatics that, under the cover of the Hippocratic oath, murder people and destroy their most legitimate tendencies. Shame on you and on your boss! I hope I will never cross your path again. So long."

He should know without a shadow of a doubt that her answer was clear and final.

For Heloise the decision wasn't hard, given her straightforward nature and her innate sense of justice. Even so, was it wise? Her puritan attitude wouldn't help much in the way of unmasking the adversary.

She had to step down from her irreproachable pedestal and play dirty. Only then would the battle be on an equal footing.

She had to concoct some elaborate scheme if she was determined to entrap the dangerous snake that wouldn't hesitate a second in seeking her total destruction.

The following day she had an important meeting with her family lawyer, Brunilda Pusher, for the reading of her father's will.

Her boss' role, outside the law firm, was still a mystery to her. Since Brutus Barker's suicide, she had looked after her family's economic interests. Had she been informed of the secret projects going on in Kaanapali? Conversely, was she aware, all along, of the illegal activities conducted by Mark Centurion and his team of scientists?

Heloise was certainly treading a dangerous path. She was surrounded by her father's closest and most faithful collaborators. Any out-of-step move could land her in a quicksand situation, from which it would be impossible to escape.

Since her car accident, Heloise hadn't had any dealings with Brunilda, obviously discounting the customary get-well and best wishes cards.

After several months, she was face-to-face with that intriguing woman, commissioned by her father to keep a close eye on her, at the time of Angie's suspicious death.

At ten o'clock in the morning, Brunilda opened the will, in the presence of Magdalene, Heloise and several CEOs, from the fast-food division to the hotel industry. She read the most pertinent passages of the important document.

The sole heiress of the immense fortune was Magdalene, and at her death, Heloise. In the meantime, Heloise would receive a substantial annual pension to be disclosed only to the interested party.

In a surprising codicil, a half-million dollars, annually, would go to a child he fathered in Italy, in the eventuality of being found. In parenthesis he wrote the name of the mother and her address. That came as a bolt from the blue to everybody, except to the mother and the daughter.

Catherine, who was absent, when she received the news, burst into tears, not for the money, but for the acknowledgment received posthumously by her father.

How much she had longed to have her father's acceptance, while he was still alive. Unfortunately, that never happened.

Anyhow, that gesture meant a lot to her. It made a world of difference. She was no longer an intruder, or a foreigner. She was an integral part of the Centurion family.

What a joy and satisfaction in that poor heart always thirsty for some fatherly affection!

Incidentally, the will had been written a year earlier. Probably, it would reflect a different spirit had it been drafted just after his daughter had discovered the abominable project.

Immediately after the reading of the important legal document, Heloise waited to exchange some ideas with Brunilda.

She did not have to make any effort, because her boss and family lawyer took the initiative of calling her.

"I renew my condolences," she said, "and I look forward to seeing you back at the office as soon as you are ready. I highly value your work, and I enjoy having you around. You are an excellent lawyer and a real asset to our firm."

Heloise couldn't process fast enough all those compliments and verify, on the spot, how much truth was in them. However, she had a few questions that could be the key to solving the mystery.

"Did my father," she inquired surreptitiously, "leave any disposition regarding the team of medical researchers working for him?"

Brunilda, shrewd to a fault, and well informed of Heloise's vicissitudes while in Maui, grasped at once what her not-so-naïve interlocutor was getting at.

Since she had nothing to hide, she replied, "I will give you a copy of the will, and you will notice that no provision had been made in this respect."

That came as no surprise to Heloise, knowing her father's knack in covering his tracks.

Pressing her luck, she moved a question forward. "Did you have any knowledge of their activities, and how they were remunerated for their services?"

In a rare moment of candor, Brunilda answered, "I know that your father had set up a special fund from which he derived their salaries. Concerning their activities I was kept in the dark. I knew of some research taking place, but nothing specifically. That is the full extent of my knowledge on the matter."

Her prompt reply, without hesitation or dubious circumlocution, gave the clear impression of honesty and sincerity.

However, she knew better about lawyers. They could be convincing and lie through their teeth.

Heloise's final question went straight to Brunilda's heart, appealing to her nobility as a lawyer and her sensibility as a woman.

"If there was anything wrong in my father's dealings, would you be willing to tell me?"

The seasoned litigator reflected a few seconds. Summoning her courage and multiple abilities, she delivered a sibylline answer. "My loyalty to your father, combined with my sworn duty to complete confidentiality regarding my clients, prevents me from revealing anything detrimental, even after death.

On the other hand, my respect and admiration for you, as Mark Centurion's daughter, and as my valuable employee, compel me to be open and honest with you.

Like any businessman and philanthropist, your father conducted activities of a dubious nature, but nothing outside our legal system. This I can assure you. If you have any other questions, I would be glad to oblige."

Heloise, deeply dissatisfied with the outcome of the conversation, thanked her boss and asked for a short leave of absence from her job to reflect about her future.

Brunilda accepted her request and bade her farewell. Heloise joined her mother. Both, in a somber mood, returned home.

The residence was silent and cold like their souls. There was no desire to comment on anything that had happened that morning. Magdalene had seen all her fears confirmed and Heloise remained with all her doubts unresolved.

Now, the moment of truth had arrived. It was solely up to her to fight the good fight and deliver the final blow to her deadly enemy. If she really believed in justice, she couldn't shy away from her fundamental responsibilities.

All she knew was that criminal organization wouldn't rest until she was eliminated. She wouldn't stand a chance of surviving their fierce determination.

Why not take the initiative and unmask their dirty tricks, possibly bringing all to justice?

She called Ercole and told him that she had changed her mind. She would be glad to have dinner with Charles Kent and exchange reconciliation tokens. The meeting place would be revealed just an hour before the actual event.

Ercole, with no surprise or emotion in his voice, conveyed the message to his boss. Charles, who had already abandoned, in the short run, his criminal plan, smirked unpleasantly and exclaimed, "Good heavens! The lonesome dove is coming to the bird of prey."

Heloise did not lose a second in setting up the trap. She requested full support from the local police. Whether the operation would be successful or not, she would pay handsomely for their services.

Their job was to install invisible electronic eyes in the dining area, in the kitchen and in the manager's office. Undercover policemen would cover the whole area, inside and outside the hotel. The officers had to keep their eyes peeled for any signs of foul play.

The unusual operation was surrounded by an atmosphere of expectation and intrigue. Heloise felt at the zenith of her detective creativity. This would make or break her as an amateur sleuth and as a woman of the world.

Her level of anxiety was very high. That wasn't a good sign. Every time, in fact, she had high expectations and her worries clouded her judgment, she had stumbled and fell. Were the bells tolling for her success or for her failure? What was in store for her?

When the set date came, as she had promised, she called Charles Kent an hour in advance to disclose the location of the meeting.

She was dressed conservatively but in fashion. Her demeanor appeared professional, her attitude extremely guarded and somewhat apprehensive.

Charles, on the other hand, exuded confidence and self-assurance. He was dressed in a suit and an impeccable white shirt.

Who had the advantage in that duel of shrewdness and artfulness? Hard to say.

When they met, they shook hands and exchanged some introductory greetings. They were accompanied to their table, located in a spacious corner of the dining area, near a window overlooking the major historical monuments of the city.

Heloise felt a kind of instinctive resistance sitting opposite her murderer physician. Anyhow, she tried to overcome her natural repugnance, in order to achieve her coveted goal.

With a nonchalant attitude Charles opened the conversation.

"I regret the past events as much as you do. Unusual circumstances forced us to act in an irregular manner. There is plenty of blame going around on both sides. It is time to put an end to this, turn the page and make a fresh start."

"Regrettably," replied Heloise, "I don't share the same view on what happened. Neither do I condone my father's projects and methods and your subservient role. Despite how despicable all that might be, we need to call a truce, which will be mutually beneficial."

"Yes," continued Kent, "we must come to a common understanding and reach a compromise. I will forget you breaking and entering the lab, and you will make no attempt to incriminate your father and I."

While Charles kept talking, Heloise was nodding her head in agreement and observing, at the same time, every movement of the waiters, every dish arriving and every drink served.

At any moment she was expecting an undercover agent to come up with some startling evidence. But nothing of the kind. The time passed inexorably, and the dinner conversation was dragging on with no end in sight.

It was well past dessert, when both agreed on an amicable truce with no strings attached. Whatever promises they made or whatever compromises they reached it would be like a gentleman's agreement, without any legal ramifications.

When they parted company, Heloise was still confident that the hidden cameras had caught some incriminating evidence.

What a disappointment and frustration after reviewing all the tapes! Nothing was found that was even remotely inappropriate.

Had she been outplayed and outsmarted by her maverick physician? All the signs pointed in that direction. That was certainly one of the worst times of her life.

Jesus, centuries before, had stressed that cunning social reality, where unscrupulous people outwit simple and honest folks.

"For the children of this world are more prudent in dealing with their own generation than are the children of light." (Luke 16:8)

Heloise felt inadequate and out of place, to say the least. Her position, in the eyes of the law enforcement agency, had been largely discredited, as had happened in Maui.

Shedding bitter tears for her dismal failure, she failed to recognize the positive outcome of her investigation. **With her brave action, she had put an end to an insane project of modifying human nature**. That was the incredible redeeming feature of all her failures.

Left without any recourse, she recoiled from the idea of pursuing an activity alien to her profession. She bent herself over in a desperate attempt to find her true identity.

The following day, miraculously, she retracted from that narcissistic posture, and as if nothing had happened, she greeted with an extraordinary effusion of love Catherine, her mother and anyone else that happened to be in her way.

It was a totally new day and a completely new life. A heavy weight had been lifted from Heloise's fragile shoulders. She was breathing again normally and looking at things with renewed determination.

The reader might be curious to know what happened to the leading protagonist of this intriguing human story.

Conclusion

Further down the road, Heloise accidentally stumbled upon the reason why her detective work had failed.

The son of the restaurant manager, where she had dinner with Charles Kent, revealed to her the puzzling mystery.

An informant from the local police department, with whom Charles had close ties, offered him on a silver platter the secret plan to entrap him.

Warned in advance, he took his precautions and behaved irreproachably.

This dismal failure, the last in a chain of unfortunate attempts, greatly disheartened the poor untrained detective, tipping the scales in favor of a radical change.

Heloise, looking at herself in the mirror, didn't see a successful lawyer, but a failed detective. Her crusade against the evildoers had encountered an enormous roadblock.

Her thirst for justice was burning her throat, and she was dying without satisfying it. The main criminals in her life had escaped justice. Brutus had committed suicide. Her father, the mastermind of the entire operation, hit by a sudden stroke, went to his grave unpunished. Finally, Charles Kent covered his tracks in such a way that nobody would ever be able to incriminate him.

In the face of such adversity, Heloise showed a remarkable spirit of survival and adaptation.

Unlike many people, she didn't give up her basic mission of implanting justice on our hostile planet; she just changed recipients.

The cause that caught her attention was the silent suffering and unbearable degradation of millions of women all over the world, being used and abused as sex slaves.

That outcry was becoming deafening in her ears and in her conscience. She decided to join a volunteer organization, dedicated to rescuing those poor women.

After breaking away from their sex bondage, they would be reeducated and reinserted into society.

That was the new face of her mission of justice. Her legal skills, her strong humanitarian feelings, and her deep empathy for those enslaved women would be a real asset for the organization.

The frigid woman, deprived of her sex drive by her own father, could understand better than anybody else what it meant to perform a supreme act of love, against her own will and against her own desires.

She was the right woman for the job. The **justice** she believed in wasn't a theoretical one, like the one she had described in Rome to the seminarians, nor an operational one full of subterfuges and deceits carried out in the courtrooms, but a live one, **imperfect** and **passionate**, always **unfinished** but always **satisfying**, made flesh and blood, and engendered during the last traumatic stages of her life.

Her new drive for justice wasn't a competition where tricks and abilities, pride and prejudice, arrogance and unfairness are put on display, but a humble and obstinate push to give back humanity to poor human beings defaced and degraded by man's brutality and cruelty.

The new face of justice had to shine in the smile of every woman freed from sex slavery, from Cambodia to Thailand, from Somalia to Sudan, from Europe to America.

Heloise had changed profession, but had retained the same inspired vocation of **pursuing justice with a renewed spirit**. The same voice of two thousands years ago would repeat to her. "**Blessed are they who hunger and thirst for justice and righteousness, for they will be satisfied**." (Matthew 5:6)

Only in this sacred mission would she find satisfaction, so sweet and so dear, that it would fill the emptiness of her femininity.

The mission of justice and human realization would have one name and one face only. That name and that face would be Heloise.

Her decision to join this fairly unknown volunteer organization affected people in varying ways.

Magdalene, the suffering mother, had been hit hardest by the news. Her heart began bleeding again at the simple thought of her daughter in foreign lands, exposed to dangerous situations, and possible vile retaliations.

Catherine had found love, attachment and new perspectives in life, and was scrambling to resettle herself in a new shifting landscape.

Brunilda, despite her ambiguous and selfish behavior, felt deeply the loss of such a valuable associate.

Charles Kent jumped for joy at the news. That was certainly his ticket to an undisturbed life, far and away from the long arm of the law.

Ercole was the only one that remained undisturbed and unmoved. Nobody would ever know the reason behind that unexplainable behavior.

The world Heloise had known and cherished in her conviction and imagination, never existed in reality. **The best of all possible worlds, where everything happens for a reason and some good can always come from evil**, was a comforting and reassuring theory, but a theory and a myth nevertheless.

The justice system she had believed in and worked for never took shape, not even in an embryonic stage. "Justice is blind," "Justice is equal for all" and "Justice is served" are cherished beliefs of our society. Unfortunately, justice is never blind and rarely equal and served. **Justice is always imperfect and unfinished**.

The family she longed so much to be part of, never materialized. Her father, the man she adored as a child, not only became her biggest disappointment but also turned out to be a ruthless criminal. No discovery can ever be as grim as that.

Simply, she had been betrayed by society, justice organization and family.

Her previous life had been a total illusion, a deceptive entrapment, an incredible fiasco.

Misfortune, cruelty and failure woke her up to a more realistic world and a more believable and satisfying mission.

Things were looking up, but in a completely different way.

Publications by the same author

1. - **Dario Lisiero**, *People Ideology, People Theology*, Exposition Press, New York 1980.

2. - **Dario Lisiero**, *My First Life*, Trafford, Victoria (Canada) 2004.

3. - **Dario Lisiero**, *Angelica*, Lulu, New York 2006

4. - **Dario Lisiero**, *José Benito Lamas, I. Reconstrucción histórica del gobierno eclesiástico en 1852-1857*, Editorial Dunken, Buenos Aires 2003.

5. - **Dario Lisiero**, *José Benito Lamas*, II. *Relectura del pensamiento y de la acción de José Benito Lamas*, Editorial Dunken, Buenos Aires 2004.

6. - **Dario Lisiero**, *Uruguayana*, Lulu, New York 2006.

7. - **Dario Lisiero**, *El Vicario Apostólico Jacinto Vera, Lustro Definitorio en la Historia del Uruguay, Primera Parte*, Lulu, New York 2006.

8. - **Dario Lisiero**, *El Vicario Apostólico Jacinto Vera, Lustro Difinitorio en la Historia del Uruguay, Segunda Parte*, Lulu, New York 2006.

9. - **Dario Lisiero**, *El Vicario de Montevideo*, Lulu, New York 2007.